D0382812

The

Limits

of the

World

The
Limits
of the
World

A NOVEL BY

JENNIFER ACKER

DELPHINIUM BOOKS

THE LIMITS OF THE WORLD

First Edition

For Nishi
And for my parents:
BEM & CWA

PART I

1.

Urmila rearranged the animals. They were homely, unwelcoming; no one was buying. Should she group them by type: elephants next to rhinos next to giraffes?

All morning, only two customers came into the shop. The first peered, scowled in confusion, then left. The second was a girl with hair stuck together in clumps, wanting to buy a dashiki.

"You want to dress like a man? Wait until Halloween," Urmila said.

"Seriously?" The girl stood defiantly on short, thick legs.

"You tell me there is anything else you like. I can find you a nice dress," Urmila offered, putting on a smile.

But the girl walked out, and Urmila was left with the animals.

Two-inch heels, slacks, and a striped sweater had seemed smart when she'd dressed in her dim bedroom, but now Urmila felt exposed like one of her zebras, alone on the plains. Then, with an arrow of hope, she remembered the latest shipment from Habari Exports, still in boxes in the back. Soapstone candlesticks were her best seller.

The messy taping was the first bad sign: the careless, tightly wound crisscrosses. There were scissors near the register, but Urmila was already on the floor, so she ripped off the recalcitrant tape with her hands, even her teeth. Pulled out the loosely balled newspaper, heart sinking. The candlesticks were cracked, every one of them! Some snapped in half, others chipped. The soft stone's pretty rose colors wrecked by black faults.

This was not the first broken shipment. She bit her thumb, strangling a furious cry. How close to the margin she already was.

Outside the store window, shoppers and mall workers walked by, ignoring her sign and her displays, the square paper she'd pasted up twelve years ago on opening day: *Authentic African Goods. Low Prices.*

Gifts. She would change *goods* to *gifts*. More high-class.

This morning, Urmila had reminded Premchand that his April transfer of funds to the store was due. She didn't believe her husband forgot; he was withholding. Sending money to their son Sunil. The two of them thought it was a secret, but Urmila had known for more than a year. Many summers when he was a boy, she had taken Sunil to Nairobi, where he'd worked with her brothers in their businesses, but clearly he'd not learned about work ethic, about savings. Sunil's upbringing had been too easy, she often thought. He didn't know the meaning of struggle.

Sunil was thirty and still in school. Too busy squandering to phone his own mother.

"Why all this schooling?" she asked him once. "You were never in the smart set." When friends asked how Sunil was, Urmila said he'd made the dean's list, a phrase she'd heard on TV.

Yet she missed him. His boyish face, his humor. He was often the only one who could make her laugh. Surprise her with tenderness; his endearing awe and curiosity. For a time when Sunil was young they'd sailed smoothly along. She guiding, he sweetly following. If she was honest, she had to admit she learned from him, too. Things about her adopted country, new ways to understand the people around her. He tried to show her people meant to be kind. He told her that people in Ohio were unusually nice. This belief was his American birthright. But after thirty-five years here, people were still rude to Urmila, and why should she not say so? She sometimes thought about visiting Sunil in Cambridge, but it was hard to get away from the shop, and he'd just put her up in a hotel, like a dog in a kennel. He had an American girlfriend now, too, and Urmila did not want to encourage things. Her visit would be an endorsement. Best to ignore the girl and let it pass. Act as if Sunil were simply flirting and would come around. Still, Urmila found herself wondering what the girl looked like, what she studied, what she wanted with her son. There were a lot of successful Indians in this country—her friends' children were doctors, lawyers, accountants—but Sunil was not one of them. The last time she talked to him, his voice had sounded worn, defeated, and it had hurt her. "I'm working hard," was all he said. Trying to teach and study and write, to embody a life unknown to any of them, and terrifying to Urmila and Sunil both, if for different reasons.

Breaking the store's quiet morning, Urmila now saw a darting movement in the back. Hangers clanged, and a long printed cloth crumpled to the floor. She stepped closer, but she already knew. She did not hesitate. She kicked off her heels. She'd always been faster barefoot.

Urmila ran after the hippie girl, hair hanging like a dirty mop; she did not know she'd been caught and was walking with no hurry toward the fountain. In Urmila's mind, her hands were claws that stretched spectacularly to snag the prey.

This was the real America, the one that thought of her as low, like the neighbor who'd asked if she wore a bra. If her husband had other wives. Was she a fool to be cheated?

Near the mall exit, the girl turned, realized she was being hunted. Clearly she knew about the security cameras, because she whipped around now and stood alert, ready. She flung the dashiki to the floor. "You can have your stupid robe!"

"Raand!" Urmila shot back, the English escaping her.

But the girl just stared. "You're crazy," she said, backing away on those stubby legs. She had pretty green eyes and a sweet pink mouth.

Urmila followed the girl outside, onto the cold concrete in her bare feet. She wanted to punch her. That saucy mouth. The revolting hair. The disrespect.

The girl floated two twenties to the ground. "Those cheap things are overpriced."

Urmila breathed in hard, the air spiked with car exhaust. Just in time, just as the girl turned to walk away, English words arrived, and she shouted, "Thieving whore!"

Surprised, exhilarated, and only a little ashamed, Urmila picked up the bills and carried the dashiki back to her store. She dusted it off and hung it on the rack next to the others.

Her first months in America, Urmila had been shocked by the height of the buildings, the clock towers always on time. And the busy-ness: people running to work, hurrying home, rushing between children and friends. The houses in the white neighborhoods so solid, leather car seats like melted ghee. All the roads paved. At first, the bright supermarket lights had stunned her, blunted her senses, but she'd caught on. Those oranges were frauds, falsely painted. And how far apart the Americans stood in line! What were they worried about, a little sneeze blowing their way?

She and Premchand had immigrated from Nairobi in 1965. Urmila had not imagined then that one day she'd own a shop. For years she'd felt so far away from all the people and things aligned, seemingly effortlessly, in front of her. Then she'd had her stroke of genius. People had always looked up to her husband, but now they admired *her*; they didn't just think her lucky to have arrived married to a doctor. Pride? Yes. She'd started something from nothing, just like her father.

Urmila's brothers had taken over their father's River Road shop in Nairobi decades ago. They never would have given her a piece of it, even if she'd stayed in Kenya. Gopal, Urmila's oldest brother, was her wholesale connection. She'd had to push him hard to help her—their sister Sarada called Gopal a *good-for-himself*—but Urmila had flattered his expertise and worldliness until, following months of her wistful *I wish I had your smarts, brother*, he'd agreed to share his contacts. Later, she wanted to work with the suppliers directly, but by then he'd grown used to having her under his wing.

Their father was nearly ninety now, in bad health, moved month to month between her siblings. She didn't talk with him often because his hearing was poor, but sometimes she heard his voice. *Stand up, bow your head, be polite, do what your brothers say.* Now that he was old and far away, she could think of his words as fatherly, not sharp and belittling.

To distract herself from the quiet and boost her spirits, Urmila checked her investments. These tech stocks went nowhere but up, there had been no massive reset or failure when the calendar flipped over to Y2K, and her heart raced at the figures. At her desk, in front of the computer, she chewed a few bites of cold potato shaak.

She also reread yesterday's email from Bimal. *Dear Urmila Foi, Here is Raina wearing your gift. She loves them very much and sends you a hug. I am working hard and must go now.* Unlike Sunil, when Bimal said he was working hard, it meant he was progressing.

Raina's fat cheeks surrounded little white teeth, and she

wore the sparkly pink sneakers Urmila had sent. She pushed her face very close to the screen, as if to inhale the girl's powdery scent. She read the words again. Bimal still lived in Nairobi, near Urmila's brother Anup and his wife, Mital, who had raised him.

She thought about Bimal often; she couldn't help it, but she'd learned not to share these longings with her husband. He didn't like to talk about it.

At closing, she peeked in a tiny wall mirror and yanked out her gray hairs. A fresh layer of lipstick. No beauty, but presentable enough for the walk to her car.

At home, she ate dinner alone. She was watching Connie Chung on *20/20* in the den when Premchand poked his head through the door. "Hello, darling." His wiry eyebrows, stern and curious, fringed his brow. In Gujarati he said, "Listen, there is tepla and potato shaak in the fridge to microwave. Also rasmalai for dessert." Except on weekends, they did not eat together. He always came home too late, even when Sunil was a boy, when her son had insisted on eating meat like a real American. Urmila had been forced to give in when her husband took the boy's side, admitting that he often ate ham sandwiches from the hospital cafeteria. How could she argue with a doctor, even when back until forever Jains were vegetarian? She cooked Sunil's hamburgers wearing rubber gloves, turning her face away while they bled and sizzled.

After *20/20*, there was a story about the civil war in the Congo—*Belgian* Congo, as she knew it. Though Africa's murder and mayhem were often in the news, Urmila wasn't sure what to do with the jolt of recognition that arrived with stories like this. Tonight she thought first not of her own childhood, the tumult of Mau Mau and independence, but of the white-haired lady who'd come into the store last week. Who'd announced, looking around, "My husband was in the war in Africa."

Urmila did not know which war she meant, but the woman did not look friendly to questions. So Urmila had showed her a long Maasai spear, authentically rusty at the point, and an accompanying leather shield. "Maasai colors. For your soldier husband."

But the woman had looked appalled. She peered into the display cases. "Don't you have any ivory?"

Ivory, of course. This was a rich woman. And so, to impress her, Urmila showed her the chain of ivory elephants, hooked trunk to tail. They marched in place on a glass shelf next to the register. "Touch the sides, so smooth," she said. The carving was precious to her, one of the fine things she'd bought for herself during her and Premchand's one visit to India. After seeing the great sites, they'd detoured to the rural town near Jamnagar, where her family was from. Where the homes were still made of mud and the Untouchables glued their eyes to the ground. Premchand had been disgusted by the lack of sanitation, and they had not stayed even one night. Her husband had preferred to sleep on the train than in one of their far-flung relative's poor homes. Secretly, she was glad, if embarrassed. She agreed with her husband that they had not escaped poverty in Nairobi only to return to the dirt in India.

"How much?" the woman had asked.

"Oh, it's illegal to sell now."

Her husband was a collector, the lady said. She was willing to pay a high price and left her phone number, and her name, Lillian Ross, in case Urmila changed her mind. She hadn't.

Urmila turned off the television and listened to the neighborhood. No jungly children, no barking dogs. She listened warily for the spring sounds of insects and mice.

In Nairobi, rats had been a problem. Every couple of years the population burst, usually during a wet season when the rice and lentils molded. When the tears in the burlap sacks appeared, the children were supposed to alert a servant, who set out the poison. Sometimes a neighbor came over to commiserate and tease Urmila for sending the rats next door: "You told them where the better food was, eh?"

Her father had lost a brother to plague in the early years, when Nairobi was just rotten railway headquarters. Bapuji had mentioned it only once, when Urmila was a child. Surely he'd revealed other things she had failed to remember, and sometimes she yearned for knowledge—memories, artifacts—of her childhood so fiercely her hands unconsciously balled into fists. Now that her father was losing his grip, and her mother had been dead ten years, there was no one left to pull up the truth of their past.

Urmila heard her husband scrape his chair back from the table and slot his plate in the dishwasher, careful not to leave a mess for her.

This house, on a curved street with narrow walks, had been their home for twenty years. It was carpeted and comfortable, the furniture bought in discounted sets from Sears, display models right off the floor. In Urmila's pantry were grains and pulses from the Asian grocer, and in the drawer next to the stove her spices cozied up next to each other like babies. Urmila could tell a good cook in an instant from how she laid out her spices. To line them on a shelf was casting them into dusty exile. Now that Sunil was gone, she cooked less, and they never used the parlor, where an old Coca-Cola stain blotted the carpet. Urmila no longer hosted parties; the cooking and the conversation tired her too much and made her feel small. When they wanted to see friends, and her husband almost never wanted, there were plenty of Indian restaurants in Columbus to dine out.

Their house used to be one of the newer ones, but now, all around, people were demolishing homes like theirs, putting up two and three stories, adding high fences. But at least it was not like Nairobi, where fences were not enough. Where you hired armed guards and still you feared for your life.

Near midnight, Premchand found her in the computer room. He was wearing his green flannel pajamas, and his hair stuck up like grass.

"I woke you?" she said.

"I wasn't asleep."

"Just lying there doing nothing?"

"I tried to read *JAMA*—to put me to sleep—but nothing is working. So I am reading the paper."

"Darling, you need a vacation."

He leaned over her shoulder toward the screen. His night breath was stale and smelled of betel nut and fennel. He'd been snacking from the jar of supari. "You are taking me to Nairobi?" he said. "That's not a vacation."

"Yes, it's a break from work! Plus I need to have a business talk with Gopal. You know they sent me another broken shipment today?"

Her husband clucked his tongue. "I did tell you."

"Just two weeks," she said. "I can't be away from the store for more than two."

He didn't answer. Instead he slipped on his reading glasses and brought the folded paper up to his chin. In English, he said, "There is a very interesting article here. It is saying we Americans are not good savers. The economy is doing so well, stock market going up and up, but it's not enough. In other countries, they are smarter, families have cushions to fall on in emergencies. We should be saving more."

"What are you talking about? We have savings account. We have retirement account." She wished she hadn't told him about the shipment.

"The store is one of these places to reduce, perhaps selling fewer items," he said, removing his glasses and pointing them to the paper the way Urmila imagined he did when showing a patient a test result. "Or maybe you prefer to save money by not buying expensive plane tickets to Kenya?"

"It's business," she said. "Tax deductible."

"Not my ticket. Maybe you should take the trip by yourself."

"This is what you always say! Last two times I have gone by myself. Raina is almost three and you don't even know her."

He sighed, ready to give in. But she hated his if-you-want-it-I-will-do-it-*darling* sigh. When he'd decided to work in USA, he'd promised that they'd go every year to Nairobi. For two years they did, but shortly after Sunil was born her husband began saying he couldn't take the time off, the airfare for three was too expensive, he preferred to spend on vacations in America. In the twelve years since Sunil had left home, Urmila and Premchand had gone to Nairobi together just once, for Bimal's wedding. Sunil had stayed behind, away at school.

"Okay, but you cannot so openly favor Raina when we go," he said. "She does not belong to you."

"I know that!"

But he did not soften. His chin lifted.

"Loving everyone equally," she said, "that is a myth!" He acted as if it were wrong, treating Bimal as her son. Urmila punched in their credit card number on the British Airways site. Suddenly, she was overcome. She couldn't wait. "It's settled," she said. "We go the first two weeks in May."

Premchand left the office, slipped through the doorway. When Urmila entered their bedroom a few minutes later, a sharp chill raised the hairs on her arms. He'd left the window open. She rushed to close it, but not before the icy night circled her ankles and pinched the nerves running up her legs.

Climbing into bed, under the warmth of the electric blanket, she had a thought she'd not had so urgently since the early years of their life in this country. It was just one word, but it said everything she wanted. It meant heat, love, life, yesterday, and tomorrow all in one.

"Home?" Gopal said. "Of course I am not home. You reached me at the shop."

She knew that. She was at work, too. She meant, *How are things at home?* But she didn't wait for an answer. "Motabhai, you aren't looking out for my interests. Those men you set me up with are taking advantage."

She heard him pull out drawers and slap thick folders onto his desk. She shouldn't feel hurt. Being the oldest, Gopal didn't listen to any of them. But they were colleagues, almost business partners. No woman she knew had come close to what she'd done. Her Columbus friends worked, but only helping their husbands in the pharmacies and dry cleaners.

While she waited for him to respond, she heard the new doorbell she'd installed after her run-in with the dashiki thief. A blond head poked through the doorway. Urmila held up a finger—*one minute*—but the head disappeared. Now her brother had cost her a customer.

Finally, he said, "Working with Africans is difficult. You know this. They say they understand but they do not. They are not completely honest. If I talk to them, they will say, 'Okay, sir, problem is solved.' But I tell you they have not understood the problem in the first place. Yes, these packaging boys are careless. But they are not my direct employees."

When Urmila visited the old shop in Nairobi, she still felt a thrill. For her father's lasting work, for the hustle bustle, for commerce—she even liked the grimy feel of the bills and the coins warm from hands and pockets. She reveled in the noise and traffic smoke. Her store, of course, was nicer. Clean and orderly and American. Gopal had never seen it. Though recently, since the embassy bombings, he'd been making noises about visiting.

A few trips to lay the legal groundwork, in case he needed her sponsorship suddenly. Africanization was rising like a flood, he said. What if their president turned on them, like Idi Amin?

"I tell you what," her brother said. "When you visit here, you can meet the men face to face. Insist for yourself."

Well, why not? She put down the phone and tried to repel the smug echo of her brother's voice in her ears. She surveyed her wares, eyeing one of the blue and black kikoys printed with Swahili words. When someone had asked what it meant, Urmila could not remember, so she'd said: *Home is where the hearth is.*

When Urmila went back home to Nairobi, she wanted to be a little celebrated, not thrown to the hyenas.

And here, in her adopted country, she wanted to feel buoyed, confident, like the American women who managed stores in the mall, but she did not.

Yet Urmila also knew that the lack of script and social order had freed her. From living with her controlling mother-in-law in Nairobi, for one thing, kissing the woman's wrinkled feet, following her orders like a slave. But these same freedoms had also built the walls of her loneliness. Raising a son in this country should have rooted her, but it hadn't.

What made Sunil so hard to talk to? So eager to condemn her high standards and her absences from his school events. The un-American things she'd done when she hadn't known any better. Running into the arms of an American girl was spite, she was sure. A way of showing her how little he cared, how well he could do without her. Urmila worried Sunil and the girl were living together, and thinking about their sharing an apartment suddenly made her feel cornered, helpless. She could lose him for the rest of her life.

What would heal the years of anger and bind them together again? There were many things she had never told him. Maybe if he knew.

2.

They were starving there on the farms of the Saurashtra, so they left. They left mothers, sisters, elders, everyone who had watched them grow. They left the paths worn by their own feet, from hut to field to stream. Paths they imagined leading to the sea but which they had never taken to the end. They left the morning birds, cobwebs they'd watched being spun. They had to leave because their fields were dry, the millet stunted, the rice vanishing. They left behind their wives and the girls their sons might have married. They weren't so lucky as my Urmila when she accompanied her husband to America.

Do you know how hard this was, my grandsons? Are you getting all this? You here and you across the ocean? How we do love to cross oceans!

My father, all the men, they were promised so much by the scouts—the Britishers sent to India to bring labor to East Africa. Our men took a few rupees, all they had, a gold bangle if they were lucky, and sewed them inside their pockets. Many died with the pouches still sewn shut.

On the stepping-stone of a promise, they boarded the dhows.

They were used to bright light, but not to ocean. Used to cramped quarters, but not to being trapped—unable to walk away from an argument, a bad smell. They knew poverty, rations of food and water, but not the stinginess of so many strangers. They did not know being away from their families. They began to count clouds as friends. Gave names to the birds perched on the mast. They dreamed—nightmares—of stars falling and drowning in the waters around them.

They were not originals, you know. From early days, thirteenth and fourteenth centuries, Indian coastal people had crossed the seas to Africa. They were traders, exchanging silk for ivory and gold. An Indian steered Vasco da Gama himself across the ocean. But our people, our family, lived on farms some kilometers inland, too far when you are counting in footsteps, and it was a long time until the chance to leave, for a better life, came to us. Until the British needed our strength and numbers.

Our people did not know it then, when they were starving, but they were walking every day on oil fields. Our old homeland is a big city now—largest oil refinery in the world! But then, then they had only their hands digging into dry earth. So they left.

They crossed.

They arrived.

They remained.

And hear this. Their names, your ancestors, are inscribed on the great iron snake stretching from Mombasa across the plains, all the way to Lake Victoria. Our men who knew nothing but the most important thing, survival, built the railroad. It's important you know this, my boys. The generations are passing.

Fareh teh chareh. He who roams advances.

3.

A modest front yard featured three young, bitten trees, barely visible at this hour. The place had been recently painted, a subtle green Sunil liked. It was Sunday, and the neighborhood of well-kept houses and straight yards was quietly active with push mowers and runners stretching in driveways. Kids on bikes grabbed the last rays of light.

The landlady was much older than Sunil expected. Unusually tall. "I was tidying up," she said and smiled, wide and toothy.

He wanted to trust the woman. He chose to ignore that he and Amy were just two prospective renters among legions, that there could be a garbage mound on the floor crowned by a giant rat and still rivals would draw blood over a well-located one-bedroom.

The woman opened the second-floor apartment and swept her arms open, as if to say, *All this could be yours*. "It was my son's place. Him and his ex-wife."

Sunil held Amy's arm. She reached a hand behind his back and covertly pinched the top of his thigh.

The kitchen offered a scuffed linoleum floor, an avocado

table, and a beige refrigerator. Beyond was a larger room with gangly potted plants. Windows faced the street, but fortunately little noise floated up. The furniture was floral, the walls hung with drawings of trees with human arms and smiling sunflowers. But the bedroom was painted a cheerful white, and the office had a large window with what seemed to be a view of a backyard. A layer of spring snow flecked the brown earth.

"No laundry?" Amy asked, looking herself like she could use a bath. Amy believed that her sweat was inoffensive, clean, and she often resented showering as a waste of time. Today, she showed up straight from a run, her clothes dry but neck still damp around the collar. It was true, she didn't smell ripe—he happened to like her undertone of old lemon—but her disregard for impressing the landlady embarrassed Sunil.

The woman said there was a laundromat around the corner. Sunil took note. Laundry was his job. Amy paid the bills and fought the credit card and utility companies.

It was a quiet block, academics and families, the landlady said. There'd be a slight reduction in rent if they mowed the lawn. "If it ever gets to be spring."

He would mow the lawn. He loved spring, the pulsing, daily greening of the world. The give in the ground, the strengthening sun on his face. Amy slipped from sweaters into fitted T-shirts, like the orange scoop neck she was wearing the day they met. Yet spring signaled summer, the dead months; he had a hard time getting work done during the limp, boneless season. This summer, Amy would need a job. And Sunil would finish his dissertation. He had to.

Sunil looked around again excitedly. They'd take down the floral art and put up pictures of Boston, artful shots of places they'd seen and been together: the courtyard of the Gardner Museum; an Old World streetcorner in the North End. Buy real flowers from the corner store and set them in jelly jars. The books on shelves instead of the milk crates they used now.

The old woman slid heavily into a chair at the kitchen table. Surely questions about their finances were forthcoming.

Instead she asked Amy to bring her a glass of cold water— "You have to run the tap thirty seconds, dear"—and instructed Sunil to pull the chain on the light fixture. "Now I can get a good look at you."

Amy delivered the water, then peered intently into the cabinets; she had already opened closets and inspected shelves. She was registering potential improvements—wedges under rickety table legs, hooks on the back of doors. Her silent inquisition made Sunil nervous that they appeared ungrateful, but she would say such inspection was their right. She was also a snoop, though she wouldn't admit it. Such eagle eyes had discovered, the first night she spent in Sunil's apartment, a birthday card from two girlfriends ago. She'd brought it to him with sly pride, like a cat delivering a bird.

As the woman looked Sunil full in the face, his hopes began to sink. He prepared himself for some good old Boston Brahmin racism. And sure enough, she said, "What are you?"

Here it was. The white person's arrogant insistence on knowing not who or where but simply *what*, as if he were a mineral or some other piece of ground.

"Indian," he said flatly. He didn't bother saying he was born and grew up in Ohio and didn't know his parents' language well enough to understand it, much less speak it. No one ever cared about that.

But the woman surprised him by nodding approvingly. "Some day all the babies will be brown, long after I'm gone. Café au lait."

Standing near the table, girlfriend at his side, Sunil was overcome with longing to sit in this room together in the mornings: reading, typing, drafting their joint lives. He held his breath as Amy slipped off the cap that made her look like a boy and gripped it in her hands behind her back.

"We love it," Amy said. "When can we move in?"

Sunil exhaled. He had worried Amy would shy away from saying what she felt. She was not timid, and if she was feeling scrutinized or defensive, she'd order enough food for an elephant, or shout at a stranger who'd jostled her. She'd told him this came from being small all her life; when threatened, she felt that she had to prove she could eat, kick, rage as hard as anyone. Yet sometimes, with him, if she sensed that he felt strongly, she pretended her own desires didn't matter in order to placate or relieve him. Sometimes her yielding did make things easier for Sunil, but more often he was frustrated by her withholding. He felt locked out. Now Amy moved closer to him. They waited for the verdict. He wondered if Amy had suspected, as he had, that his brownness might interfere. Unlike a lot of white girls in the Midwest, Amy had known him to be Indian right away, having grown up in a DC enclave packed with foreigners and immigrants. What she never fully fathomed was his distance from his family, and their so-called culture. She'd been saying for more than a year that she wanted to meet his parents. But he hadn't seen his parents in longer than that.

"A week should give us all enough time," the woman said.

Sunil swallowed his astonishment and smiled widely. "Thank you."

"This is such good news!" Amy bounced on her toes and gave the woman a quick squeeze. Hugging strangers was a behavior he would never understand.

Then their new landlady said, "Of course, you're married? Stability, that's the main thing in life."

As she said this, Sunil realized he'd been thinking it.

But what could they reasonably say? He threaded his hand behind Amy's back and felt her fingers—lively, anticipating—

respond. Then she surprised him. She slipped her small opal ring, a college graduation gift from her parents, from her right ring finger to her left.

"Engaged," she said, bringing her hand—thin, bright, trembling—into the light to be inspected.

Here was action, here was *progress*.

They tumbled to their seats inside the Nepalese restaurant, one of their favorite places. Sunil sucked on ice cubes from his water glass, and Amy crunched happily on papadum. "What do you think?" she said.

"Don't you want to?" he said.

"Of course. It makes sense. I love you. We've been together three years. But I wasn't sure. Do you think she would have rented to us anyway? As we were?"

He shook his head. "No one asks about marriage if they don't want the answer to be yes."

Amy looked at him closely. "What's wrong?"

"Marriage is scary, isn't it?"

"Why?"

"I'm just thinking about my parents. When one of them is strong, the other becomes weak. It's an awful way to be." How did couples keep their individual dignity? "We can't let our marriage be about power."

The waiter brought clean white bowls of soupy yellow dal. Sunil lifted the bowl straight to his lips while Amy blew on a spoonful.

"No, we'll be equally committed," she said. "Like inmates." Her hair mussed, her cheeks wide and lit from within. A light scrim of salt lined her temple; he leaned in and lightly licked it off.

He said, "You know, a real wedding, a big one, would be impossible given our families. Your parents wanting kosher, mine wanting their five hundred closest friends from Nairobi, London, Columbus . . ."

"Maybe a five-year anniversary party," she said. Then, after a long pause, "Actually, I think I don't want my parents at our wedding."

"Really?" He was shocked.

"They're too crazy right now." A few years ago, Amy's parents had undergone a radical and confusing conversion to Orthodoxy. Her father had been a business journalist at the *Post*, but started to crave a more consequential life. Her mother had been a free-lance architecture critic, which she decided was a vacuous profession. So they secured jobs at Elie Weisel's *Moment*, where the people around them were living the kind of exceptional, purposeful, selfless lives the Kauffmans sought to emulate. The path to such worthy lives, they came to believe, was the Torah.

Their conversion had happened quickly, during Amy's last few months of college. "I broke out into hives," she'd admitted to Sunil early in their relationship. "I was afraid of losing them to a relentless fundamentalism. So I treated them like fifteen-year-old anarchists who were going through a phase."

Sunil always had admired Amy's toughness, even though he suspected that bottling up her confusion and frustration wasn't good for her in the long run.

"Are you sure?" He hated how even low-level arguments with her parents knocked Amy off her even keel for a day or two, but he had also seen that there was long-standing love between all of them. A resilient, enduring love that Sunil envied.

"Yes. They're in Israel now anyway, and I don't want to wait."

Together, silently, he and Amy watched the young sons of the restaurant owners slide into the back booth. The boys' father sat down heavily next to his children and gestured to the worn schoolbooks on the table. For years, when he was a child,

Sunil had wanted a brother badly.

"Still, I do need to finally meet *your* parents," Amy said. "It's time, and it's only fair."

"Fair to whom?"

Amy raised her eyebrows, which lifted the boyish cap off her ears. "Don't you think I need to know what I'm getting myself into? I've given you a full disclosure."

Sunil groaned. "That's exactly what I don't want."

He believed that Amy could handle his mother's abrasiveness and his father's unsettling quiet. What worried him was what dark behavior Amy would suddenly see in *him* when they were all in the same room.

Sunil tried to push these thoughts away. He looked at Amy across the shiny Formica table, and saw the future. Of course she would meet his parents, but they would marry without either the Kauffmans or the Chandarias present. He ripped a naan in two and gave her the larger half. She ate greedily, and demanded another from his hand.

The next morning, Sunil woke singing one of his blurry, half-awake love songs: *Amy is my cuckoo clock, and I love my cuckoo.*

The coffee was already started when Amy emerged from the bedroom and slipped down the stairs barefoot, in short shorts and sleeper T, to get the *Globe*. Sunil wove into his song her grumpy expression and slept-in hair, her nose reddened from the morning cool.

Amy read every square of the front page, then the travel section. Over yogurt and granola, she mockingly read aloud the last paragraph of the pro-Bush op-ed. Some conservative was arguing that Dubya had significant foreign policy experience because Texas was a border state. A few minutes later, Sunil left to work in Widener, leaving her the kitchen table, the only available workspace in the apartment. Amy—who ran and biked and swam in all the public health charity athletic events (good health, good networking)—always, irritatingly, urged him to walk to the library because he didn't get enough fresh air and exercise.

An hour later, Sunil was back on his street; he'd forgotten a book. From outside their apartment door, Sunil heard Amy on the phone, "He works so *slowly*—I'm not even sure what he does all day at the library. How could he not have made any progress in six months—maybe more?"

More. It was more. But she didn't know that.

He pushed open the warped door. Amy was sprawled on the floor, phone to her ear. He fetched the book and waited until she was done. "Who were you talking to?"

"Monica," she said. "I realized I couldn't get married without my sister, so I called to invite her."

"Don't change the subject."

"I'm sorry, love. I didn't mean for you to overhear that. I just feel like I can't ask you what's going on because you're so stressed out. But I should've just talked to you."

"And said what?" He pressed his heels into the cracked floorboards until his toes tingled.

"That you seem to be reading endlessly to keep from writing."

"You know what I'm doing is really hard, right? Coming up with something new to say after two thousand years of analytic philosophy. It's not like we have new data to work with, like in medicine. Philosophers have to think up something new using the same evidence we've always had." He winced as he heard himself speak, adding "analytic" like an ass.

Data, in fact, was a point of contention between them. For Amy, "I looked it up," was a favorite, argument-ending phrase. Like her journalist parents, Amy believed most answers were out there in the world to be discovered. Like he *used* to think about moral truths.

"I know it's really hard, but if you just keep at it, the writing, the words will come." She paused. "I wish you had a course to teach. Teaching was so good for you."

It had been. Sunil's scholarship, earmarked for minorities, did not allow him to teach, unlike almost everyone else at Harvard, who'd been TFs, teaching fellows. But last fall he had begged Bernardston, the department chair, to let him do so for just one semester. Bill James, Sunil's adviser, had strongly discouraged the idea: Sunil needed to devote all his time to his dissertation; teaching was a distraction. But Sunil had persisted. And Lieberman, who could be credited with planting the seed of his dissertation, had supported him; she agreed it would be good for Sunil to explain material to students, and to know if at least the teaching part of the academic enterprise was something that he could be good at.

Bernardston could not bend the rules of his scholarship, but he had offered Sunil a chance to sub for him while he was off at Oxford giving a series of lectures. It would be the most difficult of any teaching situation, at mid-semester, but Sunil had immediately accepted.

The morning he was to lead the class, Sunil threw up his breakfast. His hands shook. Bernardston normally wore jeans and a sport coat to class. Sunil didn't own a jacket, so he wore his nicest button-down. At some point halfway through, he realized his shirt was misbuttoned, one side dragging lower than the other. Heat flushed through his entire body, but he forced himself to think *It could be worse* and kept going.

He discovered that it was easy for him to create simple, stark paradoxes for his students. He could make them understand why personal identity was not a simple matter of a singular brain yoked to a singular body. What if brain and body were cloned, was You2 still *you*? What about memories? If I don't remember what happened yesterday, is that yesterday-person me? Students had arrived in the classroom with low visors, droopy eyes, yet he had been able to induce many of them to *think* for fifty minutes. There were awful moments of demoralizing, vacuum-packed silence, but by the end of the class, his prodding had yielded results. Hands in the air!

At the end of the semester, Bernardston had called Sunil in to his office. "I have to say you've set up something of a problem for me. Because of the class you taught, now my students are asking for more discussion."

"So, they got something out of it?"

"I don't know, but they liked it." Bernardston smiled.

Now Amy said to Sunil, "When you sit down to write, can you pretend that you're teaching someone? Could that be a way to reboot?"

"I don't know," he said. "But it's a good idea." He kissed her on the cheek, and headed back to campus.

Later that day, Sunil sat in on an ethics seminar. It was taught by the abrupt but persuasive Rivka Lieberman. Sunil had taken this same seminar two years ago, during Lieberman's first year with the department, and the questions it raised had burrowed inside him. Sunil had felt mentally sharper during that class than any other time. Philosophy became urgent.

It had started with J. L. Mackie, an Australian ethicist writing in the 1970s. Mackie asked why there was such variation in moral beliefs among different cultures. Why, for example, did some cultures believe in monogamy and others polygamy? It couldn't be, Mackie argued, that one culture simply had a better ability to grasp moral truths than another. It didn't make sense that one culture would be somehow more attuned to what was good and what was bad. This had led Mackie to argue for an antirealist view: the view that moral truths did not exist independently of our beliefs about them. That is, certain actions, practices, and desires were valuable only because humans *thought* them so: monogamy was good because humans valued the practice, not because it was objectively the right way to live. Sunil had thought Mackie's reasoning valid, but he was bothered by the premise. Sunil didn't see such wide variation in moral beliefs. He instead saw strong uniformity and thought that the differences philosophers pointed to were superficial. Didn't the uniformity mean we were all attuned to the same moral reality? The human burden was to acknowledge and follow moral scripts.

But then, one day in her office, Lieberman had challenged Sunil. She asked, "If, as you say, there are widely shared moral beliefs, what's the origin story that explains them?"

It was a good question. For several moments he sat in silence. The tick-tock feeling of his college pre-med classes crept up on him. That unbearable scrambling for the answer. And then, for the first time, one of these courses came to his aid—his class on evolutionary biology, and Robert Trivers's paper "The Evolution of Reciprocal Altruism." Trivers argued that reciprocal altruism—"I'll scratch your back if you scratch mine"—was not simply a human social nicety but necessary to facilitating the survival of the species. Sunil realized that if evolution could account for this kind of behavior, then evolution could also be responsible for the universality of moral principles. He explained this thought to Lieberman, concluding, "Just as the human species has developed ears because hearing is evolutionarily advantageous, in that it promotes survival, humans have developed certain moral judgments that advance the gene pool."

"Good. Now forget about Mackie, and start at the beginning," Lieberman said. "Tell me the problem without jargon."

Sunil took a deep breath. "Okay. So, Mackie aside, let's take the standard example of torturing little babies for fun. Most of us don't think it's wrong because our society *thinks* that it is wrong; rather, we believe that torturing babies for fun is wrong because it *really is* wrong, that it would be wrong *even if we never thought about it*. So we act as though we have moral antennae that can detect what's right and what's wrong. In abstract terms, we believe that our moral judgments are about a moral reality that is independent of us, not a reality that is created by us."

She nodded. Sunil continued. "However, we also believe in evolution, which means we believe evolutionary forces have had a big role in shaping our moral judgments. If evolution had gone differently, and the world itself were different, if we were, say, *shumans* instead of humans, our moral beliefs would be different. If torture actually made babies stronger, maybe shumans would think it's okay to torture them for fun."

Lieberman waited for Sunil to bring the two points together.

"But once we realize that our moral beliefs are shaped by evolution, we can't trust that they're correct. Because evolution only cares about what's reproductively advantageous. Evolution doesn't care about the rightness or wrongness of torturing little babies; if torture gave us a survival advantage, as absurd as that sounds, evolution would be okay with that."

"Can you give me an analogy?" Lieberman leaned back in her chair, balancing precariously on its hind legs.

Sunil looked out the window, listened to the traffic noise. He briefly recalled a scene he'd witnessed on his walk to campus—an older woman, exasperated, leaning over the open, steaming hood of her car. "I've got it. It's like Evolution is a used-car salesman. He says to you, 'Hey, come drive this efficient, eco-friendly car'—what we'd consider a *good* car—when really he doesn't care if the car is good, or if it's a total lemon. He's just out to make a buck. He's not necessarily sleazy, he just doesn't care one way or another. The end result is all that matters. When you realize this, you distrust everything the salesman has told you. You can't trust him to have provided you with a good car. So in the case of evolution, evolution is concerned with perpetuating life itself, and this may or may not provide an accurate guide to moral truths."

Sunil paused. Too casual? Had he lost her with the used-car salesman?

Landing her chair on all four legs, Lieberman said, "So your point is that your moral beliefs start to unravel when you realize their source is not guided by the truth." She paused and looked at him directly. "At the metaphorical level, what you say makes sense. So now you need to put it in concrete terms."

These terms were what Sunil had been working on the past two years. At first, as he continued to push back against Mackie's premise, he believed he was defending moral realism. It was therefore a great and terrible irony that Sunil discovered that his view about evolutionary pressures on moral beliefs led him to the conclusion that moral truths do *not* exist. Or at least that we have no idea if they do or not. This skeptical implication had destabilized Sunil's project, so much so that his writing had stalled.

He was now revisiting Lieberman's course in the hope that Mackie, or someone, would get him going again. Lieberman was not on his dissertation committee, of which Bill James was chair, but, having helped him shape his project, one she had suggested was uniquely promising, she claimed to be invested in the outcome. She periodically checked in with him. But the spring semester was now three-quarters over, and Sunil had nothing but his verbal contributions to her class to show for it. After a promising prospectus, his dissertation had flatlined.

After class, Sunil found Lieberman waiting for him outside the seminar room. Animated, pushing her hair back to show dark brows and a fine, straight nose, she said, "Sunil. Stop and talk to me. What is the problem."

She was so unnerving. It was disorienting the way she asked questions without the question mark. The way she asked also made Sunil suspect the faculty were talking about him, which rattled him further.

"I don't know what you mean."

"You stopped talking in class. You think I wouldn't notice? First eight, nine weeks you're jumping in and objecting, you have the books in your hand, I see the marks. But then, the last two weeks, since the readings on antirealism, you don't say anything and I think that I have made it unbelievably boring."

"I've taken this class before," he reminded her. He wanted to tell her that he always learned from her, but something made him hold back. He squirmed under her gaze. She was large-boned and large-breasted, with wide hips and a flushed neck that embarrassed him.

Then he surprised himself by saying something revealing, setting free the worry on the tip of his tongue. "It's just that this view is messing with my head. It's making me doubt some pretty fundamental things—like whether we're justified in holding people accountable for their actions."

Lieberman nodded. "You're terrified. The skeptical worry is taking over your life."

"Yes." He realized how much he wanted to impress her, to prove correct her faith in him.

"This is normal," she said, then tilted her head to look at him quizzically. "Do you believe our philosophical views should guide our lives?"

"Yes, sometimes." His stomach began to turn.

"Then you should prepare for a revolution, my friend. Perhaps for anarchy." She was teasing, in her unfunny, Israeli way. She smiled like a wolf.

Sunil was convinced that evolution provided a cohesive universal story about how humans came to share a set of moral principles, but the conclusions were dark and left him feeling alienated, unmoored, and nauseous. He was not ready for revolt.

He should take this opportunity to talk with Lieberman. Because the anxieties about his project seemed only to be relieved by airing them in conversation. Not by working alone and writing. Writing was supposed to be cathartic, as he believed it was for his closest friends, his professors, and probably for everyone else writing philosophy everywhere. His friend Erik was even writing in his second language, Norwegian being his first. But writing was not cathartic or clarifying for Sunil. It was hard and horrifying. Words on paper were non-negotiable; they had to be absolutely sure of themselves. Which his were not.

But now, instead of inviting him into her office, she said, "When you are ready, let me know."

He nodded.

Then she added quickly, "Your passion is inspiring," and turned and walked away.

Earlier in the semester, she had stopped him in the hall to tell him she'd been thinking about something he had said, and the intoxicating pride and excitement had carried him for hours. Now her abrupt goodbye left him standing alone, useless.

He had to get out of here. Sunil hurried down the hall toward the common room, where Andrew was waiting. Halfway there, Sunil passed James. Sunil waved and smiled; he was meeting with his adviser tomorrow. But James walked right past him. Of course he did.

Sunil panicked. The combined punches of Lieberman turning her back and James's snub skyrocketed his insecurity. He had to fetch Andrew, but Sunil couldn't bear the nervous energy of the other grad students. The hall smelled of photocopy paper, microwaved soup, and steamy anxiety. Sunil barged into the buzzing common room and signaled urgently for Andrew to leave as quickly as possible.

"James is kind of blind, right? Those thick glasses," he said as they walked out and away from Emerson Hall.

Andrew shouldered a smooth leather bag and wound a scarf around his milk-white neck. "Sure, the guy is old. He sits in the front row at talks and still cups his hands behind his ears. Why?"

"He just walked right by me."

"Well, he must hate you."

The cold air struck Sunil in the face. He bent his head and the wind knifed his scalp. Amy was always reminding him to bring a hat, and Sunil was always forgetting. Andrew and Sunil were in the same cohort, but Andrew had an adviser who thought he was smart. He was nearly done with his dissertation and didn't seem to have struggled writing it. He was not who Sunil wanted for company right now.

Daily, Sunil saw examples of what he'd turn into if he didn't finish his dissertation. They were the slight, ghostly figures of the Double-Ds. Harvard was notorious for letting people continue for ten or eleven years. One guy had entered the program in 1985, fifteen years ago. Another had bragged to him that he was able to live on two dollars a day, which Sunil disbelieved until he saw the man picking through trash cans. Sunil and his friends mocked the Double-D grad students behind their backs. Yet at the same time, Sunil and Andrew and Erik were afraid of them. The older guys—and they were all guys—knew a lot, they'd read a lot, they'd been to countless talks and dissertation defenses. They knew how to argue. Sunil envied their alacrity and sharpness.

Years ago, toward the end of his sophomore year of college, Sunil had called his father from a pay phone. *I quit!* he'd yelled over the beer pong being played down the hall. He'd enrolled in the pre-med track (where he'd studied evolutionary biology) to please his dad, but he had hated the classes, found them stultifying and difficult. To be a doctor, he'd discovered, you had to have many webs of detailed knowledge at your fingertips. You had to render a response in seconds. Sunil had not been able to summon whole biological processes at once, was minutes behind his classmates in arriving at an answer. Everything was so damn fast, and it made him feel trapped and stupid. He had grown to hate the word *answer*, the word *evidence*. He instead felt compelled by philosophical inquiry, one in which our most fundamental impulses and assumptions were questioned and explored. In which *progress* meant intellectual discovery, rather than a body of knowledge learned, or even a life saved.

Rosie's was strewn with peanut shells and smelled sour, but there were free pretzels and three-dollar pitchers before four. Their beer arrived with mozzarella sticks, courtesy of their waitress, a mousy undergrad. Sunil wasn't hungry, but he ate. It was his mother's ingrained injunction: food wasn't worth eating when it cooled past piping. He swallowed roughly as the cheese sticks scratched his throat.

"Forget it," Andrew said, picking up their earlier conversation. "James doesn't snub. He might not like people all that much—and by 'people' I mean everyone—but he wouldn't do something to make you—and by 'you' I mean anyone—feel bad."

Andrew's face could change from sincere to mocking in a flash. Now he was sincere—eyebrows hiked up, mouth in a wide, soft line. The luxurious confidence that came from growing up rich. Yet Andrew deserved every academic award he received. It was right that his friend would progress and Sunil would stagnate. Sunil sweated into his shirt, the nice white one he'd worn out of respect for his seminar, for Lieberman. She had once commented approvingly on his dressing up for class. She'd then complained that as a woman who had to garner respect, she felt compelled—at least until she got tenure—to wear suit jackets, which she hated. Sunil had never before thought about how women needed to dress better than the men, several of whom taught in T-shirts.

"Today I ran into Double-D 36," Andrew said. They'd discovered Doug Berman's age by grossly flattering the department secretary. "He was pulling hard-boiled eggs out of his pocket and peeling them—*eating* them—on the street." His face turned gleeful. He patted Sunil on the shoulder. "Don't worry, I won't let that happen to you."

"At least poke your head into my cardboard box, check my pulse." Sunil drank his beer, shifted in the hard wooden booth. Then he announced, "Amy and I are getting married." It was the first time he'd said it out loud, put those striking words together in a sentence. But he didn't get the charge from them he'd expected. He still felt awkward, nervous.

"Hey! That's some good news! What did her parents say?"

Andrew had been the one to point Amy out in the café where they met. Blond, petite, color in her cheeks and forehead. Playful. In the thick of a spirited game of timed Scrabble with her roommate. She was five years younger than Sunil, but driven, ambitious, certain. When he was her age, he'd been flat, directionless. Amy's dreams had shape and promise.

"She doesn't want to invite her parents to the wedding. She's worried a civil ceremony would only offend them, so we're not going to tell them until it's done. It's the first major decision she's ever made without her parents."

"Won't that be worse? Them finding out after the fact?"

Sunil nodded. "Probably. Especially because she wants her sister to be there. Which means her parents will feel even more slighted. It's just conflict avoidance. Amy hates fighting with her parents. Their conversion made her angry, but she doesn't want to show it because she's worried it will put more distance between them."

"It sounds like disagreements with the Kauffmans are inevitable," Andrew said. "I'm thinking of that 'anti-God' conversation you told me about."

"Exactly," Sunil said.

The Kauffmans liked Sunil—Ariel affectionately called him "duckling" because of his boyish face and out-turned toes—but he wasn't a Jew, and they were skeptical of his moral compass. During a bitter spell this past winter, over a meal at Legal Seafood, Ariel had said to Sunil, "I know you are an ethicist, this is what you study. But what do you *believe*? I've read that Jains aspire to 'the three jewels': right belief, right knowledge, and right conduct. But you say you're not an observant Jain."

Sunil had told her that he did not believe in transcendental codes—laws that came from a divine power. "So you're both anti-God *and* amoral," Ariel said. "Because morality comes from God's commandments."

Sunil had responded, gently, that he could not be against something that didn't exist. And before he could address the charge of amorality, Amy had exclaimed, "Mom, how can you say that!" The meal had ended with a no-hard-feelings sharing of crème brûlée, but Sunil was left with a worrisome taste in his mouth. He didn't know whether the Kauffmans had felt the same.

Sunil slowly shook his head. He said to Andrew, "I have no idea how this is all going to go down."

"Well, they are out of the country, right? Aren't yours, too?"

"They left for Nairobi a couple days ago. They'll be gone for two weeks."

"Maybe that's your excuse?"

Sunil sighed. "Not one that holds much water."

Walking home from the bar, having reached the bottom of the

pitcher and the end of happy hour, Sunil felt a clammy tight-
ness in his chest. He was starting to fret about money, about his
ability to succeed at what he'd set out to do. Why couldn't he
be calm and focused like his father, who every morning ate the
same bran cereal with applesauce. Who woke and went to sleep,
taking all that came his way, with the same mild expression on
his face. Premchand could go days without even talking, leaving the house early on weekend mornings without telling them
where he was going or when he'd be back. This mute stoicism
had made Sunil worry that his father was so unhappy he'd leave
them, and because of this, he had hated his father's absences.
But most of all he had resented being left alone with the livid,
changeful emotions of his mother, who had ruled their world
and made Sunil feel powerless. He knew he was hard on his
mother, but she had been hard on him. He couldn't quite summon the same anger for his father, whose reasons for leaving
the house Sunil had always understood. And despite his father
being gone a lot, Sunil couldn't help but admire his steadiness,
as well as his dedication to his profession, to work that he found
fascinating.

Sunil remembered the day he'd been admitted to Pick
Academy. He had not been a good student, but Pick needed
pleasant brown faces for their catalogs, and he'd been elated to
leave public school, where he was trailed by kids who tapped
their mouths to make *ow-ow-ow* sounds.

Private school had been his father's idea, and his father had
helped him with the application. But his mother had also come
to the admissions interview and asked if they could they pull
Sunil out and get their money back if the teachers were not
able to improve him very much, if they were unable to provide
the structure needed to guide a lazy boy's mind. When his father
insisted that it was worth paying money for good teachers and a
better quality of classmate, she'd exploded. Why didn't he care

as much about her, and her happiness, as he did about their god-forsaken, do-nothing son? Sunil had just turned ten.

Sunil didn't remember, did not in fact know, the exact phrase she'd used, but it was a curse worse than *buckwass*, worse than *benchod*, which he'd been slapped once for mindlessly repeating.

He knew now that his mother had been cursing out his father, not him. When he'd brought it up, years later, she'd been embarrassed. But when his father's car had pulled out of the driveway after that fight, headlights sweeping across his bedroom window, Sunil had felt as though the whole neighborhood had tuned in to the immigrant family who could not get along.

Sunil had finally escaped to college, but still he shouldered a collection of injuries and insults, a clumsy sack of brittle sticks. He had not known how to exist in the world as a steady person who could carry his own load with eyes ahead and an even step. Who could appreciate and love other people and be entirely loved in return.

As an adult, he could not simply hurl his sticks at whatever threatened him. He had to use reason. And to unfurl the empathy he'd kept tightly pressed to his chest.

Over the past year, Sunil had made numerous attempts to cast his worries aside and tackle his dissertation. But every time he tried to articulate his argument, several serious objections reared their heads, and Sunil abandoned what he'd begun. Sunil possessed his mother's ferocity, but he lacked his father's sureness and discipline. At every stop he felt his weaknesses, his lack of entitlement to the elite position he now occupied.

In the apartment, he found Amy in yoga clothes, surrounded by boxes. Her hair was pinned up in a ridiculous mess, fine hairs falling loose as she danced to Janet Jackson on a small travel radio. She flipped her elbows and knees out and in like the Tin Man in a chorus line. Breasts compacted by a sports bra, thighs and butt bopping to the beat, her whole glistening body unself-conscious and exuberant.

"Hey, crazy hair," he said. He looked around at the taped-up cells of their lives. She'd packed most of their clothes, plus her books and photo albums. His books lay scattered around the apartment still, as well as a few old pairs of shoes, not yet worn enough to discard. The one thing they'd bought together, the toaster oven, was still on the counter.

"I'm going to need these cool moves in our new apartment, don't you think?" she said. "I'm so happy we're moving."

"I can tell. You must really hate this place."

"Loathe it. Abhor it. Execrate it."

The rusty water that sometimes emerged from the taps gave Amy's hair a brownish sheen, and two of the four burners on the stove had been broken for a year.

Amy turned the radio off and said, "I'm starving. What did you bring us?"

With just three days left in this warped and worn place, they'd stopped buying groceries. Sunil remembered he was supposed to pick up sandwiches on his walk home from campus.

"Shit, I'm sorry. I spaced. I'll go back out."

"You forgot our dinner?" While she had been home packing. She growled. "Don't bother. I'm too hungry." She opened the freezer and pulled out a carton of ice cream, which they ate with sliced bananas and salted nut mix. Amy served herself more than she could possibly eat—nearly the whole half-gallon—to show how put out she was by his forgetfulness.

Sunil started to tell her what he'd been thinking about on the way home, but she cut him off. "No," she said, "you don't get to forget dinner, then hijack the conversation."

"You're right," he said. "Tell me about your day."

Today her project model for addressing multidrug-resistant TB had passed departmental approval. She simply needed to write up the final pages describing existing community resources. Then she listed the job applications she'd sent to public health research orgs and nonprofits all over Boston. She thought continuing TB work would be interesting, because it was localized within certain intimate populations, like prisons, but she also wanted to work with immigrant women.

"You're looking only in Boston?"

"Are you trying to get rid of me? We're engaged, remember?"

He smiled. "I remember. I just don't want you to limit yourself. You always said you wanted to work at the NIH." Amy's grandmother had been a biologist and was one of the first women to head up her own research team in the forties, during the war. He did not know how he could live alone, without Amy, but she was too young to restrict her options.

"Someday," she said.

But it bothered him that she refused to own up to her own ambitions. It didn't make her desires less real, just less transparent.

After dinner, Sunil washed and dried their bowls and spoons, and they sat on the couch, looking at the room, empty except for the TV—the NBA playoffs had started. Amy lifted her feet into his lap. He was tired and bloated from the ice cream, but she wiggled her toes insistently.

"Do you think being married will change anything?" she said.

"I won't love you any less," he said. "Plus I'll get to call you the old ball-and-chain."

"What am I supposed to call you? The ball-peen hammer? The Phillips head?"

"I don't even know what those things are."

"I know. That's why it's funny. How about 'the old rusty pitchfork?' Or just 'the tool'?" She was quiet for a moment, then she said, "I suppose we are following a long, proud line of prac-ticality. My parents married because my mom was pregnant. Your parents' marriage was arranged. We're doing it for a good deal on an apartment." She said this breezily, happily, then closed her eyes to enjoy the pressure of his thumbs on her feet.

"We're *not* like them," he said. "Neither of them. Why would you say that?"

"Say what?" She opened her eyes.

"Draw our parents into this. You really think their exam-ples are that relevant?" The thought terrified him.

"Of course they are. You know they are."

"But their values, their wants, what makes them happy or unhappy—we don't have to deal with any of it. We can start fresh. That part is really important. We don't have to take their baggage with us."

She withdrew her feet from his lap and placed them firmly on the floor.

He wished he hadn't raised his voice. He thought of how his father turned his head and showed his profile when taking on his mother's fury, and her own rapid headshaking when she was overcome.

"We're not. I'm the one who said I didn't want my parents at our wedding," Amy said. "But we can't erase our upbring-ing. Our parents are the closest examples of real marriages we have."

Sunil sighed. "Yes, of course, I just don't want to be like them. They don't, they aren't—" He couldn't finish.

"Listen, love. Whether your parents love you or love you enough is not the only fact about them. It's impossible for our parents to be irrelevant. What matters is how we deal with them."

He was silent for a moment. "I agree with you. Maybe I'm just trying to prepare you. I don't think you've met anyone like my mother. She is deaf to me—so unbending. And she can be mean, explosive. She's not going to accept you easily."

Amy nodded, as if trying to ready herself. "Even so, we're the children. We're the ones who have to imagine, and believe in, good outcomes," she said quietly. "As much for us as for them. C'mon, philosophers excel at thought experiments."

"So we say." He leaned in, embraced her. Inhaled her. Did not let go.

Yet Sunil still felt that Amy didn't understand how important it was for the two of them to be unconstrained, to be able to love without holding on to the obligations of their parents.

Yes, he had his idealism—he would prefer to call it having *standards*—and perhaps that tainted his view of his childhood. This idealism sometimes gave rise to self-righteous anger. But didn't anger make him good at philosophy? Isn't that what Lieberman meant by his *passion*? He had ideas, good ones. He wanted to think about these things for the rest of his life; he wanted to teach, to make progress. There were good people on his side. He would not let them down.

Amy said she had reading to do, and went into the bedroom. Sunil turned on the TV and watched the end of the Lakers game.

Three minutes left in the fourth quarter, the Lakers were down by eight. Sunil leaned in, sensing a momentum change. Something was about to happen. Then Kobe rolled off a pick, received a pass, shook his defender with a crossover dribble à la Tim Hardaway, and shot from downtown with a hand so close to his face he could've licked it. Twenty seconds later, Kobe scored again. Sunil swore happily and muttered the triple double, *25-10-11*. Commercial break.

The phone rang, and Amy padded to the kitchen to answer it.

She appeared in front of him with wide eyes, covering the receiver with her palm. "Your mother."

He grabbed the phone and jumped around Amy to see the resumed play. "Mom? Are you all right?"

"There was an accident," she said. Her voice was thinner than he remembered. He hoped it was a bad connection.

"You? Is Dad all right? What happened?" He gestured for Amy to turn off the TV.

"Yes, yes, fine, fine. It's your brother."

"Slow down. Who? You know I never understand that cousin-brother stuff."

"Bimal, he has been in a terrible car accident." She started to cry. Noisy, heavy sounds. So loud that Amy stepped closer, but Sunil held up his palm.

"Is it serious? Is Dad there?" He'd get better information from his father. He wished his father had been the one to call.

"No."

"Dad isn't there?"

"I want you to come here," she said. "I will buy you the ticket."

Sunil sat, stunned.

Amy watched him, tentative.

"Mom, I'm really sorry, but I can't just go to Nairobi. I have a lot of work here. Bimal's going to be okay, isn't he? He's conscious and everything?" Bimal was the cousin closest to him in age, and the one Sunil knew best, but they hadn't seen each other since they were young teenagers. Sunil pictured a skinny, shirtless boy on the beach waving to a low-flying plane.

"That is what they are saying."

"What? What are they saying?"

"That he needs to stay in hospital for a while, but he will survive. Please, please come."

His mother never begged. She demanded, she threatened, she guilt-tripped, but she had never said *please, please*. She was crying harder. Amy was moving her hands and mouth, but he couldn't read her. Was she saying to accept? Or just to take a deep breath?

He took a deep breath. "If I go there," he began, "Amy has to come too."

"What's this, your girlfriend is not family. This is serious!"

He tried again, but his voice was overrun by a barrage of sobs mixed with words that he couldn't understand.

His eyes on Amy, he said, "Mom. Listen to me. Amy is not just my girlfriend. She's my wife."

This silenced her, for a moment. "Liar," she said.

"No," he said softly. "I'm telling you the truth. We got married. I just haven't been able to tell you before now."

"Why do you insult us? You think we are just some after-the-fact thoughts?"

Sunil wound the phone cord around his wrist. "You're the first person we've told. It just happened."

"—anything you want, and we were so proud . . . and Harvard . . . but we are your parents! Heartless, just like your father. No one in our community has ever done such a thing."

"I find that hard to believe."

"True!"

"Can I talk to Dad?"

"No."

"Then let me talk to Sarada Aunty."

"Everything is my fault, chho? You think I have caused this accident? No. It was fate. Now you listen to me. I am going to tell you something." There was a strange pause. "Bimal is your brother."

"Mom! Don't say stuff like that just to get me to come. I'm really sorry about Bimal's accident, but he's going to be all right. And I haven't seen him in fifteen years."

"I am talking about brother-brother, blood brother!"

Was the shock making her confused? He walked into the kitchen and back to where Amy lay on the floor doing anxiety sit-ups. She stopped and looked at him for explanations.

"I am telling you, Bimal is your one hundred percent brother. Born before you, in Kenya. It was a bad time. We gave him to your uncle. We thought it was the right thing, but you—*you*." She swallowed what came next, but Sunil was sure he heard the word *mistake*.

"What are you talking about? You said you only ever wanted one kid. You always said that's why I am your only child!"

"No," she said gravely. "You are not my only child. I have two children. Two sons."

Sunil gripped the phone with two hands. "You lied to me? For thirty years?"

"Yes, I lied to you. I had to lie. If you come to Nairobi, come home to us, I will explain. I will tell you everything."

Then his mother was gone. Sunil stared. He shivered. He reached for Amy, who embraced him with both arms.

"What's going on?" she asked. "Who is Bimal? Why did you tell her we were married?"

"Because we will be." He pulled her down with him until he felt her warm breath on his neck, and the weight of her pressed against his quavering heart. "And then we'll go to Nairobi."

4.

Every night, under open sky, lions invaded their camps. Lions with an appetite for human flesh prowled around the Commiphora with snapping jaws and vicious claws. They snuck up on the sleeping men so fast—like *that!*—the jaws unhinged. Eaten to death. Crunchy bone and bloody tongue.

They called those lions *Ghost* and *Darkness*. Because the men did not believe they were animals. The lions were demons wearing fur. Ghost and Darkness could not be killed. The Englishmen tried with their rifles, but the demons always escaped. When a man was taken, ripped from his tent, dragged from the infirmary or a railway car, there was a debate: Who was the murderer? Ghost left tooth marks in the skull. Darkness ate the belly and left the head alone.

This was in Tsavo, one hundred miles upcountry. The name is infamous now.

My father arrived from Jamnagar in 1898. He was recruited by a firm promising a better life, and he was one of the "free" Indians, unrestricted by the government. Left to accept whatever deal he could find. He was an adventurer. He was truly desperate, okay? Not many of our Jain people were coming to Africa then. Mostly he worked with Punjabis, some Sikhs, many Muslims.

The men working the rail line were sick all the time: malaria, scurvy, jiggers hatching in their feet and hands. On any day, half the men were laid out flat. When the water is strained from mud, what can you do? It is a miracle anyone survived.

Maybe you have heard of one of the heroes of that time, Pir Baghali? This man ran so fast he could catch a peacock and was so pious and kind he could put a python to sleep. He spoke the language of animals, and his powers kept his people safe from the lions. They even said his kerai full of sand and cement floated a few inches above his head. When he died, they made a monument to him—now it is a mosque, I think—near Mackinnon Road, on the rail between Mombasa and Nairobi. The trains slow down and whistle when they pass.

Fear kept the men awake, but it also brought them together. On the dhows, the men had shared their nightmares—of crashing stars, drowning, giant jellyfish. Here, on the plains, in the *nyika*, they stayed awake and vigilant at night by telling stories, the stories of Shiva and Parvati and Ganesh. (After all, here they were, surrounded by elephants.) My father told of the Tirthankaras, who conquered the cycles of birth and death. Around their fear, they wound words like bandages.

Those who survived the night were so relieved in the morning that they broke into sudden, insane laughter. They joked about the lions choking on their turbans before finding a soft, juicy bite. And the killings were not all bad. Some were merciful. When the men taken were so weak they wouldn't have lasted two more days. What did the sahibs care about the workers? There were so many more to fill the place of the dead. Every week, more Indians arrived. The sahibs were always calling for more carpenters, more blacksmiths, more dirt diggers.

On the nights the lions took one or two or three of the men away forever, my father prayed so hard for sunrise. All the men prayed for hammers and nails and more workers to speed the pace of the rail. To be done and finally see the waters of Lake Victoria, where they could lay down their tools. The Hindus wished for arms stronger than Shiva's, our people wished for the patience and renunciation of Mahavira, and the Muslims prayed for who knows what from their prophet—their God is a vengeful one.

Is it a surprise, then, my father was so devout? So strict. You can't understand a war against nature until you have survived. Survived in order to be born into the next life, a better one, by meditating so deeply you are dry of all karma, and perhaps you can taste just a little bit a possible end to the eternal cycles.

Yes, the lions ate whites and savages, too, but our men—the masons, track layers, water carriers—were most exposed.

The lions ate twenty-eight in all.

And yet, there is reason to be a little grateful to the lions.

Because of the killings, word of the men's courage spread back along the rails. Reached the ears of their cousin-brothers in Mombasa. Newspapers in London printed their misfortune. Members of Parliament read out gruesome accounts to the floor. Their story began to be told.

Because you know what these men did? They mutinied. Refused to work until the lions were slain. Refused to pound steel nails, shape tools, carry the earth, and even to fetch water. That is the way to get the bosses' attention!

These men never meant to stay in this country. *Who is remaining in this rotten desert-jungle?* they said. *Not me!* But first they owed their labor—there was always more steel to bind, another fishbolt to secure—and when that was done, they had no money to go home. The scouts, you see, had counted on their death. If you were "free," you were not protected, not guaranteed a return. Some five or six thousand Indians remained in this place of heat and rain and sweat, squeezed between the whites and the savages.

Now, turn that recorder off and tell your aunty to bring the two of us tea. You over there, so far away, you have some, too, and think of us.

5.

In the kitchen, Sarada pointed down the hall to where Prem-chand sat reading a newspaper. "What is going on with him? He slept all day. He isn't like this in Columbus—only here, isn't it?"

Sometimes Urmila wished her little sister did not know everything, that she hadn't confided and relied on her so much over the years. Urmila was the oldest daughter, not counting the two who died as babies, and she'd worked alongside her mother since she was four, patting flat endless rotlis, stirring dal, fry-ing samosas, washing clothes in the cast-iron pot, taking her siblings to school and cleaning up after them. Yes, her husband had fallen asleep in the waiting room of the hospital, so what? He had given her worse embarrassments. "He is the same as always," she said.

She peeled the skin of a ripe mango away from the flesh and bit in. The rush of sweetness calmed her. Juice slid down her fingers. She took in the swept tile floor, the sparkling appli-ances and stone countertops. The new gas stove. In a dim room next to the pantry, the housegirl made chapatis. Urmila drifted to the window, where watery light spread through leafy branches.

The weather had been drippy and cool since they arrived, and her room upstairs was chilly.

Where was the sun of her childhood? The baked-clay smell coming up from the earth and the sky blown with cooking smoke? Previous visits, she'd stepped off the plane and felt at home; the old rhythms had come back, settled into her arms and legs.

Urmila had felt such relief when Bimal opened his eyes after surgery, but now she could think only of his face, how it was pulpy thick, bloody and bruised. A jagged wound slashed from the corner of his mouth across his nose and eye, up to his hairline. They were taking turns watching over him.

Sarada put Urmila's plate with the mango peels and the hairy, sucked-clean pit in the sink, then looked at her, fists on her hips. "This is a tricky time for you, sister. You have to be careful not to get in the way. Tomorrow I'll take you to the Oshwal Centre."

Everyone was talking about the Centre. The beautiful building made from imported stone, the top-of-the-line sound systems, the commercial-grade kitchens. *Why doesn't Columbus have something like this?* they asked. It was so good for the community, especially the young people, keeping them away from the bars and clubs, where they drank and mixed with all kinds.

"They have some classes, a little yoga, a track for walking. It will be good for you. So you can breathe when Sunil arrives. I agree with you, bringing him here. It has been too long since we have put our eyes on him. Times of crisis, a family needs to be together."

Then Sarada handed her an onion and a towel to cover her clothes. Urmila had dressed for dinner, her emerald green sari bordered with pink. She hadn't expected to be put to work in the kitchen. Trying to keep me busy, she thought.

Urmila slipped off the skins and cut the onion in her hand, slicing the blade toward her palm.

She said to her sister, "The other day, this American woman came into the store. She wanted my advice on starting a business. Now she is dental hygienist, but she wants her own shop. She is jealous of me."

Sarada nodded and listened as she chopped potatoes.

Urmila had first met Maddy a month ago when she'd bought two pairs of sandalwood salad tongs, then last week the woman had found her at the Wok n' Roll, where Urmila liked the egg rolls. Maddy had reintroduced herself, then sat down across the table.

"You're lucky, you know," Maddy had said. "Your own business. For years I've wanted to start a greenhouse, but my husband always said it was too risky. Now we're divorced."

"Oh? So you are fighting a lot and then all of a sudden it's over? Or he cheats on you or what?" Divorce was a topic that interested Urmila.

"No cheating. We didn't do that. We married too young, grew apart, wanted different things. You know how it is."

But Urmila didn't know. She didn't know a single person who'd divorced. She'd heard of only one, the niece of a cousin-sister in London. Perhaps if she'd seen a divorce up close, she might have had the courage to get one.

Learning that Maddy's son was also in Boston, Urmila had boasted about Sunil. For a moment she had tried to imagine him at the university—how did he fit in? Did he have friends? What did they talk about in his classes? How was it possible he'd gone all the way to Harvard? She wished she had a photograph so she could carry him around, show him off, and see him in his place. What did the buildings look like? Did he have a car? She did not allow herself to think about the girl. Yes, she told Maddy. She was proud.

The way Maddy smiled at her, sweetly and with trust, had made Urmila feel her own accomplishments were unshakable.

The rest of the afternoon, she'd almost felt sorry she was leaving for two weeks. She had hesitated before locking up and taping up the sign: *Gone to Kenya on Business: New Items Upon Return!*

Urmila told all this to her sister, then said, "So, I am going to help this woman with her business plans."

"What do you know about flowers?" Sarada said.

"It is just selling, like any other."

Urmila had told Maddy, *You need something of your own. Women do.*

"Yes. Like your son and his philosophy," Maddy said. "Not everyone can do that. I don't even know what it means."

Sunil used to ask so many questions—to insanity. Unlike most boys, who pulled the wings off insects and found dinosaur bones in the yard, who asked, *Where does the rain come from? How many stars in the sky?* Sunil would dig down hard. If they were watching TV, he would ask, *Why didn't the man beat up the robber? What makes that woman keep her secret? The detective says he knows, but how can he know for sure?*

"There is another thing," Urmila said now, slowly. She had to tell someone.

Sarada's face stilled while her hands continued to peel and dice.

Her voice dropped to a whisper. "He has married an American."

Sarada's knife clattered to the counter, loudly to the floor. The housegirl rushed in to pick it up, rinsed it, wiped it on her kikoy, and handed it back.

"Who is the girl?" Sarada stopped short, knife pointed at her sister.

"I haven't met her," Urmila said.

"What? No one has met her?"

"After everything we give him." Urmila bit her fist until

it hurt, the onion bitter in her mouth. She couldn't bear it, one son in critical danger and the other farther away than she'd ever imagined. "This is how he poisons us."

"He is unusual. But he is sweet! I remember him as a little boy."

Her husband, too, during Sunil's unruly high school and college years, had tried to convince her: "Look, he is young and focused on his studies. He cannot be thinking of us all the time. Let him grow."

But Sunil grew only more distant.

"What do you know about her?"

Urmila tried to speak, but even the girl's name was hard and threatening in her throat.

"What does he think?" Sarada's knife swiveled toward the living room.

Urmila did not answer.

"Wait, you are telling me your husband does not know? What kind of seeds are you sowing?" Sarada wiped her forehead with the back of her arm, careful not to mess her hair. She pulled the potatoes into a metal bowl, added the onions and spices, and handed it to the girl. Washed and dried her hands. "This is a deep hole," she said.

"Sunil does not love us." Urmila wished she could cut out her son's marriage like a rotten spot from a peach.

"What will you do when she arrives?"

"Naa. She is not coming. I forbid it."

"Are you going crazy? Losing your marbles? Your son takes a wife and you forbid her? These are not the old days. Young people do what they want."

Urmila's insides turned to water. "I want only him," she said. "That is all."

Sarada hugged her fiercely, gold necklace pressing hard into Urmila's chest. She said, "You believe in your heart of hearts that your son is going to arrive alone?" She pulled back and held

Urmila's face, hands cupped around her chin in a gesture so firm and intimate and ancient Urmila nearly melted in a heap of tears. "Have you forgotten who raised him?"

Her sister smelled of lavender, which she claimed was soothing. Urmila tried to inhale, but her breath was scarce and thin.

6.

When Bimal was fifteen, Sunil fourteen, the two boys shared a bed in a Mombasa motel room that reeked of smoke and mildew. It turned out to be Sunil's last trip to Kenya—finally he found a way to get himself kicked out of the country.

The Diani Beach Bungalows were sandwiched between the dirt and the ocean, across the road from the Shan-e-Punjab restaurant. Sunil was old enough to realize that his family knew only their own kind, the East African Gujaratis—the Chandarias, Shahs, Patels. When his mother said *we Indians*, this was the group she meant, whom she cared about. The ones who scraped their way and had made good. Made money was what she meant.

"This is nice for you boys, yes? No more sleeping alone," Mital Aunty said the first night. Because they were just a year apart, the cousins were always thrust together when Sunil and his mother visited. When they were young, Sunil had enjoyed this; Bimal treated him as something of a celebrity, coming from America, and Sunil had the pleasure of presenting his cousin with shiny Matchbox cars and gleaming white baseballs, which his cousin accepted gratefully, even though no one in Kenya cared a thing about the major leagues.

Nearby was an airstrip, and they woke repeatedly to the thunder of planes. By the third morning, Sunil stayed in bed to sleep more when Bimal and their mothers left to lie on the beach, but a cleaning lady marched in with a bucket of muddy water and squished a mop across the floor.

Up from their cabin were the whitewashed chalets where the real Americans stayed. But it was low season, the scorching middle of summer, and the shore was nearly empty.

He found the shade of a palm tree. Wearing a baseball hat, long-sleeved shirt, and shorts, he sat and hugged his painfully lengthening legs to his chest. He despaired at the empty time stretching ahead: he was being walked down a long dry plank, at the end of which was another plank. Bimal was acting like a baby, not wanting to stray too far, not even down to the fruit juice cabana. Sunil had thought they'd get up to some adventures, but instead his cousin basked in the attention of the women. His mother was always particularly attentive to Bimal. Now Bimal splashed around close to shore, dumb pleasure on his face. Knee in the air like the Karate Kid. Sunil wondered if his cousin had seen any movies besides the Bollywood imports at the Shan, where Indians sat in the front and Africans in the cheaper seats at the back. Along the water's edge was a ridge of half-dried kelp like the scum that accumulated on the handle of his mother's toothbrush.

His mother called over. "It is hot like anything! Go jump in the waves."

Like anything. She couldn't be bothered to compare the heat to something particular, just to *anything*.

He was scared of the ocean, hated the heat, and she knew it. This dump, unlike the nice hotel where they'd stayed in Florida, at Disney World, didn't have a pool.

The advantage of family trips, though, was that Sunil was no longer alone with his mother. By the time he was thirteen, his father was receiving fewer invitations to speak, traveling less. But his father stayed out later now—paperwork, he said—and was withdrawn at home. It took effort to get him to crack a smile—a delay between the joke and the reaction, and sometimes no reaction at all other than "Hmmn, is it?" In response, his mother wound up, spun like a top, and found ever-increasing opportunities to voice her displeasure. Sunil thought he understood. It wasn't fair that his father should have stopped traveling only to be out of the house or silent. But his mother couldn't let it go, couldn't carry on as she had in his father's extended absences. She needled him, provoked fights with both her husband and her son.

But worse than his parents' fighting were his mother's confidences. While he ate dinner, instead of dreaming up schemes bound to be a hit in the Columbus marketplace (a samosa delivery service, self-cleaning water fountains), as they sometimes did together when his father was away, she listed his father's faults: he was never home; he didn't listen to her opinion; he was too cowardly to ask for a raise; he didn't sleep in the same bed with her. Once Sunil had pressed his palms over his ears and said, "I'm not listening! I'm not listening!" She'd wrested his hands away and shouted back, "Life is not sunny and perfect! You have to learn this sometime."

Now Sunil was discovering that being with Mital Aunty and Bimal was not the balm it used to be—didn't diffuse his mother's concentrated power. Worse, he often felt that his mother and aunt were colluding against him, sharing secret meaningful looks. But Sunil was getting older, stronger, and he hoped this meant that his life would be different soon.

Bimal called to Sunil, "Come fight with me! Show me your karate kicks!"

Sunil shook his head, though his cousin probably couldn't see him past the ocean glare. Through the palm leaves, his eyelids burned, and he didn't feel like moving. His stomach rumbled. He hadn't eaten more than a bag of chips and a mango. Yesterday his mother had spent most of the hours before dinner quizzing Bimal about his recent exams and saying to Sunil, "See, this is how a boy studies!" Sunil knew that Bimal's exams consisted mostly of rote memorization, while his were five-page papers, but he hadn't wanted to embarrass his cousin by pointing this out. So Sunil played along and humored both of them, even though his mother's repeated comparisons abraded him more deeply than he cared to admit. There was something uncomfortably insistent in her tone that Mital Aunty also noticed, Sunil believed, based on the forcedly placid look on her face, the slight turn away of her head, but sometimes it was easier to simply let his mother rant on and not stand in her way.

Bimal, still in the water, suddenly let out a scream. Sunil scrambled to his feet and ran down to the ocean.

"Pick him up," his mother said.

"He's way too heavy for me." Sunil was broader and taller, but only by an inch and five pounds.

"He is nothing but skin and bones!"

The skin of Bimal's foot was a raw reddish pink and there was a thick mess stuck on. "Jellyfish?" Bimal said.

Sunil, gawking and repulsed, echoed his cousin. "You didn't tell us there were jellyfish!"

"They are everywhere! Don't you know anything?" Urmila said.

Mital Aunty turned Sunil around, and, with a surprising burst of strength, hefted Bimal onto his back. Sunil staggered forward. "Crap, you weigh a ton."

"Sorry," Bimal said, clutching Sunil's throat with salt-sticky monkey arms.

When he set his cousin down in a chair, Bimal's foot had puffed up like a red balloon. The front-desk man brought a bucket and a large jug of vinegar. Urmila hovered, ready to criticize the treatment. Sunil wanted his father. His father would know what to do. His father who treated death and injury clinically. Who insisted that Sunil, too, become an organ donor when he passed his driver's test. And who had extracted from Sunil a solemn promise: "When it is my time, you will not pray over me. This is important. You are to keep your strength and remain rational, do not give in to hocus pocus."

In a small voice, Bimal asked, "Will you need to cut off the foot?"

The hotel clerk laughed like a donkey. He could have been forty or seventy-five. He told them with pride that his great-grandmother had once cured the District Commissioner's earache with a vial of urine. In Gujarati, he said, "You will be okay," and gave Bimal an antihistamine.

Urmila suddenly remembered their beach bag and sent Sunil to fetch it.

No one had touched it, but when Sunil picked it up with the towels, a small boy popped out from behind a palm tree. His head was shaved to the scalp, and his only clothes were a pair of ragged shorts, the pockets torn away. He perched on one leg, like a flamingo. The skin on his ankles was torn and raw.

The boy spoke in Swahili, and when Sunil didn't answer, he said, "English?"

Sunil smiled. He said gently, "What do you want?"

The boys' eyes popped wide as if he'd been waiting all week for the opportunity to speak. "Hello, my friend! My reward please, sir."

"Reward?"

"Yes, sir. I stand here when you go away. No one steal." He spoke the words without inflection, as if memorized. The boy shifted legs, and Sunil saw another patch of peeling skin on his calf.

"Where did you learn English? Do you go to school?"

"Yes, sir. English! My friend!"

So this was the boy's job. Sent out onto the beach to collect from tourists. The boy, or his handler, was smart to approach Sunil. His mother and aunt would've shooed him away. Inside his mother's wallet were mostly shillings, and Sunil didn't know what the exchange rate was. The denominations were large, in the thousands. He fingered through until he found dollars. He handed five singles to the boy, feeling both shy and important. "Here you go. Thanks a lot."

"Thanking you much, sir!" The boy took off across the sand, toward a row of tin shacks down near the juice stand. Sunil glanced back at the hotel. No one in the doorway, no one sweeping the tiny patio. No one watching. He withdrew the fistful of green bills and shoved them in his pocket, leaving only a few Kenyan shillings in the wallet. Then walked casually back to the lobby, depositing the load at the feet of his mother, who sat in a bamboo chair, her floppy hat on indoors, drinking out of a coconut.

"How's Bimal?"

"Oh, he will survive."

That night, the street air pulsed with a distant reggae beat. An ice cream vendor sensed Sunil's hunger and leapt on his hesitancy. "Something you like?" The tops of the metal tubs were askew, sticky-looking. The scoop immersed in a tub of creamy brown water. The man came closer.

Sunil walked quickly away. He was not brave enough to go far, but he'd seen a shop where he could buy sodas and a snack. What he really craved was a hamburger with real Heinz, but the poverty of his options was soon clear. The snack shop was farther than he remembered, and by now he'd walked a long way from the bungalows. He fingered the money. He tried to appear relaxed, as if he knew where he was going.

Passing an open doorway crowded with batteries and flashlights and tin-can lamps, he grew more aware of the darkness. His body hugged the shop walls, most of which were padlocked. Things scurried past his feet. His hunger battled his fear.

Then a round, fleshy man draped in a smeared apron appeared in a gray halo. Sunil walked hopefully toward him, but the man frowned when Sunil stood in the doorway. The man's black eyes bulged. "The night is late," he said. Behind the man was a tiny food stall.

"Are you open?"

"I make you something before I close. You should not be walking around."

While his fear of unknown food welled up, and his hunger fought to push it down, the man told him he'd graduated from an American university with a math degree. His name was Tom. "You know this part? Alabama? All the African people live there." He compared racism in the South to the way the Kikuyu in Kenya treated the other tribes. Sunil didn't know who the Kikuyu were. "But over there you have so many peoples, the Asians and the Spanish." He popped off the cap of a cold Coke and slid it down the counter to where Sunil perched on a metal stool.

A sizzle on the grill. The air steamy, sweat formed at the man's hairline, trickling down his forehead furrows. He was tall and bulky and serious-looking, like an African superhero. "I picked the name myself, after Tom Mboya. He was a big man in the Old Man's government. You have heard of Kenyatta? Mboya was loyal, but still he was assassinated. In that year I took his name to honor him."

"Did you work for the government?"

Tom shook his head, smiled. "In the old days, I did dream of it." He turned the meat on the grill, and strands of primally delicious smoke swirled in the heat. "Who is your hero, boy?

Aside from Mr. Ronald McDonald." Tom laughed, a thin, sad laugh for a powerfully large man.

Sunil didn't have a ready answer.

"I know, Mr. Magic Johnson. Big and tall but quick. You know Kenyans have always believed in magic, but it takes a black man from Los Angeles to make Americans know that it is real." He laughed again.

"You watch basketball?" Sunil couldn't believe it. For a moment, he was thrilled, an electric hug. But Tom's comment was also a jabbing reminder that Sunil was here, in miserable nowhere, instead of in his comfortable room at home watching the NBA playoffs. At home he didn't need friends or family because he had TV. Right now Sunil was missing the Lakers play the Sixers. Magic against Dr. J: behind-the-back passes, jump hooks, and windmill dunks.

Hungry, lonely, Sunil did believe in this moment that basketball was a kind of magic, because when he watched, he effortlessly disappeared.

When the burger was ready, meat between squares of spongy bread, glaringly white, Sunil didn't bother with condiments. In five wolfish bites he ate the whole thing, and when his plate was empty, he was embarrassed. Tom had gone to so much trouble. He couldn't explain that if he hadn't eaten so fast, he probably would have thrown up. "That was really good. Thank you."

"You would like some ice cream?" said Tom who had a degree from an American university and was here flipping burgers.

But Sunil was tired now, from the sun, from walking, from unease; a sudden, hopeless fatigue. He was so far away from home. He asked how much he owed.

"Do I look like a man running a business? This place belongs to my brother. He will never notice a little food given to a child."

"But I have all this money." Another night Sunil would have rejected being called a child, but tonight he felt like a young stray.

Tom chuckled, as if he knew where it had come from. "You spend that to take a taxi back to your bungalow. I find one. Someone I know, you understand." Tom cocked his head and narrowed his eyes as if the two were partners, but Sunil was thinking about how he'd never imagined getting something for free could make him feel so bad. He wondered how Bimal was doing, if he was continuing to sleep. His cousin had been so terrified, and Sunil had felt such pity for him as they together looked at the grossly swollen foot. Bimal had always been a happy, confident kid—much more so than Sunil had ever felt. But there was also a fragility to him, a tragic, bewildered expression that sometimes took over in moments of conflict.

Clouds rolled in from the ocean and suffocated the moon. If Sunil squinted, he could see the orange-yellow haze far off that could be the beginnings of the sun coming up, the lights of the Old Town, or something else, some flash of the future.

There was a gasoline smell and a honk, and Tom pointed to a car so low to the ground Sunil expected Fred Flintstone to get out and pedal. He got in the car and rolled down the window to wave goodbye to Tom.

Dark slips of people walked along the unlit road—women in short skirts and men carrying hefty sacks on their shoulders. The outlines of skittish dogs nosing the ground for trash. As they bumped along past everyone going somewhere, Sunil idled on the island of homesickness.

He paid the driver twenty dollars for the five-minute ride and wished he'd spent even more. The money was slippery in his fingers. He tried to whistle walking toward the bungalow, but his lips couldn't find the shape.

He cracked open the door, surprised to see a light on. Sunil felt the air snap as his mother immediately scrambled to her feet. "Where? Where did you run?" She shook his shoulders, her eyes livid. The nutty smell. She was the closest—and only—reminder of home he had here, and for a second, the most fleeting instant, he considered letting himself fall into her embrace. To be bundled up in her arms, like when she used to stuff him into snowsuits in the winter.

But instead of drawing him in, his mother pushed him away.

"You smell like animal!"

"Why did you take me here? Why do you hate Dad?"

When the flat of her hand made contact with his cheek, he was not surprised. He was by now almost as tall as she, but she was not afraid of him. Her arms were stronger, her center of gravity lower. It was not clear who would win a true fight.

Instead, he shouted, "I should have a job—my own money!" From his pocket he pulled out the leftover bills and flung them in her face. "And so should you! Without Dad, you'd have nothing."

She could drag him across the world, but she couldn't watch him every second. She couldn't make him want to be with her. She couldn't make him respect her. Nor could he fix her problems. His relief, realizing this, was enormous.

It was then Sunil understood something else, something profound and long-lasting. The fury he was capable of had grown in scope to match hers, and one day it would dominate. His fury would be more than force, more flexible and sophisticated. He would have reason and knowledge of the world on his side. Not only against her, but those like her who took advantage; he was old enough to know that they were everywhere. Tonight, though, he could do nothing to change her mind.

While his mother sobbed on the bed whispering, "*His* son. *His* fault," Mital Aunty comforted her with stiff back pats.

Sunil was sent home early the next day. Though Bimal

must have said goodbye, Sunil's last memory of his cousin was his thin sleeping body splayed on their shared bed.

Sunil had not flown internationally since that ruined trip. As they boarded the plane to Nairobi in the Frankfurt airport, he thought of Bimal's tiny wrists and ankles sticking out from underneath the covers. He tried, too, to conjure the boy's face, to scour it for familial resonance. Clues that would speak to their indelible connection. But he could not see his brother's features clearly. Too much time had passed, and he could remember only his Karate Kid posture in the waves, his guile and innocence, and feel the way Bimal had clutched at him and pressed his tear-stained face to the back of his neck. Bimal, bashful and eager to please. No wonder their mother had openly worshiped this son, especially given Bimal's recent success in business—he'd started his own company, Sunil remembered—and the birth of his daughter. It made painful, obliterating sense now, Bimal as the gold standard. Like a fool, a dupe, a pawn, Sunil had not known that this boy, half a world away, whom he had been compared to his whole life, was his brother. And he had to admit that, by any standard, Bimal had done so much more with what they both had been given.

Amy clipped her seatbelt and gave them cough drops to clear their ears during takeoff. She'd insisted on bringing salt-water taffy from Boston and buying fancy German chocolates in the airport for his parents, aunts and uncles. Sunil was little help with the gifts. His mother had always brought suitcases brimming with clothes and small appliances to Kenya, but these were specific requests and sizes. Sweets would be fine. Though Sunil could not imagine handing them out in an open show of goodwill given the betrayal he felt, knowing that all of his relatives had kept to themselves a piece of knowledge so personal and important.

Amy had been too stunned to believe him at first. She'd insisted that there must have been a good reason to keep him in the dark, perhaps to protect Bimal? Maybe there was some social stigma? But this was bullshit and she knew it.

"I doubt anyone in Nairobi wanted them to keep quiet about it," he said. "I was too far away to have any impact."

"It sounds like they were embarrassed," Amy said. "Didn't your mother say 'It was a bad time'?"

He nodded. "They were immigrants, given the chance for a blank slate. I can understand that—at first. But then what about later, when I'm old enough to *do* something with the information."

"What would you have done?"

"Maybe nothing," he admitted. "But I did always want a brother, and my parents knew that because I used to complain. At least I think it would have changed how I thought about my life. I would have felt less alone—just the idea of a brother, even if we didn't have anything else in common." He looked at Amy, whose eyeliner had smudged during her nap on the previous flight. In her lap were all the extra snacks she'd purloined from the flight attendant's unattended basket. "You would have had a bake sale to raise the funds to fly over right away, if this had happened to you."

"Hah. No. I'd just have asked my grandparents for the money." She looked at him with a soft smile. "You could have used some tough Russian Jews. To introduce you to vodka on your fifth birthday and teach you how to recycle rubber bands." She sighed and squeezed his leg sympathetically. "But really the saving grace has been my sister. I can't imagine my life without her. All the conversion crap with our parents—at least we always have each other."

Sunil nodded, his eyes full and stinging. He looked around at the other passengers while the flight attendant made them aware of all the things that could go wrong. Seated were several other Indians, and a small handful of whites, but mostly the plane was full of Africans. He laughed at the fact that he was so rarely surrounded by other brown and black people. He had long ago stopped noticing that he was the only minority in the room because it happened so often. Sunil took a deep breath and felt Amy's hand on his knee, the press of her fingertips through his jeans. They wore nice clothes, Amy in a sweater and skirt longer than the usual minis and which gave her a lovely waist, because they'd go straight to a family dinner from the airport. His father would meet them. Sunil's throat caught. His father was the easy one, relatively speaking, and yet he, too, had kept silent all these years. Sunil wrestled with the metal clip of his seatbelt, pounding it with his fist. Amy now made him promise to be civil, as relaxed as possible, until they knew more, which might take a few days.

"What if they're not civil back?" he said.

"Do you really think that will happen? They're going to be happy to see you. If they're really being bastards, you can dole out one punch in the face each, but that's *it*."

The first time Amy had taken his hand in a dark movie theater, she had audaciously thumbed the inside seam of his jeans. Once they began sleeping together—which she had initiated, taking ice cream bowls out of their hands and straddling his lap on the couch—he could not get enough of her lips.

Then there was the moment on the street. Amy had stopped abruptly, obliviously, to tie her Keds in the middle of the sidewalk, causing an avalanche of bodies to stack up behind her. As she apologized and gathered up the oranges and paper towels tumbled from bags, she had managed to make everyone laugh at her folly, at their joint chaos, until they all were standing and smiling and shaking hands and Amy appeared like the ringleader of a small, beautiful circus of the everyday.

When Sunil had learned that Amy had run—and lost—a bid for class president in high school with the slogan *'A' for Amy, 'A' for action*, complemented with a two-fisted sky-punch, Sunil was smitten.

With her jokey comment about punching his family, Sunil realized he was taking his wife into a battlefield. He had given Amy the option of staying home, but she had refused. They had to do this together.

So he laughed and agreed to her plan, even though the wound of deception felt larger than could ever heal. But he would try. He took two Dramamine and knocked himself out.

7.

Premchand looked for his wife first in the bedroom, then the bathroom. He found her at the small table in the kitchen, shoulders hunched under her black cardigan, bare feet clasped under the chair. She had disappeared after dinner. Premchand was moved by the brown lines of his wife's soles, calluses worn with age. It was a miracle of modern science how long people lived now. If he'd had a life like his parents, he'd welcome an early death, but in today's world he could still see patients, still learn, even at his ripe old age.

"Darling, what are you doing?"

Urmila startled, and as she turned, she wiped her mouth with the back of her hand.

"You are eating the shrikand."

"Just tasting. You know how my sister sometimes makes her desserts too, too sweet. I came into the kitchen for a glass of water and decided to be a help to the chef."

"You have eaten fully one-quarter of the dessert."

Urmila looked at the bowl. "Not true." But her expression was doubtful, her mind somewhere else.

"I know what I see. Now hurry and fix it so the damage

is not so obvious. This is the problem staying here. You don't eat good food, only the fry and the sweet. What you eat affects mood, rest, everything." He said, "Bimal is going to be okay, you know. Broken bones heal."

He remembered how gently Urmila had held Raina at the hospital the night of the accident, how her body had filled with ease and joy.

She said, "You have that pink liquid with you—the soothing one?"

"Yes."

"Well, will you bring? I am in need."

"Because you ate too much shrikand!" But he pitied her. In some ways she did not belong here any more than he did, despite her closeness to her sister and her business connections.

"How many more days are we staying?" she asked.

"First you make the tickets for two weeks and now you ask about leaving? Sunil is arriving tomorrow." Premchand was eager to see his son, but he was nervous. Already Urmila was on edge, and he couldn't imagine how his son was feeling, coming back to Kenya after so long. Having just learned about Bimal. Premchand touched the beating pulse in his temple with his fingertips. He was relying on Sarada to help make the visit smooth. There was a time when she was the daughter that he would marry, but Sarada had preferred someone else, or was already engaged, he could not remember now. Urmila, too, once had another prospect, a man in Mombasa who owned a chain of tourist hotels.

"Just bring me the pink." Urmila waved her hand. "It is hard to keep track of the days."

She took the Pepto-Bismol; they said good night to the family and got ready for bed. Soon Urmila was asleep beside him, lightly snoring, but he stayed awake, remembering.

The first year they lived in America, Urmila had stayed

up until he came home, in the middle of the night, to make sure the food he ate was hot, nourishing. The second year, she was more often asleep, both when he woke in the morning and when he returned. He ate congealed dal standing up at the two-burner stove at two, three, four in the morning.

After three years, she had had enough. His wife wanted to go back to Nairobi. But he couldn't. He'd come too far. One day early in 1969, a few months after they'd moved to Columbus and were trying to start afresh, Urmila began packing. She would go back on her own. Premchand had believed this was the end of them. He would live alone in USA. Then, three weeks into their separation, they learned of Urmila's pregnancy. She didn't want to return to Columbus, to him, but she could not raise a child on her own. Her family made that clear. What should they do? Premchand had seen it as a stroke of luck that Anup and Mital could not conceive, could take the child as their own, but Urmila had been the one to carry him, to birth him. She had given him up unwillingly, then flew back to Columbus, to try to restart her American life. She had not been consoled, as Premchand was, by the birth of their second son ten months later. Regret had invaded his wife and stayed.

Baggage claim was a swarm. Clamoring reunions in all languages, hawkers pushing flowers, phone cards, newspapers. Beyond picking out the Arabs in dishdashas and the lanky Maasai with their red blankets, Premchand couldn't identify the tribes anymore—the Kikuyu, the Luo, the Kalenjin. Not the way he could now tell from a patient's name and appearance if he was Vietnamese or Thai, Somali or Ethiopian.

Premchand hoped Sunil's presence would break the monotony at his sister-in-law's. After so many days, conversation had been scraped down to the bare bones. The family and classmates who'd stayed behind in Kenya had regressed, he thought. They lived in nice houses with modern appliances, but their thoughts were staid and backward. It was a world without science.

Last night, Gopal had gone on about snakes and their mystical qualities. He had recently fasted, for the first time in many years, and it had led to a purity of mind, he said. "We are all striving for moksha, are we not?" The night of the fast he'd dreamed of a snake and then, the next day, he'd come across an old photograph of his mother. This was a sign that his mother's spirit was unwell. That she wanted something from her children. Then a cousin-brother had launched into a story about a Japanese dog who waited for his master at the train station every day, but the day the man died of a heart attack in the office— "because the Japanese work too hard, yet that is why they are ruling the technological world"—the dog stayed home.

Premchand was sensitive to not overusing his physician's authority, but he could not let the absurdity go on. He'd thought momentarily of Sunil, pursuing a doctorate at the most prestigious university in the world. Even if he never finished his degree, attending lectures, keeping his mind sharp was the main thing. Premchand had cleared his throat and pushed his voice over the table to assert, "There is no relationship between one ridiculous tale and another ridiculous tale. People die. We cremate the bodies. End of story."

But his victory was short-lived. The conversation ran to the American political contest, but that, too, derailed when Premchand tried to ask about Kenyan elections. "Every citizen should vote," he'd said. His wife had rolled her eyes, and Gopal said, "What we say doesn't matter. The African majority looks out only for itself. They all want to be big men, go back to their tribes, and get another wife. Even in your country the big money wins."

Premchand had acceded to the last point and went to bed early, but he had not slept well.

As he waited for Sunil to emerge, his body fought fatigue.

He felt pressed thin and lifeless as a gauze bandage under the terrible airport lights. Premchand's brother-in-law, Ajay, stood beside him, rocking back and forth on his heels.

"Dad!" Sunil's hand waved high above the other black-haired heads, and he walked toward them. He looked tall, thin. The collar of a wrinkled button-down shirt opened over a navy sweater, and his jaw was speckled with black.

Premchand squeezed Sunil tightly, quickly. Here he was. Solid, in the flesh, with the beard of a grown man.

"Dad, this is Amy. My wife."

Premchand inhaled sharply. "Who?" A wife? He held his breath while the girl—how old was she?—came slowly into focus: slight and pale like vanilla cake. Disheveled from travel but lively. Eager and nervous and holding out her hand. She gripped Premchand's palm and gave it a shake firm enough to snap the neck of a snake. "Dr. Chandaria. I'm so happy to meet you." She looked from him to his son. "You look alike," she said. "Your hair is wavy and Sunil's is straight, but you have the same eyes and nose."

"Sunil is lucky," Ajay said. "The gray hair comes late to the doctor's family."

Premchand suddenly realized that his brother-in-law had not been surprised by the girl's appearance, the word *wife*. Urmila must have known and told Sarada, who told Ajay. Everyone had known and kept it from him. Ajay's silence he could at least understand. His brother-in-law would want to see the effect of the surprise; he was always needling Premchand, hoping for a spectacle. But his own wife? Premchand crunched his fists into his pockets.

"Dad, are you all right? How is Bimal?"

"He is recovering, yes, do not worry. Everything will be just fine."

Passengers with taped-together suitcases streamed around

them. Skinny men with high foreheads, fat men with yellow eyes, broad women with skirts and headscarves in wild, bright patterns of blue and green and red and yellow. Everyone else moved, but the four of them stood still.

"What are we waiting for, eh?" Ajay said, adjusting his belt to fit better below his belly. "Come, strong man, pick up these bags so your newlywed does not think we are barbarics."

They wheeled the suitcases across the parking lot, weaving in and out between the cars. A few were sleek Mercedeses, but most were dented, collapsing, crusted in dirt, paint barely visible through the rust. Ajay proudly drove a brand-new Audi. Premchand offered his son the front seat, but Sunil wanted to sit in the back with Amy.

Cars on the access road slowed to a crawl. Women and children gestured at their closed windows with bouquets of rolled newspaper. So many looked lost, like they needed help.

"She didn't tell you, did she?" Sunil said to him.

Premchand ignored this and pointed out the window. "Groundnuts," he said. "The Africans are very fond of them. They resemble peanuts."

"Dad—"

But Premchand, stifling irritation, waved his hand. "We will talk about everything after the meal. You must be hungry."

The vendors multiplied and merged. In the dusky light their torn clothes faded into their skin. Women carried stacked plastic buckets on their heads; men shouldered string bags of bananas. He looked over their heads to the jagged skyline, the new high-rises lit up with the last rays of sun. From the back, Premchand heard only low, fierce, whispers.

Then Sunil said in a too-loud voice, "This is awful traffic. Is it always like this?"

"Twenty-four hours, seven days a week!" Ajay said cheerfully. "And the matatus." He pointed to one passing, bags stacked high on top, the fee collectors hanging off the running boards. "You can see, they are so filthy crowded. Every such distance stop and stop and soon they are all hanging out the back like monkeys. You can't believe how they live."

"Like monkeys?" Sunil said.

"No, he doesn't mean that," Premchand began. He looked at Ajay, but the man was oblivious.

"What are matatus?" Amy said.

"Buses for monkeys, apparently," Sunil said.

"Minivans," Ajay said.

Premchand shared a look with his son, who was shaking his head.

As he drove, Ajay told them about Nairobi's population explosion, segueing, unprompted, into Idi Amin's expulsion of the Asians from Uganda in 1972. "This is the fear we are always living under. Ever since independence, there's Africanization. The government can take away your business at any time. It's not right, but there is nothing we can do. They want the locals to have all the power and all the money. We are an oppressed minority."

"I thought Asians owned lots of businesses," Sunil said. "Mom told me that. Don't Indians have more money than all the Africans put together?"

"But there is no political representation for Asians," Premchand interjected and then wondered if this was still true. Kenya had been a democracy for almost forty years.

Ajay did not contradict him. He was smiling at Amy in the rearview mirror.

They drove through the darkening city, past skyscrapers and weary petrol stations. The pastel greens and purples of the older concrete buildings were barely visible, though Premchand picked out the steel bars bolted across the storefronts. In the daytime, when the city's trees unfurled, Premchand would tell Amy about Nairobi's old nickname, The Green City in the Sun.

Obviously, Urmila had known about the marriage. But Premchand was sure she hadn't arranged for the girl to come along. How would she react? And how had his son paid for the trip? He knew that even with his own contributions, Sunil barely scraped by.

He knew, too, that he had not fooled his son. He sighed. Already there was a wrong to right. And who was this girl? What was she like?

"When can we visit Bimal?" Sunil said.

"You are eager to see your cousin-brother, eh?" Ajay said.

"I'm worried about him." Sunil paused, holding something back. "What exactly happened? Mom wasn't very clear."

The night of the accident, the phone had rung, and then in a great *whoosh*, the women had swept up their purses, the men started the cars, and suddenly there they were, at Aga Khan. "We did not know much, only that Bimal was in critical condition and the other driver had died on impact. Head-on collision on the Outer Ring Road."

"The other driver died?" Sunil said.

"Yes, it was very unfortunate."

"He was an African," Ajay said. "Bimal was not at fault."

"Then you waited around the hospital all night?"

"Yes," Premchand said. "Anup and Mital, and Bimal's wife, Sheetal, with their daughter, Raina. We were all crowded together in the waiting area like a bowl of gulab jamun."

Sunil laughed, and Premchand felt a spark.

"We waited for many hours until Bimal emerged from surgery." Premchand did not tell his son that he had been so jet-lagged that after this he had fallen asleep. After a while, he'd felt his arm moving, a woman crying. "Tell me it is going to be all right, Uncle." He had struggled to come to the surface. Something was expected of him, but he didn't know what. He wasn't even sure what language people were speaking. His whole life he'd spoken English and Gujarati, switching easily between the two, but then all he could say was, "You are speaking . . . English, beti?" And then he hadn't heard anything at all.

Craning his neck toward the back seat, he said, "You know I used to work at Aga Khan."

"When you were back here repaying your loans?"

Premchand nodded. His tuition to B. J. Medical College in Ahmedabad had been paid by two Nairobi Asian organizations, who required that he spend three years in Kenya practicing and training others.

"Did you like living in India?" Amy asked. She leaned forward in her seat to better hear him, one hand on Sunil's knee.

"Yes, very much." Premchand had thrived in school. "Finally I could identify the 'fevers' everyone was suffering and dying from in Kenya. Cholera, dysentery, malaria, meningitis, encephalitis, schistosomiasis." He'd even seen rabies, a disease that destroyed like a demon. "I had excellent classmates." Ravenous young men, hungry for fellowship and knowledge. They worked up appetites during long walks and endless nights of cards. Premchand read crime novels and saw movies, shopped back alleys for interesting old coins and miniature chess pieces.

In those days, he carried in his pocket a jade knight he'd bought in a tiny shop near Gandhi's Sabarmati Ashram. The knight was his favorite for its ability to jump, for being the only piece that could attack a king, queen, bishop, or rook without risking reciprocal attack. The knight was gallant and a little mischievous.

He patted his right pants pockets. The jade knight he'd lost long ago, but here was the tiny plastic one he carried most days. Its neck was beautifully curved, like a seahorse. The ears worn down to soft nubs over so many years.

"So why did you go to the States?" Amy said. "You could have stayed here or gone back to India, right?"

"Oh, well, here there was Mau Mau, instability. The others"—Premchand forced a nod in Ajay's direction—"had more backbone. They were less afraid of what would happen when the British broke and withdrew."

"At least under the British there was some order," Ajay griped.

It was true that when the Africans took charge, everything was up in the air. But Premchand cared more about privacy than power. In Ahmedabad, Premchand had discovered he liked being a stranger. He could count on one hand the number of times he'd returned to Kenya in the last thirty-five years.

"We stayed through independence, but in sixty-five we left. There was a training job in Jackson, Mississippi." He'd toiled twenty-hour days in a crumbling hospital with dozens of other Indians, Pakistanis, Brazilians, and Argentines, a force of brown doctors-in-training caring for a vast sea of black patients. He became an infectious-disease specialist and was invited to Columbus by a Ugandan Gujarati friend who'd been two years ahead of him in Jackson and before that in Ahmedabad. A small train of pioneers following medicine from one country to the next.

"The doctor was ambitious," Ajay said. He slid into the next lane, barely avoiding a moped. "He always wanted to live in USA. He was not truly made for this country."

Premchand was irked by this dismissive tone, but he could not disagree with the words. He had never in Nairobi felt like he belonged.

Sidestreets vanished into dimness. They passed a mall where, earlier in the day, they'd bought home-care supplies for Bimal, and soon they were in front of Ajay's gate, waiting for

the askari to open it. The guard smiled broadly, teeth shining, hands loosely on his gun.

Sunil looked up at the house, which loomed tall and wide in the dark. He said, "I hope something looks familiar in the morning."

8.

Some men returned to India with small riches, quickly spent. But most remained in Africa, and the stories of opportunity grew and grew. Must be good if some are staying, no? Better than famine at least, which was all across the Saurashtra. The dhows set out for Mombasa in November, when the sweet weather began. Sailed with the monsoon winds. Men who had never even seen the sea trusted their lives to the nakhodas, who took on no freeloaders. Even the crew were one-way passengers. For food and shelter, they swept the deck, jiggered the sails, and secured the dhows through the storms.

The storms! Sky shaking, waves pounding. The boats over-flowed, and they emptied with buckets, rain slashing their faces. Tied everything important down with rope, sometimes themselves. The dhows set out in groups, seven or ten at a time, and it was not unusual for one or two to be lost at sea.

To keep up their spirits they would sing, *Salavo, salavo . . .* one man leading and the others following, *We are here, sail on!*

They ate boiled gram, chapatis, a few grains of rice. One cup of water per day.

Women, too, began to come. They lived entirely below deck, cooked with kerosene in circles of hot stones, breathing the soot-filled air. Up into the light and sea breeze only to use the toilet, a dank box pitched over the waves. If you were a tall one, the others could see your head.

Your grandmother arrived when she was twelve. Her body was cramped for so many weeks she forgot how to walk. Her parts grew crooked, too—that's why two of our children died in their first weeks of life.

Some, of course, died at sea. Of fevers, weakness. There was nothing to do with the bodies but pitch them overboard, and this has always, always haunted me. Where are their souls now?

Do you know what I am saying? Without the funeral pyre, the soul is in limbo. We used to sing about the golden pyre, the silver body, *a golden flame is burning, silver smoke is rising to the sky*. The soul needs to be released. Fire allows the soul to detach. Flames prevent new life from growing in the body.

Promise me you'll take care of my body in the proper way, when the time comes?

After all this horror, the Mombasa skyline was a glorious sight. It was thick with fruit trees and shade, the colors soft and pleasing. You have been there, but you have never seen the city from the sea, as I have, coming back from a trip to Zanzibar— the island that smells of cloves. From the sea, you think you can grasp the city in your hand, scoop in your palm all the trees and mosques and white coral houses that glitter like grains of rice. You hold your breath, dreaming of fresh coconuts. You are a sailor, an explorer. Land!

In the harbor you look around at the other dhows, trying to read their stories from their weathered skin. These boats, they feel like family. You feel relief. Also regret, because some sights are once in a lifetime. The instant you see, you know you will have to keep the picture in a little warehouse in your mind. It is funny, isn't it? I have never lived in that city, but I miss the ocean, the sea breeze. Asians have lived there for so many years, we are part of the air, the stones and streets.

Mombasa was, and still is, a mixed-up town. When my father arrived, the city was filled with Swahili traders. The Asians here then were Muslims, but they spoke our language, and they soon surpassed the Swahilis. You have seen their folded turbans and wide beards? They were clerks, middlemen, loan officers, they made things happen. Whites relied on them. Colonials gave these men letters of recommendation and soon everybody knew them. Merchants like J. M. Jeevanjee and Allidina Visram—you know their names, either of you? They grew rich. Owned hundreds of shops here and across Uganda.

Ivory was the big trade, of course. The Swahilis sent parties to the plains to shoot, then sent tusks back to the coast in long caravans. It took months, braving the savages and hostile lands, wild beasts. In Mombasa, whites snatched up the precious bone and posed for pictures with the long tusks crossed high above their heads.

They traded slaves, too, until the Queen abolished.

But this was not for our people, this business of killing and owning. *Ahimsa* requires we treat every living thing with respect. Even the tiniest creatures that flit in the air and live in the ground.

The lions? Oh yes, killing them was terrible, but it had to be done. Finally, the sahib, Patterson, got them. When the bodies of Ghost and Darkness were paraded around, my father wept. He almost forgave sahib the punishing pace he'd exacted from the frail men. Almost. Fear had eaten not only their flesh, but also their hearts.

9.

He remembered a night years ago, when she'd stood in the living room in a long purple vest and pants, stylish platform shoes. Black hair pulled up, twisted. His parents were going to a friend's house to practice disco dancing. The woman Sunil saw now, in an expensive sari, hair short and frizzed, didn't look upright or keen or confident, but shrunken and sad.

His mother embraced him fiercely, and he smelled the coconut oil in her hair, a scent he still associated with being bawled out. He nearly drew away in an act of instinctive self-preservation, but she gripped his arms and swaddled him so hard he couldn't even hug her back. Was she crying over him, over Bimal, from exhaustion? It was awful to see her black mascara tears, her distraught face, and he wondered what comfort he could offer her.

She pulled out of him something he had long tried to keep in a dark, airless place.

Then his mother surprised him by grabbing Amy, too—so fast it was more a thump than a hug. Then Sarada Aunty took hold of Amy, exclaiming, "Look at you, as pretty as a doll!" Big mistake, Sunil thought, but things were moving too fast to correct it. Soon everyone was hugging, jabbering, asking questions. Sunil began to introduce his wife, but she didn't need his help with formalities. She managed grace in the scrum, standing at just the right angle to include several people at once, repeating her name—not Jamie like James, but Amy like . . . Amy. He saw her strain to catch their accents and keep a smile. His cousins' English was good, clear; his aunts' and uncles' accents were stronger. Sunil's younger cousin Meena threw her arms around both of them at once. She had Sarada Aunty's wide nose and wore sunglasses to hold back her hair. "So happy to see you! Our long-lost American cousin." Her energy and animation and sleek black hair were just what he remembered of his aunt when she was younger, though Meena's voice lacked her mother's sharp imperiousness.

His family had waited hours to eat—it was nearly ten— and Sunil and Amy were sent to wash their hands. He'd forgotten how the bathrooms here were like those at restaurants, with the sink, soap, and trash bin in the hall and only the toilet closed off, a tiny room just large enough to sit. Sunil used the toilet, and when he emerged, Amy was on her knees peering into the cabinet under the sink, a small pile of cleaning supplies and sanitary napkins next to her.

"What are you doing? Get out of there. Someone might see you."

"Looking for the hot water pipe. Only cold water runs from the tap. It's freezing."

He couldn't see her face but he knew that she'd been snooping. "Sure you were," he said. "If you're cold, you can borrow something from Meena."

Amy quickly replaced the items she'd removed, stood up, rearranged her hair, and pressed her skirt down, trying to stretch out the wrinkles and make herself taller. She ran a damp towel around her neck and under her arms. "Do I stink?" she asked.

"That's a first for you," he said.

"Nerves smell different than exercise. Proven by studies with rats."

"Uh-huh," he said, then leaned down to smell her neck and collarbone and shoulder, their almond sweetness cut faintly with sweat. "You're fine. Just don't give any monster hugs."

"I was thinking of arm wrestling your uncles."

It occurred to him, for the first time, that Amy's nosiness might be a nervous compulsion. Because he could see her withdrawing into herself tonight. She had nailed introductions, his family swirling around her circus-like, just like the people on the street when she'd caused a pileup. But sometimes those moments of elegant orchestration were followed by clamming up, uttering only the blandest comments. He had seen her do this around pushy strangers, as well as her own parents when an Orthodox obligation or prohibition was mentioned. "You have to promise me something," he said.

"What?"

"Don't shrink."

"I'm not." Her shoulders stiffened.

"I mean it. Be you. I don't want them thinking I married you only for your looks."

A tiny smile turned the corners of her lips, but her rigidity remained. "I asked questions in the car," she said.

"Two."

"It's loud in there, and I can barely understand what people are saying."

"You said you wanted to come, that you would be up to this. You'll be manipulated if you aren't strong, and you won't get to know anyone, which is what you wanted." Amy often struggled to say things that might appear mean or insensitive. Her humor had come out only gradually as they were dating. When she was a girl, her comments intended as jokes had been taken as insults, and she'd become hesitant.

"Let's just relax and let things go easy this first night, okay? We're all tired. I'll be fine." Then she added, a touch cruelly, "You don't remember them all, do you? You have that uncomprehending smile."

"I didn't even know I was smiling."

He knew she was still annoyed at him about the plane ticket: he'd refused to ask her parents for a loan and instead had charged a credit card they couldn't pay off. He said he'd get the money later, from his father.

"Good thing you're along to tell me how I feel." He was teasing, but he meant it. Another breath, taking her hand, then, "Ready?"

She exhaled. "Ready."

They sat at a table the size of the room, squeezing in around every inch. Sarada Aunty passed an endless number of dishes, each introduced with a flourish to Amy, who eagerly and insistently piled food on her plate until it threatened to overflow. Sarada would have been cooking for days. Chakli, bhajia, pulao with vegetables Sunil didn't recognize, chana dal, moong dal, chutneys of pineapple, mint, and mango, multiple salads. Every few minutes a servant carried in hot parathas, pooris, and stuffed naan.

While they were eating, tasting, nodding, appreciating, Ajay Uncle told them there was a restaurant in Nairobi Sunil and Amy had to try. "Famous. The best. All the Americans like to go." He looked at Amy. "You eat meat, yes? Because at Carnivore's, they cook what you can't imagine. Crocodile, zebra, gazelle . . . waiters walking around with meat on long sticks, these spears used by the locals."

His uncles' black, thick-framed glasses from the seventies had been replaced by frameless or gold-rimmed ones, and their temples sprouted gray. Their forearms had thickened; wrists bared fat watches. Anup Uncle, Bimal's father, was the slightest, his thin wrists barely visible beneath his too-long sleeves. They all wore dress shirts, some with sweater vests, and smelled of cigarettes. Sunil was touched by the sharp, pressed clothes, and his aunt's huge spread. Diagonally across from him was his cousin Prakash, looking glum and soft and saying little, taking one more paratha every time it was offered. Sunil remembered him as fast, sleek, sprinting down the driveway and diving for obscure corners during hide and seek. Was he the one whose depression had caused him to take off from school? The one who went to seek treatment from specialists in the UK? Someone else had spent two months at an ashram in India, but he couldn't remember who that was.

Sunil never believed he'd be back here, so he'd never prepared for this moment. Now he felt protective and incredibly nervous. Especially when he saw that Amy alone used a fork. True to form, she was packing it away, proving she did not have the appetite of a delicate doll. He wanted to protect her, but also to share her. To make his parents, at least, see who she was. Here was a moment that neither Amy's evidence nor Sunil's a priori reasoning could have prepared them for. None of this was a controlled experiment. Between Sunil and his parents, patterns had been set, Amy had pointed out before they left, patterns they could—and should—seize the opportunity to alter by providing different inputs. Sunil wanted his family to know Amy as he did, to see her as the sharp interlocutor he knew her to be. But he did not know how to draw her out before his family. Based solely on their encounter with her at the dinner table they'd be justified in thinking she was another blonde American girl with an eating disorder. A "California type" the Indians he'd grown up with would call her.

Sunil's mother now put a hand on Sarada Aunty's arm and looked directly at Amy. In another family, it might be time for a toast—he had brought his bride!—but Sunil had never seen a toast at any gathering of Indians, never mind from his mother, and his throat tightened. Urmila announced, "Everyone loves my sister's cooking. She spares no expense, no effort. At the market she picks out the best of this and that, the very freshest. Oh, you should see her negotiate! She is very economical. And you just wait until the dessert." Though her comments were directed at Amy, she spoke in a brassy voice that silenced the rest of the table. Just like his mother to start with a brag.

"We Indians are vegetarians," she continued, shifting her gaze to Sunil, then back to Amy, whose jaw had begun to jut in a hard line. "We eat just these vegetable dishes and some rice and these breads and we are satisfied. I have been telling my sister that probably you do not get this kind of food where you live. I know Boston is a big city, but my sister does like nobody else. And the issue of meat, we understand if you need to get some outside the house, like my brother said. He has done this all his life." She pointed at Sunil's father. "I think you'll see we are very open-minded."

As if soothing a child, Sarada said, "They will see, Urmila-bhen, don't worry."

"They're here now, we have to teach her. Him too. They don't know anything. Even with all his tip-top schooling."

Sunil felt the buried bitter capsule break open and seep into his blood. They'd traveled three thousand miles to be found wanting. The age-old worry that his mother was ashamed of him was already gnawing away at his insides, his mother who always wanted him to be more like his Nairobi relatives.

One fall Saturday when he was twelve, his mother came into his bedroom, turned off the TV, and said that if he wasn't studying, why couldn't he review for an exam? And if he was done with schoolwork, there was the yard to mow. Didn't he see that, yet again, his father was not there to do it? Sunil put on a hat to shade his eyes and mowed quickly, striping back and forth. Back inside in time for the next episode. But while he was taking off his shoes in the front hallway, a boy he knew from school, Chris Altman, had called to ask if he wanted to meet at the mall arcade. At first his mother had said no, she wouldn't drive him, he wouldn't waste his afternoon, but then the phone rang again, and his mother spoke in Gujarati, then she told Sunil she had to go out anyway and would take him to meet his friend if the boy's parents brought him home.

Getting dressed, he changed his shirt three times. Wore his jeans with the ragged cuffs. Girls he knew might pass by the arcade. Or, better, girls he didn't know.

His mother appraised his clothes, the cuffs, but said nothing.

When she turned left instead of right at the Methodist church—*Welcoming All God's Children (since 1967)*—he thought they were driving the long way around. But Sunil soon realized they were over by the high school, passing the bleak, off-the-grid railroad tracks where he'd hang out with degenerates a few years later. They were on the opposite side of town from the mall and spinning farther away every second. They passed signs for the airport. Panic swept in, slowly at first, then, with each plane passing overhead, with such urgency and force it left no room for doubt. At last his mother turned to him and announced that she was shipping him off to Kenya because she couldn't stand his indolence anymore. She'd told him several times that week how messy and slothful and ungrateful and stupid he was, how unlike his Nairobi cousins. In the back seat was a British Airways duffel bag. Couldn't be more than a few changes of clothes and a toothbrush in there. He was too terrified to speak.

Would he have a chance to escape once his ticket was taken? Maybe he could hide in the bathroom. Had his father approved this plan? He checked his pockets for change for a pay phone and found only pennies.

Sure he hated his life, but he didn't want to grow up in *Africa*.

When they pulled into the driveway of their family friends, the Savlas—where his mother was presumably stopping to pick up a suitcase of the shoes Ramesh Uncle got at a discount from managing the Payless, to ship with him to Nairobi—Sunil rolled out of the car and took off. His shoe caught on a twig, he fell and scraped his knee, scrambled again to his feet, and kept on running, pumping his arms like Carl Lewis. Behind him, adults shouting. Ramesh Uncle's voice carrying, "Hey!"

Sunil sprinted to the edge of the yard and kept going, across the next yard and the next, dogs lunging at leashes, cars braking suddenly and drivers swearing, anger whipping in his wake like hungry flames, afraid if he stopped or even slowed his intestines would unclench and release everywhere. He had never tested well in the timed mile in gym, and he'd chosen today shoes with worn, slippery bottoms instead of sneakers, but he ran as if it were his singular gift. He skirted mothers and sons and sisters and giggling girls. He didn't care if they laughed. More dogs on leashes, a stroller, two strollers, and then the sidewalk ended and gave way to a main road and still he sprinted, kicking up pebbles. After many minutes—ten? fifteen? *twenty?*—his thighs ached intensely, his ribs collapsed into his chest, and he scoped out fences and parking lots and gas pumps. Where could he hide?

Soon he ran out of steam and fell, spent, bottomed out, treads-worn-down-to-the-foot-balls, against the wall of a Kroger's.

The cashier came out. *Clara*, her name tag said. Pink-streaked hair cut across her eyes; she stepped over him on her way to the bathroom around back, then looked again at his dirt-lined face, grass-stained knees, and changed her mind. Went back inside. Emerged with Orange Crush, handing it over wordlessly.

He savored the soda, tasting it gently, furtively. His gratitude was bottomless. He dared not set it down on the ground but wrapped his fingers tightly around the can and enjoyed the sweetness sip by sip, until his mother found him.

Ramesh Uncle was driving. He looked as if he didn't know if he should scold or laugh. "Never have I seen a boy who hates mowing lawns so much he runs away!"

His mother got out of the car. Her pants swished furiously. Time grew shorter, and shorter still. He was too tired to run any farther. He'd have to learn both Gujarati and Swahili in a hurry. Who would he live with? Would he even recognize his relatives at the airport? His mother's face melted then reformed, sharpened. Then she grabbed his collar and he could smell the coconut oil in her hair. "What is wrong with you? Just after I praise you to the skies for the job you did on our grass? Ramesh Uncle calls and asks for some help and then you run away like a scoundrel thief!"

"You said you were sending me to Nairobi."

"Just a little joking!"

Sunil felt sick to his stomach. "I didn't know," he whispered, and collapsed further into himself.

"Come now, Urmilabhen, take the boy to play," said Ramesh Uncle. "Look, he is terrified, like we have tried to kidnap him." He swished his hand through Sunil's hair.

His mother was caught. She thought the boys at his school unserious, bad influences, and the arcade games too violent. "Okay, first you mow the lawn, then I take you to the mall."

"Forget about the lawn," Ramesh said. "I have two perfectly good legs."

His mother sighed and gave in.

But Sunil couldn't imagine facing Chris Altman now, after his mother made him so late. There was no way to explain, and Chris Altman never called again.

That night, Sunil sat in continued misery at the end of the dining table and watched his father eat. With one hand, he flipped the pages of the paper and nimbly ate with the other. Adam's apple rose and fell. Once his father looked up to catch his son's gaze and nodded politely, like to a stranger on a train.

After dinner, Amy perched quietly on the edge of a chair in the sitting room while the women chatted in Gujarati. He tried to catch her eye, he wanted to somehow telegraph: *Go ahead, interrupt*, but she was looking intently at his mother and aunt, as if trying to follow along.

Beside him, his father traced the rim of a glass with his finger. "This traveling," he said, "it is exhausting. You are really not too tired?"

"I am. Wired, too. Being here feels very strange."

The television turned on in the next room. "Probably they are watching the cricket match," his father said. "Sri Lanka versus Zimbabwe. Go join your cousins. No need to stay here and talk with me."

"But Dad, I haven't seen you in two years. I want to stay here with you."

"Has it been that long?" His eyebrows lifted.

"Yes. It has."

Sunil glanced back and forth between his mother's animation and his father's stillness. Which of these had been funneled to Bimal? Which of them had he, Sunil, become? Who was Sunil compared to his brother, other than the lesser son?

"How is school?" his father asked.

Sunil was glad he asked, but he realized he wasn't ready to talk about the problems with his dissertation. "Remember when I called to tell you I'd quit pre-med? I was so worried you'd be upset."

"What makes you think of that?"

"When I see you I remember how I wanted to try and be like you."

"Why would I have been upset?"

"Because I rejected your career. After failing at the most basic things. I still don't know if I can succeed in philosophy. It might be years before I even have a job."

Premchand shook his head. "Medicine is not for everyone. We just want you to be happy."

Meena's brother Nikhil came to fetch them then, putting Sunil on the floor and Premchand in a chair carried in from another room. All the men were now watching the game while his female cousins, mother, aunt, and Amy remained in the sitting room with the tea and the barfi, their voices carrying laughter and admonishments, Gujarati and English bleeding into each other, dominating and receding. His childhood returned to him powerfully in this heady mix of sounds and smells. But Bimal, his hopeful ally, was not here, causing a spring of worry despite the reassurances that he was improving.

On the television, Sri Lanka was bowling. Sunil had loved playing cricket with his cousins; it was the most fun he'd had in Nairobi. The matches ran for days, a lot of easy taunting. The grass was green and lush, the pitch a rectangle with the boundary marked by rope. Sunil was a better bowler than batsman. His aim was sharp and his fingers liked the hard leather seams. Except that in cricket, Sunil liked to take a long run-up and rely on speed and strength. Bimal also bowled, but he was a spinner, tossing the ball in a high, deceptive arc.

His cousins cheered, and Nikhil turned to smile encouragingly at Sunil. Sunil smiled weakly back, his head nearly too heavy to move. The room shifted if he looked around too quickly.

During a commercial he whispered to his father, "What about my grandfather—how come he isn't here? Isn't he the oldest one left?"

"Better ask your mother. She says he is suffering from dementia. We have not seen him." Then his father pulled a small shiny object from his pocket and spun it in his fingers. Brought it to his lips then put it back in his pants.

"And when are we going to talk about Bimal? Can't you imagine that it's eating me up?"

His father looked at him with concern, almost pity, and said, "Yes, I can imagine. But again we have to wait for your mother."

"Are you saying it was her decision not to tell me?"

His father shook his head. "No, that is not what I am saying."

Sunil could see his father would not say more tonight. "Can I tell you something then, Dad? Something true. I'm finally happy. I got married and I'm in love with her."

Premchand smiled with genuine pleasure then, the silvery hair of his eyebrows flickering like little stars in the glow of the TV.

The day they married, Sunil had surged with joy. The morning after his mother's call, they woke early, called City Hall, and summoned Amy's sister from DC. Air crisp, sky cloud-tufted, a cream of yellow light over the first tree buds. Monica had brought her sister a silver-blue backless dress and pulled Amy's hair back into a single sweep tacked in place with pins. That neck. Those ears. Amy looked pearly like the secret interior of a shell.

Sunil had worn a pinstriped jacket and a stain-covering silk tie, both borrowed from Andrew. He and Amy held hands before a judge. "Tether me," he said to Amy. "Or I'll float away."

"With pleasure." He felt her hold him fast with her eyes and hands, her knobby knees.

Promises exchanged, they signed the paper absorbing their

damp fingerprints. After a round of scorchingly expensive whiskeys, also courtesy of Andrew, at a bar near the courthouse, Monica took the newlyweds to a fancy French restaurant. Sunil had pointed, open-mouthed, at the prices.

The sisters had laughed. Amy kissed him. Champagne and hot, crusty bread. The women chatted and shifted comfortably in the cushioned chairs. Monica and Amy knew silverware rules and how to toast in several languages. The birthday parties and Diwali buffets of Sunil's childhood were in the dingy basements of community centers. His parents and their friends didn't drink. He felt momentarily lost at his own wedding dinner, as if he lacked the tools to celebrate, to join the world of adults. But all he had to do was find Amy's face. "I'm your beacon," she said, tipsily. She was ready to lead them, because she knew how life should be lived.

Everything glowed. The blue plates, the wine, the creamy foie gras with cherry sauce, all of it shocking Sunil's tongue, which had grown accustomed to peanut butter sandwiches, fried eggs, and Indian takeout.

In the mirror behind Monica's head, Sunil had caught sight of his father's straight nose and brown-black eyes against the white of his shirt. White was a good color for his skin, dark brown with hues of purple. Like Indian corn, Amy said—the other Indians. With the backs of his fingers he brushed her yellow-pink arms. He wanted to put his mouth in every fold of her skin.

Amy said, "Husband, you look like you're in shock. Let's have a smile. A joke."

"A philosophy joke? How about the one about the dog from Minsk."

She rolled her eyes. "Definitely not. It's a crime to even call that set of words a joke."

"It's so sad," he said. "You just don't get me."

"That's the wrong inference, my love."

Monica watched them, smiling, shaking her head. "You dorks are made for each other." Monica, who had brown curly hair and hazel eyes, looked far more Jewish than Amy, but the sisters resembled each other around the nose and mouth. For hammy laughs, they made wild, exaggerated faces, stretching their jaws and tongues and throwing their eyes into corners.

Monica said, "Mom and Dad are going to be furious with me."

"Because you should have stopped us?" Sunil said.

"No, you're right. They'll be furious with you. I don't envy you breaking the news."

The Kauffmans were back from Jerusalem on Friday. On Sunday, Amy and Sunil would visit them, then fly from DC to Nairobi.

"I keep going over how to put it," Amy said. "Truthful but not hurtful." She flipped over a fork in her fingers, then pressed the tines, hard, into the spotless tablecloth.

Monica took her sister's hand in hers, then pressed a palm on Sunil's to form a warm triangle of love. A family.

Amy shook her head. "I didn't know that acting on your own—being an adult, I guess—meant disappointing your parents, even if they disappointed you first." He saw how much this pained her, this mutual disappointment; it drew down the corners of her eyes. In this moment, Sunil loved her more intensely than he'd thought possible. What she'd said about her parents wasn't meant to be a bold strike, or a bid for sympathy. She was saying exactly what she meant, putting it in a way he'd vaguely sensed but hadn't had words to say. This was how they would learn from each other, grow together.

The restaurant door opened, and the cool spring air, which they'd been ahead of all day, now caught up to them. Thin blades across their bare throats. "It's inevitable," Sunil said. "That disappointment."

Amy looked unconvinced.

"And your parents?" Monica said. "I guess we already know your mother's reaction."

"At least Amy isn't black," he said.

Monica looked shocked.

He grinned, playing with Monica's discomfort. "From her point of view, I mean."

She shook her head, skeptically. "Sunil, be serious. Did they ask you that?"

In Kenya, there was no mixing. It wasn't tolerated, he explained. "When my mom asked me what kind of family Amy came from, I think she was relieved by the answer. She said that Jews put their kids' education first, just like Indians, which is ironic, given my mom doesn't even want me in graduate school."

"She's just worried you won't finish," Amy said. "That's how parents are. Philosophy isn't exactly a sure thing."

He was thirty; how could it still hurt him that his mother didn't believe in him, didn't ask him questions about school, still asked what was wrong with being a doctor like his father? He knew she didn't talk about him with her friends because whenever he was home they said, "What are you doing with yourself these days?" But what, really, could he complain about? The other Indian kids he grew up with, they were still leashed, fulfilling their parents' scripts. He was doing what he wanted, his father helped him out, he'd married a woman he loved. He would finish school, get a job; Amy too, a good one. They'd be happy.

"Another toast!" Monica said.

"To choices," Amy said.

On the second floor of Sarada Aunty's house, Amy washed her face and brushed her teeth, but she did not get into bed. His mother had cornered Amy after dinner. "She said I need to *warm your cold shoulder.*"

His stomach lurched. "What did you say?"

"Nothing."

"Why not?"

"I didn't know where to begin. What she said was so vague."

"That's how she talks. You have to pin her down. Don't worry, I'll talk to her."

"No," she said. "Let it go. We agreed to give it a few days, remember? She's obviously stressed. Her words just feel so intense—there's this emotional tidal wave behind them." Amy tugged at her cuff. "She loaned me this sweater." An acrylic brown cardigan with fake pearl buttons. She glanced around the tall-ceilinged room. "It's a big house. Big piece of property. I think I was expecting an apartment, or—I'm not sure what I expected."

Sunil listened and did not push her.

Amy changed into thin cotton pajamas and put the sweater back on. "I like your aunt. She asked about my degree, though she seemed to think the jobs I applied for are unpaid because they're at nonprofits. You know, I should hear back from the Welcome Group soon. Is there anywhere I can check my email?"

Sunil thought most of the jobs Amy had applied for were beneath her skills, and some of the places were so underfunded they didn't even know if they'd have a job for her, but she was optimistic—about the Welcomers in particular. They had been excited about Amy, her grad-school-fresh skills, and she thought she could improve their data gathering and community outreach.

Sunil squirted toothpaste on his finger and rubbed it around his mouth, too tired to walk down the hall to the bathroom they shared with his parents. "I'm sure they have a computer. We'll ask. You can't just wander around Nairobi, it's not safe." He patted the bed. "Let's get some sleep."

The night was cold, the linens rough. Despite their fatigue they kept turning, pulling the sheets and blankets in opposite directions. They tried to press close, his arms around her, which felt good but didn't help them sleep. Sunil repeatedly woke to unfamiliar walls papered with pictures of flower-strewn Indian temples, family photos taken on a beach with palm trees, and strangely patterned ceilings. Creaks in the floorboards, in the walls, startled him. Shook him, again, into this new-old part of the world. He reached for Amy and found her warm arm. He imagined them as old as his parents, loosely holding each other's wrinkled hands.

This morning, the sun was out, and Amy's side of the bed was empty. At the window, she cupped her hands around her eyes, and he thought of all the mornings he'd woken up to her, her hands cool, the tip of her nose and toes touched with red.

My love her name is Amy, and she is in Nay-roh-bee, he began to sing, but then he stopped. Not here, he thought. His silly songs were for home.

Here was the smell of hot milk, of cumin. Air-conditioning buzz punctuated by car horns. At home they kept the windows open. They heard bicycle bells ringing up from the sidewalk. Sounds that drew him to the window in a welcome break from his work.

Before they left Cambridge, James had given Sunil an extension—a final extension. A chapter of his dissertation was now due two weeks after they returned from Nairobi.

But Sunil had no idea how he was going to continue writing. There was the age-old problem of getting something wholly new down on paper, but even more worrisome were the implications of his view: the conclusion that if there are moral truths, we can't know them. Maybe not as stark a conclusion as Mackie or Nietzsche, not all the way to nihilism, but just as bad.

For all we knew, evolution had foisted on us the powerful illusion that there was a moral reality in the first place. This was unpalatable to someone who felt justified in holding himself and others accountable, as Sunil did, and with more fervor than many.

The day before he and Amy had left for DC, Sunil visited Lieberman. He wanted her to tell him how he could shake the paralyzing skepticism. He sat in a chair in her office, its walls newly painted yellow. In one corner was a small shelf supporting an abstract swirl of blue glass. Her father was a glass-blower who made only useful things, she had told him. This was the only piece of art he'd ever produced. "I like it because it looks melting—*molten*, this is the word. And in Israel, it's all desert. Things dry up but they do not melt. My father had an imagination after all."

It had never occurred to Sunil to wonder if his father had an imagination. His father was nothing like that loop of colored glass; his father was the neat tiny shelf hammered into the wall.

"I'm stuck," he said. "I don't how to keep going."

"It's very hard to help you if I can't read what you're working on." She sighed. "Send me an email from Kenya if you want. I will read it. Have a good trip." She stood to usher him out.

He was grateful for her support; her interest did buoy him. But she was unpredictable. In one moment she told him about her father and her own attempts to be a painter—and then, with a regretful, suspicious expression, she stopped and changed course. Encouraged him to speak, then cut him off.

The light coming into the guest room grew cloudy now, and Sunil pulled the bedcovers around him. Began to crawl back underneath them.

"Sunil, I'm talking to you," Amy said. "Didn't you hear me? There are people outside. What are they doing?"

"Love, get away from the window and get dressed. People can see you. Did you sleep there, standing up?"

"What? No. There's a girl—no, a family, hanging wet clothes on a line. Drawing water from the well."

"Servants are a fact of life here. Even poor families have them."

"They're not black. They're Indian."

Sunil got out of bed. "You must mean the neighbors."

"I *don't* mean the neighbors. I mean those people down there. Are they related to you?"

A row of buildings huddled against the wall at the back of what he assumed was his aunt's property. The thrown-together houses were made of corrugated tin, patches rusting. Electrical wires crisscrossed above. A girl, eight or ten, maybe younger, whipped clothes in the air, then clipped their corners to a line.

"My god," he said. "Sarada Aunty is a slumlord."

"They don't even have running water back there."

"How can you tell?"

She pointed to the hand pump, to the girl now raising and lowering it. Of course. He'd seen it but not known what it was. He knew nothing about the real world.

"It's pretty bleak. We just ignore them?"

Sunil shrugged. He was trying to be more like most people, people who said it was healthier to laugh at the absurd and ignore unfairness that you can't change. But suppressing anger was always hard for him, extremely so when it was justified.

"What were you thinking about just now, before looking out the window? Your face was all tied up."

"Lieberman," he said.

"The professor of your ethics seminar?"

"I met with her before I left."

"I thought James was your advisor."

"He is. But she . . . she was trying to help me make progress."

"Do you need her help?"

"No. An old genius who ignores me is who I deserve."

Amy wanted to point out that's not what she asked. Sunil saw it on her face, but they were late for breakfast.

When Sarada heard them opening the cupboards, she sprang into the room like a rabbit. "You slept so late, it's nine o'clock!" She inserted her body between Sunil and the cupboard. "You're the guests. Sit down. No cereal today, something hot. Alice will make you tea and pancakes."

Alice, smooth-faced, head wrapped in parakeet green, shuffled in moments later carrying a teapot and steaming brown discs. They ate quickly, something deliciously sweet and nutty in the batter, maybe coconut.

After they ate, Sunil heard his aunt telling Amy the sightseeing plans. Sarada was carefully dressed in a blue sari, her hair up. A small diamond stud in her nose. She was taller than his mother and more bustling, used to bossing around employees and his horde of cousins.

"What's the rat pack?" Amy whispered when Sarada had left the room.

"The what?"

"That's where we're going tomorrow. First stop today is a temple. Swamisomething."

Sunil smiled and tapped his ear. "She said 'giraffe park.'"

"No!"

"Yes."

Amy sighed. "What if on the last day I'm still just nodding and smiling?"

"That would be a miracle," Sunil said.

On the stairs, they ran into his parents. "Good, you're wearing the sweater!" Urmila said. "It is too cold here."

"Today, you see the city," Premchand said. "Very interesting place. The natives, the colonials, the temples."

It was both odd and funny to see his father play up the city he'd fled as a tourist destination.

"When was the last time you were here?" Amy asked.

"Oh, it must have been——"

"Eighty-nine," Urmila said. "These doctors are so busy."

Premchand nodded vaguely. He said, "Darling, Anupbhai is expecting us."

His mother turned to Amy and said, "Did my son tell you these names we have for mother's brother, father's sister, mother's brother's wife?"

Sunil said, "But I don't know them. Growing up everyone was just 'Aunty' and 'Uncle.'"

"So now both of you can go to school and learn Gujarati lessons!" his mother said brightly.

Sunil was surprised, impressed. He gave in. "What time does class start?"

"Oh, the hours are long." His mother laughed. "You know even I am learning every day?"

10.

*T*ipe tipe saraver banthai, kankre paar banthai (Drop by drop the oceans are filled, stone by stone the mountains are built.) That's a saying from the old days, from India. I always think of it when I remember my father and all those poor men building the Lunatic Express. Tie by tie, mile by mile.

When it was finished, he needed work. He stayed with the locos for a while, carrying bags for travelers—something I did, too, when I was young. Other men became Babus, stationmasters. By then there were of course railroads in India, also built and maintained by the British. But many of our people were from small villages where they didn't have these beasts, and they fell in love with the locos. The opportunities along the rail stretched far inside the country, along the trails of the early traders. We built towns at Voi, Tsavo, Kibwezi, Thika, Nyeri, Naivasha, Nakuru, Kisumu, all of these names so foreign on our tongues.

In these places I have met dukawallahs selling this calico, Amerikani, plus handkerchiefs, hurricane lamps, cooking pots, tea, condensed milk, sugar biscuits. Fundis built scorching forges to make metal things for the settlers who were so helpless on their own. The early traders had established the caravan paths into the interior, and we conquered those roads. It was like India there. Everybody used the rupee. We had Indian postal service and Indian laws. We were the clerks and managers. We worked seven days. At home, the fire was always burning for the women to boil water, wash the clothes, stir the dal. You children, you don't know how hard it is to build up something where before there was only bush.

We traded with the Africans. We clothed their naked bodies and gave them the tools to become civilized. You, Amerikana, you can think of conquering the Wild West, the explorers lifting up the natives. We were the first to buy what they grew and made, maize and millet and beans; sesame, chilies, groundnuts, ghee, beeswax, hides, and skins. And cotton, so much cotton! We brought the white puffballs from the fields to the ginneries. Built mills with water power to grind the maize. And wagons! Imagine! We introduced this crude vehicle to the interior, showing Africans how to carry goods and mail. Roads were thick with our carts and donkeys.

It would have been easy to dismiss the natives. Easy and foolish. Because they were acquisitive, wanting everything the whites had. The tools, the calico, things their people could not find even in their dreams. All along the rail, we built dukas of wattle and daub stocked with goods from Europe and India. We started small, but it did not take long. We'd survived the lions. And with each year, the Saurashtra faded more and more in our minds. We faced forward, faced the blood drinkers, who relied on us for cowrie shells.

I have seen with my own eyes these savages eat their meat raw. Some have teeth filed down to sharp points. For clothes, they used to wear a single shred of zebra. My father was embarrassed to tell me about the women, but I have seen their hanging teats. I know some men who found them irresistible.

Fortunately, the mixing of races has not been the story of our people here.

By the time your grandmother arrived, we were setting ourselves up at the 327th iron mile, Nairobi. Just a swamp the British decided to make railway headquarters. Plague struck five times in the first two decades. Bodies piled so high on the wagons, the dead faces bubbling green. Denied the healthy Highlands, we were given the most unhygienic place to live. They had ten thousand miles. We had thirty-two! They told us where to live, where to set up shops. Whites thought we were dirty and carried disease, but they had put us in a bog already thick with mosquitos.

I was born in 1910, the third child, but the first to survive.

[02 h: 13 m]

The British were enthusiastic about us in the beginning. Indian settlement was encouraged. They saw a place for us, you see. They praised how we got by on the tiniest of profits. We were *very thrifty* and *satisfied with a comparatively low standard of living*, they said. What did they know? I found these old words in the library, where Gopal used to drop me on a Saturday, before my ankles swelled and those tubes in my heart got thick.

Soon we outnumbered the whites. We could have squashed them if we were not a peaceful people. If we had in mind upheaval and casting out like the natives would do a few decades later. But we preferred to invest in ourselves. Turmoil would not have served us in early years. After the first big war, the schools for Indians grew. At first we had to fund them ourselves—not my family, but the rich ones. Then the government began to invest, and finally I could attend one or two years. Already I knew reading and writing, mathematics enough. But I was too old to be spared from the shop. My comfort was that our children would have educations. By the time your youngest uncles were attending, schooling was compulsory for Asian boys.

Whites came down to the bazaars to buy supplies for the farm and for safari—water cans, tents, boots, puttees. Bapuji helped outfit Sir Winston Churchill, the story goes. It sounded so marvelous to me as a child, before I was old enough to see how terrifying this country really is. How the same tree that shades you during the day houses poison snakes at night.

The colonials were the ones with guns, the ones who hunted, who carried weapons to protect themselves from animals and their own servants. And yet the white ladies thought we, simple shopkeepers and clerks, were a threat. They were so frightened they cabled the Queen for assistance fighting the "terrible Asiatic menace"! This is 1920, 1921, after we won the war, Asians helping Britain fight the Germans. And some of these European ladies are too strong. Probably you know about the Danish lady who tried to grow coffee here, who shot a lion herself, but I am talking about the snobbish ladies who sent their houseboys into the shops, as if we might close the door behind them and do something terrible.

We tried for the Highlands for years, organizing petitions, writing papers. Jeevanjee traveled to London to make our case to the imperial government. He tried to get us representation. Indian associations traveled even to Delhi and showed that all British subjects were not treated equally.

The British lied all the time. They tried to tell us that the Africans were against us and wanted to keep the Indians out, to keep more of us from coming to this country. This was not true. Africans who knew us, liked us. They said that next to missionaries, we were their best friends. We were between two fires. If we are nice to the natives, the whites think we are dangerous. If we are aloof, the natives say we are doing nothing to help their country.

I was sorry to see the natives lose their land. Then they

could not be farmers, and business was beyond them. But as Churchill said, no man has a right to be idle—and the African native is no exception.

In the end, we were kept off the land and out of government. We got a few council seats but the end result was a continuation of the past, the same disabilities. I remember one letter from the *East African Standard*: Mr. Indian, don't ask for more than is good for you. Be a good boy; sit on your proper rung of the Empire ladder and we shall all pull together very well.

Honestly, I did not follow all the ins and outs. The men advocating to resolve the Indian Question were good men, but it was a lost cause. The colonials were never going to give in.

Did we all agree, all the Asians? It is a good question. No, I suppose we did not. We are so many different kinds, and it is not always easy for Hindu, Jain, Ismaili, et cetera to see the same side.

What I know is that since I was three, I worked in the bazaars, and by twenty I partnered with an uncle to start a shop. One classmate became my supplier, another my accountant, a third my banker.

They say it is capital that turns a town into a city, and we possessed it. We suffered through the big depression in the thirties, but with education we became professionals. We began to build and operate on a larger scale—sisal, sawmills, construction—everything at a higher level. We held tight together, worshiped our own way. When my father died, he knew his escape from the lions had not been in vain.

11.

A long one wall of Gopal's shop was an old, dark chest of drawers. Urmila had always believed it came from India, but now she doubted: how would Bapuji have had the money? Everything in their apartment growing up had come dented and bruised from the bazaar.

Next to their River Road shop—a narrow storefront of matches, soap, occasional spices—had been Valjee shoemakers. Way in the back, they had an old gramophone that Urmila had twirled to when no one was looking. By the time Sunil was in middle school, Gopal had moved the shop to a new location. There, Americans and Europeans poured in for souvenirs, asking about the materials, the tribes, the artisans. That's what they'd called the natives—*artisans*.

These tourists had inspired Urmila to open her own African bazaar, because she knew what buyers wanted: authenticity. To keep a connection with the real place they had been. She understood. She had bought her beautiful chain of ivory elephants in India. There was nothing shallow about a souvenir.

The hard part, she'd learned, was creating desire when her buyers had never been to Africa. She was selling exotic trinkets, not mementos, and Columbus shoppers had fewer worldly desires than she'd counted on. Perhaps she could market herself better, but first she had to settle her problem with the supplier.

The men had arrived on time and courteously shaken hands, but Urmila did not trust the look of them. They were fat from cheating honest, unsuspecting clients like her. Their English was very good, though, which made them look superior and put the lie to Urmila's excuse for needing Gopal here to translate her poor Swahili. She was like a little girl whose father was looking over her shoulder. But it would have been unwise, she told herself, to meet alone with two strange African men. You never knew what could happen.

The president of Habari Exports asked how he could help her. He stood upright, regal, with his palms clasped in front like a politician.

Urmila thrust forward the fractured halves of a candlestick she had carried from Columbus. "This is sloppiness. What will you do for me?"

The president took the halves and turned them over slowly.

"There, there, and there," she said, pointing to the cracks.

"I am very sorry to see this, madam," the president said. "But with all due respect, without seeing the full contents of the box we cannot verify the rest of the broken items."

She crossed her arms, bangles rattling. She had worn her nice jewelry and Western clothes. "You are expecting me to bring the whole box so many thousands of miles to prove I am not lying? This is absurd!" Her brother shot her a warning look. But she had seen Gopal act exactly this way.

"I am appreciating your circumstances, Madam. I do not say you are fabricating. I am communicating to you the difficulty of lack of evidence. You are an important customer and because we want to continue business I say we will send you the next order free of shipping charge, a considerable savings. What do you say?"

"I say nonsense!" It was because she was a woman. They would not treat a man with so little respect. She sensed there was some solution hovering just outside her line of vision, some lightbulb of understanding that, if she were a man, would now illuminate. But she turned and turned and could not see it.

What she resented even more than their discrimination, though, was her brother's failure to defend her. Gopal, too, had grown fat and smug. He still smoked heavily, and she could smell the afterburn of his cigarettes on his breath. The shop itself smelled of old tobacco and burned plastic, as if there were frequent electrical fires. If this were America, the process would be simple. She would make a complaint, and her money would be returned.

She asked her brother in Gujarati, in supplication, "What do you advise me to do?"

"Try what you said to me on the phone. Threaten to take your business elsewhere."

She hated feeling weak, being stared down by a man with beady rhino eyes. So she put to him her ultimatum.

The president's son looked eager for resolution, tired of wasting his time. He wore a dark suit, sweat-stained under the arms. But the father was slow thinking; he weighed his options in his fleshy hands. After some moments, he said *No*, he could not refund as she wished. The son appeared surprised, but he said nothing.

She managed to stay put until they left the store. Then she fled to the street, into a crushing tide of chatter, laughter, music, matatus. It smelled of garbage, damp asphalt, and rank human perfume.

Clutching her purse under her arm, she walked blindly for several blocks. She had no idea where she was. On the way here, they'd driven past the old Duke of Gloucester School, where Premchand had graduated, but now, standing at the corner trying to hold her ground against the surge, she wasn't sure. The sidewalk was crumbling, and cars skirted around the choked traffic to graze her side. The sun reflected off a tall glass tower on the corner. She looked down to see that she was standing on a heap of banana peels.

Urmila was weary of depending on her siblings—not just to fix the problem at her store, but having to be driven everywhere, needing translation. Bimal's accident and Sunil's marriage pushed extra tension into every moment. Now the girl, the wife, was here.

Since he went to college, Sunil had begun to corner Urmila with his talk. When she forgot what he'd said about his classes, he would say she did not pay attention. She made him repeat himself every time they talked, he said. He questioned her motives—sometimes asking if she really cared, or if she only wanted to appear so. She cared! But his world was so far away and foreign to her. Was she supposed to write it down, all his details? "I just never know if you're even listening," he said. It infuriated her, to be doubted like that.

Sarada warned: if you pull too hard you will push him away. But Sarada had not raised Sunil. She did not know where he would give and where he'd stick. Urmila knew they all needed to relax, to get comfortable with each other. Sunil needed to see that his family were not strangers. But she did not know how to do this. She could not even outwit a slow-moving African or convince her own brother to help her.

Gopal found her scraping the bottom of a plastic take-away bowl of coconut ice cream and leaning against the window of a wig shop. He spoke to her in an even, patronizing voice. Urmila looked at the wigs while he talked, the straight black bobs, the wild curls, the tangles of tiny braids. How did women wear them—a different one for each day, depending on one's mood?

"You knew they would not accept," she said.

"Urmilabhen, you are not fooling me. I know the state of your business is poor. You're going along only with your husband's salary. I am not saying this is a bad thing—a husband can do this for his wife, to keep her busy, happy—but if you want to be truly successful you have to address the difficulties in your plan. The problem is not the supplier. Put this on the back burner until you have sorted matters out. This is my advice."

In her mind, Urmila bought all three wigs. She would use them as disguises, to avoid anyone she was ashamed to confront.

Bimal was asleep when they arrived at the hospital. His broken leg was bound in gray plaster; his bare toes bony and forlorn. The slash in his face had begun to stitch itself together, but it was still terrible to look at. Urmila drew the sheet over Bimal's toes then held his dry cool feet, her palms against his soles. The nurse had told her that most of the time Bimal lay in a thick fog of pain medication.

"I think I will get a cup of tea," Sarada said tactfully, as soon as they arrived.

Their brother Anup would arrive soon, with Mital. Urmila had only a few minutes alone with her son.

She did not expect him to reply, but perhaps he could hear her. So she told him about her life in Columbus, her few friends (the Savlas, mostly), her routine. Her pleasure in donating to the temple at the end of the year so she could see *The African Bazaar* and her name printed up in the lists of patrons. She recounted the books she read, biographies of Margaret Thatcher and Indira Gandhi. On Saturdays and Sundays, Premchand took long walks and read the paper for hours. They hardly saw friends anymore, and over the years invitations had dried up. "What am I supposed to do with myself?" she'd asked her husband. He mentioned card games, jogging, bicycling, volunteer work—things done by the wives of the doctors he worked with. "That is what Americans do, this leisure. That is not for me," she said to Bimal, who continued to lie very still, only his chest rising and gently falling. "What will we do when he retires?" At the very thought, her mouth gummed up, dry and pasty. Thankfully that time wouldn't come for many years.

But then, as if he were there to help her with her problem, Bimal's eyes fluttered open, and his head rolled drunkenly toward her. "Aunty," he mumbled.

"I should call the nurse?"

He shook his head. "No more drugs. Sleepy."

This would have to be enough for now. She nodded. "Rest now, just rest."

Urmila tidied up, threw away plastic cups, and refilled the water pitcher. Shook the crumpled blanket and folded it. Using tissues from her purse, she absorbed the sweat on Bimal's brow and wiped down the metal guardrails. As she cleaned under cups and vases, she began to feel better—industrious, necessary.

The room in order, her breathing calmed by the regular rhythm of Bimal's, she took his hand, warm and giving. If they could not talk, she wanted him to feel her. She spread his fingers against her collarbone, pressing the tips into her skin. *There, my son.* But there was no change in the quality of his touch, the tension in his skin. So she lifted the collar of her sweater and slid his hand down the slope of her breast, the heel of his palm flat above her nipple. Had she been the one to breastfeed him, as nature had intended, he would have felt exactly this skin as a baby.

"Mom," said a soft voice. Startled, she dropped Bimal's hand and spun around to see Sunil. In the flesh! She would not have been more surprised to see a rhinoceros. "What are you doing here? You are alone?"

He shook his head. "I wish I could be that brave, to come

here alone. No, I asked Anup and Mital to take me. I insisted, actually. They are waiting in the hall."

She was relieved that Sunil's wife hadn't accompanied him. "Come say hello to your brother."

Sunil nodded, though he looked afraid, hesitated.

Bimal rustled under the sheets and murmured something.

"Look you have woken him up! Do not tire him. He needs his rest."

Sunil said to Bimal, "How are you feeling? I couldn't wait any longer to see you."

Bimal slowly opened his eyes as wide as he could and said in a scratchy voice, "It is a little painful to talk with the tube in my throat . . . please stay five minutes. Seeing you is like a dream."

Sunil shook his head. Clasped his hands on the bed's metal rails that Urmila had just cleaned. "All the way over here I was thinking about what I would say, and now I can't think of anything! I really just wanted to see for myself that you are okay. It's hard to get details in this family, you know?"

Bimal nodded with a small smile that tugged at his scar. "But there are plenty of opinions, as many as you like."

Sunil laughed, and Urmila, who was standing gingerly at the foot of the bed and looking back and forth between the two, astonished at their proximity after so many years apart, felt her knees turn to jelly.

Bimal said gently, "You look yourself like you have had an accident."

"Just the shock of my life! Seeing you recovering makes everything better."

"Welcome back, bhai."

Sunil's face flushed right through his date-colored skin, and Urmila felt her pulse quicken, as if watching a hawk and a chicken make friends. At the sound of her brother Anup's voice in the hall, Urmila hurried out to shush him. "Calm your tongue! The boys are in there! My prayers have been answered."

Her brother put a hand on her arm and said, "Mital will be here in ten minutes; she is getting some mango juice at the shop. I told her—"

But Urmila had already turned back into the room, rejoining her sons. Sunil was asking if Bimal needed anything, and the one in the bed was shaking his head apologetically; he was tired now and needed to sleep.

"Of course," Sunil said. "Mom, we should go."

"Don't forget," Bimal said with effort.

Sunil nodded solemnly. "I won't." Urmila saw something then: the eyebrows! Both boys had weedy strips above their eyes, just like their father.

"You go," she said to Sunil.

"We both should. He's tired, Mom, plus Mital Aunty and Anup Uncle are here. They want to be with their son." Urmila would have contested these words except for the appearance of Mital on the other side of the bed. Her sister-in-law's frown cemented Urmila's desire to stay. She would not be pushed aside in this important moment. The reunion of her sons!

Sunil looked at her, then at Mital, sighed, and left the room.

"What a good boy," Urmila said, loud enough for her sister-in-law to hear.

Mital, who wore a neatly pressed sari and a faded vermilion part in her hair, handed Urmila an open bottle of orange cola and several pieces of pistachio barfi. "Hardly he is alone in this room," she said, gesturing toward Bimal, whose meds had tugged him back into a deep sleep. Gradually they would lighten the drugs, though they wanted to keep his breathing comfortable given his cracked ribs. Then Mital folded her arms, her expression hard to read; the skin of her horse-face sagged.

"We are trying to share the burden—you can't be here all the time," Urmila said.

"A mother is very strong. She can withstand almost anything for her child. Don't you think so?"

"Of course." Urmila sipped the warm cola, *pop* they called it in Columbus.

"You know, my husband never stops praising your mother? How she raised you all with so little money, arranged all the right marriages. You all were dressed so nicely for school, your faces scrubbed and socks pulled up tight. Coins in your pockets for the beggars. A real sadhvi!" Mital paused. "I sometimes wonder what she would think of this younger generation, the way they stray from their homes, marry outside, lose the language. Or your father, who still lives and breathes."

"I hope you are not suggesting something," Urmila said.

"Only that holding on to your son is hard. There are risks in America. So much temptation. Who can say who or what is to blame? I think of you often with sympathy." Mital ran thin fingers down the length of her braid, pulled off the tie at the end where the strands had frayed, and rebraided.

"You! Saying these things about me after all I have given you?"

"I never asked you. You were desperate. You would have left the child on the street. Or worse! I know you considered worse. I remember you from that time. You did nothing but complain about your husband, and now you march back and try to reclaim what you never wanted." Mital leaned forward, lips pulled back in a snarl. "Listen carefully, sister. I refuse you. I repudiate you. My son doesn't need you, he never has. Get away from here. Go home."

Thirty-one years ago, Urmila had left her husband in Columbus because she could not live with such a rigid man, not in a city of strangers so far from her family. He was too busy, and even the most industrious housewife could not make all the time go by. She had taken little jobs doing office work—they would not let her answer the phones—and once a job as a crossing guard at an elementary school, where she marveled at the huge rucksacks strapped to their little backs. She had no one to tell these things to, though, and the phone was much too expensive for more than once every few months. She disliked writing letters; they reminded her of school. She could not put her feelings in them. Her husband resisted meeting other Indians, always too tired. He encouraged her to take courses, English or arts and crafts, but she had never been handy. What she wanted was her sister, the all-day back and forth, being heard and speaking. Even quarreling was reassuring, she realized, when she did not have it in her life. She had thought that even if she could not divorce, could never start a new family or be a mother, she would at least be living with people who knew her, loved her. She came back to Nairobi planning to take up her old job teaching primary school. Live with her sister and help raise her niece and nephew.

Then Urmila had discovered she was pregnant. For a while, she believed she could keep the child and live under her sister's roof. In America, people lived like this all the time. But her family told her it was impossible. Her father, especially, was emphatic and prescriptive. Single and separated was one thing. Single mother another. She'd wept against her sister's shoulder.

"He is yours," Urmila had said to Anup. That was all. They never discussed names or how Mital had prepared the house. They took him straight from the hospital.

Without husband or child, she was unwanted, like a cup of cold tea. Her best chance at her own life, at a slice of freedom and maybe even love, lay with Premchand in America. In the end, no one exiled her from Nairobi, but not even her sister had encouraged her to stay. When she boarded her flight bound for London, then New York, then Columbus, she had felt she was fleeing.

She reentered Ohio as if she'd never left. No one asked about her year away.

When Sunil was born, just one year after Bimal, his head thick with dark whorls, they'd skipped all the ceremonies. She was too tired, no one from Nairobi could come, and then what was the point? She did apply oil to his hair when she remembered.

Now, again, Urmila felt forced to flee from people and a place she'd once thought would care for her, defend her.

Urmila cornered her younger brother in the hallway. He gave her a handkerchief for her tears, gingerly touched her shoulders. Mital has been under great stress, he told her. Her mother was ill and she was on rough terms with Sheetal, their daughter-in-law. All this in addition to Bimal's slow recovery.

"You can override," Urmila said. "I must be allowed to see my son."

His body was skinny, but her brother's face was wide across the cheekbones, like hers, but without firmness underneath. Soft like a baby's. Now the flesh of his cheeks twitched. He said, "Your own son is healthy. He is here. He is brave, you know, he took a taxi back on his own. You should be spending time with him and his wife, Urmilabhen."

A trio of nurses in purple uniforms pushed a squeaking metal cart past them. The women sang softly, braiding their voices.

Then Anup sighed. He said, "In a few days, Bimal will be enough recovered and will come home. You can talk to him more then. Though I think you will have to compete with your Sunil for his attention! Don't worry. Everyone will feel better in a few days."

But would she feel better? What could be made whole? In America they had ideas about marriages as partnerships. She had never expected this glossy dream, nor had she been fooled by Bollywood movies about romance. What she had wanted was companionship, and a comfortable life with some luxuries. She had gotten some much-loved comforts (her own car, a microwave), but the isolation ate at her. Where was the second chance they promised you in the novels and TV of her adopted country? Yes, she saw now, there was bringing Sunil and Bimal together. This was a good start. She was not so sure what to do with Amy, but she would think of some way to bring her round.

Sarada drove her back to the house. Urmila paused on the stairs leading to the second floor; faint starlight crept in through the windows. The immigrant families living in the back were quiet; still many hours until sunrise. Outside Sunil's door Urmila paused, pressed her ear to the wood. No one stirred. She turned the handle and the hinges creaked. Her feet slipped over the threshold. She should not be doing this. But her need grew arms and she pushed open the door.

What she saw: two bodies under a heap of blankets, a small white foot poking out the bottom, a brown arm curved over a hump of shoulder. Blankets furled around and over them like silk. The back of Sunil's head was so thick and dark she knew she must have rubbed in the oil every one of his infant days.

12.

Day four: the Karen Blixen house. Sarada Aunty ushered them out of the house to the minivan, where the driver and his father were waiting. "You must be stifled spending so much time with us old people. When Meena comes back, the young ones can go out." And soon Bimal would be home, where they could visit him with ease. His aunt put her hands on his shoulders. "I am so happy to see you, after all these years."

Sunil smiled. He saw the effort she was extending to welcome them. Then they rolled out of the driveway, past the guard, down the residential streets, and out into the clogged roads and roundabouts.

Sunil told Amy about his latest anxiety dream, a comic nightmare, in which James had been running after him through a field with a pitchfork. His clock was running out. He had to email his thoughts to Lieberman, so he could write them up more fully, with her feedback, when they got home.

Amy turned to look at him, skeptically. "I thought you didn't need her help."

"I think I was wrong." How could he possibly work here? His family crowded out all other thoughts. He needed to get reacquainted with his brother. And yet Sunil could not ignore the dire position he was in. If he did not make progress, and soon, the department could take away his funding. He wished he could share his troubles with Amy, but the problem felt too big, and too much his own fault.

Amy pulled at the plastic pearl buttons of his mother's sweater, which she'd been wearing for days. She'd taken on some color, but she didn't look happy. For a moment after breakfast, in the bright kitchen, his mother and Amy had stood side by side in matching cardigans, sharing some discomfort, looking like an advertisement for a multinational pharmaceutical. But what would they both be selling? Valium? Blood-pressure meds? He thought of Bimal in his wrinkled hospital gown, the purple splotch on the back of his hand where the IV attached. When he told Amy about his visit, short as it was, she had been ecstatic. He had waffled for nearly an hour before resolving to go to the hospital. He had been scared, when it came down to it, to face his mother's favored son. Bimal had shown, though, that he had a sense of humor, which counted for a great deal. His brother had also, without providing a reason, extracted from Sunil a promise: that he see their grandfather. He was old and his mind was struggling, but he still had moments of clarity, and would want to see his American grandson. "Maybe he will tell you some things you do not know," Bimal added. Bimal referred to their grandfather as *Nana*, which was new to Sunil, who thought of him as Bapuji because that's what his mother called him.

Sunil would have to convince his family to take him to the old man, but now he forced himself to focus on the day ahead, outward instead of inward. To being here together. "You read *Out of Africa*, right?" he said to his wife.

"I loved it." Before they started dating, Sunil had not read much beyond the news, but Amy had begun reading stories aloud to him. She particularly liked Isaac Asimov, who appealed to her scientific side and was a favorite of her Russian grandfather's.

"Good. Today should be okay." Reassurance meant as much for himself as for her. Because as they drove through the snarled lanes of cars, Sunil felt increasingly that he was returning to the scene of a crime. He kept remembering his childish infraction from half a lifetime ago, when they'd gone with Bimal and Mital Aunty to Mombasa and he'd run away to be fed by a stranger—Tom who knew of Magic Johnson—fistful of his mother's money in hand. He still felt the shiver and tremble of their fight, which was at heart about their claims over each other, about power and obligation, and where had his father been in all this? Outside the fray, as usual.

The stunt now pained Sunil. He would have stayed, kicked around a football, whatever would have drawn the boys toward some fraternal bond. Maybe Bimal could help him understand how on earth his mother had come to have a child here and give it to his uncle and aunt to raise. Until now, Sunil had lived his life as if his—and his parents'—past in this country did not exist. As a result, he didn't understand this place any better than when he was fifteen. On the surface he could see that the city had transformed. The ration shops were now big grocery stores. Moonlit Chemists, where his mother used to buy a special skin-lightening face cream, had been swapped out for some chain.

But the old Indian bazaar? Sunil had no memory of it. He didn't know how the neighborhood where his family now lived fit into the old city or the new one.

Worse, what he saw and heard didn't line up with what he was told. Bimal aside, the old stories about intelligence and ambition pulling a whole community up out of the malarial mud—they were so vague and hyperbolic, Sunil couldn't form a solid picture. To him Nairobi was just a polluted, corrupt, Third World city like dozens of others. Around the sightseeing, his family skirted each other edgily, with small talk.

Into this booby trap, Sunil had brought Amy. She was

determined to come, but he still felt selfish because he needed her so much.

Amy scanned the traffic and the trees, vacantly knocking her knuckles against the window glass. "Do you notice how dawn and dusk happen instantly here? The sun just appears and disappears. There should be more warning." He saw that she looked unnerved, tense.

"No," he said. "What else? Tell me." What else did she see that he didn't? What did her eyes discover and not forget?

The women selling groundnuts in the road. The kids living in the backyard. Meena's pretty accent. The sandstone Jain temple that was both humble and elegant. Dance music pumping from the matatus. "There's a lot I think I'll never forget."

Stalled at a light, they watched a flock of green-black birds on a sagging electric wire. "I can't wait for the safari," she said wistfully. If a flamingo should appear at their window right now she would jump on its back and fly away.

This was something new, announced to them last night. His father had bought them a wedding present, a three-day safari in the Maasai Mara. Sunil knew it had been bought out of guilt, but it was still very generous. Amy was thrilled.

"Privacy," he said, in a low voice.

"Sex," she whispered and squeezed his thigh. "I mean, all the beautiful, wild animals."

They'd started kissing ferociously, scratching, taking off clothes, once in the past several days, but they'd been too embarrassed, too nervous about interruption. Amy took his hand now, but Sunil released it, indicating his father and the driver.

The road started to rise, and more bushes and trees appeared. The sky grew closer.

"We are beginning to enter the Highlands," Premchand said. "There are no Indians here."

"None?" Sunil said.

"Not that I am aware of."

Amy said, "Premchand, you told us when you came to the States, but you didn't say why. Will you tell us?" Amy had stopped calling his father *Doctor*.

His father paused for such a long time that Sunil thought he might be trying to remember himself, or perhaps he was forming a story because there wasn't one.

"In November of 1961," Premchand said, "there was heavy flooding in Nairobi. Everyone was caught off guard, stranded at the hospital. It rained and rained and the rivers swelled. Patients arrived covered in mud, wet head to toe. During those three days I saw the hospital for what it really was." Again he paused, slowly shaking his head. "People there treated it as a vacation, an excuse to take it easy, okay? They changed schedules, bent the rules. I couldn't stand such laziness."

Here, in the car, watching the scenery change as they eased away from the tumbledown city into the wider, wealthier, greener spaces, it seemed shocking that his parents had moved across the world. His father's immigration story was self-serving, but Sunil believed in it. There was something inflexible in his father; it would have been hard for him to accept conditions less than optimal. This was a virtue because it inspired ambition. It was also a failing: the inability, the refusal, to see things outside the idealized frame he'd constructed.

Unlike many of his grad-school classmates, Sunil was not a seeker, someone who sought a grand unifying theory of the universe. Nor was he a debate-team champion out for blood, more interested in combat then ideas. Sunil wanted to understand not the greater workings of the universe but the logic of human beings. A business so much messier than he had naively expected.

What questions would Sunil ask Bimal when they met again? He didn't know yet, but he felt an urgency begin to swell inside him.

Premchand cleared his throat and continued, "Some people say it was a big risk moving to USA. But I'd already learned how to be brave, how to defend myself by growing up in Nairobi." He turned to look meaningfully at Sunil.

This was unusual. His father had never been a storyteller. Was he performing for Amy? It seemed she and his father were beginning to take a shine to each other, which relieved and gratified Sunil. In contrast, standing next to his mother and exchanging small talk this morning was as close as the two women had gotten. Urmila didn't come sightseeing with them, and she left few conversational spaces during meals. She seemed to disappear with Sarada during the empty afternoon hours when the older people napped and he and Amy lounged with books in the dim living room, or sat on plastic chairs catching sun in the backyard.

There were some "bad types" where he'd grown up, Premchand now said. "Gangs, hoodlums, and one of these criminals had the name *Big Tooth*, because he lost most of his teeth in a fight. He was supposed to protect our little neighborhood, but he was also very jealous so any competition he had to snuff out."

"Dad, did you see this in a movie?"

His father smiled. "It is the stuff of movies, I agree." The weapon of Big Tooth was a big knife, he said—there were no guns, not like in America, or like Nairobi today. "We would see him walking the perimeter of the compound, tossing his blade, and I grew very curious. I shouted questions at him from behind the bushes. At first he didn't mind because I wasn't a threat, I was too little.

"But I grew older and I asked him things—*How did you lose your teeth? How many men have you killed?*—and he got annoyed. It was a kind of joke because he called me Big Mouth—and he was Big Tooth, okay? But one day he got tired of my big mouth and sent some thugs to shut me up, not to hurt me, just send a message. These men were fierce, big arms and scars on their hands. They followed me menacingly. At first I was scared, but then I grew used to them. And so when we moved to USA I was never worried about the bad neighborhoods. Ask your mother."

"You stood up to gangsters!" Amy let out a full, open-mouthed laugh.

"Yes," his father smiled. "A real tough guy."

"Dad, you never told me about your time as a crime fighter."

"I never thought of it. Being here has brought it all back." He pointed out the window at a tree with corkscrew arms and leaves large as footballs. Beyond, in the distance, were blue hills nestled under the clouds. The light was golden and thick and hung all around them. "Look," he said, "some things here are still beautiful. You hardly see views like this in America."

13.

Perched at the end of a long drive, surrounded by palms, pointy trees, and trimmed hedges, the house was smaller than he expected. Red tile roof and white window frames. Very English. There was a long shaded porch where Premchand imagined colonials drinking their cocktails. Inside, the floors were dark, everything swept and shiny.

"This is all from the movie," Amy said, looking at the furniture and Chinese ceramics.

"But they are in much better shape than the originals," Premchand said. He pointed to a flattened animal skin. "This is real lion."

"Real," Amy smiled, "but not the one Karen Blixen really stepped on." She wore sneakers and khaki shorts, his wife's brown sweater. Hair in a ponytail. She bounced lightly on her heels.

"Do you suppose this was a man-eating lion?" Premchand said. When Sunil and Amy looked at him questioningly, he added, "You haven't heard about them? They ate men like candy."

"Sounds like another tall tale, Dad. Those gangsters really pulled your leg."

Premchand smiled. He couldn't remember where he had

heard about the lions. Was it in the movie? He and Urmila had rented *Out of Africa* one night when Sunil was out with friends. Meryl Streep's white suit and white hats, curly brown hair: *Doesn't it matter to you I'm another man's wife?* He couldn't remember what Robert Redford had said in response, only the hazy yellow-green plain behind his head. The silly upswell of music that Urmila had thought romantic.

Clouds slid over them and shaded the grassy expanse behind the house. Sunil squinted toward the horizon, and Premchand watched the way he moved gracefully through the museum, jaw pulled back in thought, arms crossed, then his hand on his wife's arm, leaning into her ear, a flash of smile. The way his thumbs rubbed against each other when he clasped his hands behind his back. He felt he'd never witnessed his son's life in this much color and detail. Premchand now saw this person, this being made from himself, the black stubble on Sunil's face, with sudden clarity and curiosity. He was also seeing his son in love, his son married, intimate glimpses that he would likely not witness again for a long time.

He tried to remember: who had been Sunil's first girlfriend? It would have been during the period when Premchand was traveling, giving so many talks. He had little memory of home life then. That had been the high point of Premchand's career. He missed talking to an audience. He also missed sticking his face behind a microscope, entering the tiniest of worlds. Helping patients was gratifying, but their suffering exhausted him.

If he had been paying attention back then, years ago, he would have known Sunil wasn't cut out to be a doctor. His son had found exam rooms claustrophobic and shied away from instruments and needles. He liked looking at things under the microscope, until he was told what they were—bacteria, amoeba, *C. elegans*. Premchand's own absorption—his gratitude that medicine had given him a vocation and an escape—had made him lose sight of the fact that in America a child could grow up to be anything. He had not presented his son with any options. Premchand had not known himself what they were.

Now he would follow the moments as they presented themselves. Each detail deserved his attention.

Amy gestured with her camera at Premchand and Sunil, told them to stand against the dark-paneled fireplace for a snapshot. "Say, *gastritis,*" she said, laughing. "A public health joke, right, Premchand?" Then she headed outside to take more pictures. Premchand liked this small curious girl, her raucous joke, her outsized appetite. Around him, he noticed, Amy had begun to relax, choosing to sit next to him at dinner and ask questions about his practice in Columbus, where he treated a large number of international refugees. Premchand did not blame Amy for remaining quiet when the larger group of relatives gathered. He often felt ambushed when he spoke up, unless he had been careful to prepare a big voice and forceful line, which was usually too much effort. He had the feeling that his son wanted his wife to act with confidence, and Premchand was rooting for her, too. For them.

After Amy went outside to take more pictures, Sunil said, "This museum. We never came here when I was a kid."

"Oh? What did you do during the summers?" He had missed this part of his son's life, too.

"We worked in the shop. We had foot races in the driveway, swam at the pool. I went with Bimal to a summer chemistry class. We exploded volcanoes and made borax snowflakes with pipe cleaners." He paused for a moment. "Bimal was so enamored of it. But his crystals didn't grow very well. I really lorded it over him. Then I gave him mine when I left. I just remembered that.

"Those summers were hard, though. Mom was always embarrassed I couldn't speak Gujarati." He touched the wooden bedpost and the delicate glass shade of a lamp. "Why didn't you ever come, Dad?" Sunil hovered next to the bed smothered in leopard skins. A pair of earth-colored pants and a white linen shirt hung on a closet door. But Sunil seemed to be only glancing at the objects; his gaze had turned inward, to the past, to his frustration. He now looked around and then impulsively stepped over the rope meant to keep visitors from brushing up against the artifacts. Premchand looked for a guard, but there was no one. He felt a rush—the prickling novelty of being alone with his son.

"It was hard to get vacation time," Premchand tried to explain. "I wanted to take you to the American things. Do you remember the Grand Canyon?"

"Of course. You and I and Anup Uncle were the only ones brave enough to ride donkeys down to the bottom. We drove across country in that big van. Ajay Uncle lit the back seat on fire with his cigarette."

"Your uncle is a little careless." Premchand moved closer to his son, but stayed behind the rope. "You know your mother wanted you to come here, very badly. She misses you."

Sunil crossed his arms and looked down at the leopards, then up at Premchand. He said, "The last week has been pretty long, you know. First telling Amy's parents, now being here."

"They were unhappy with your news?" This was the first his son had said about their days in DC.

They'd told the Kauffmans as soon as they arrived, Sunil said, all of them sitting in the backyard. "I remember staring hard at this bush beside me, I couldn't focus on their faces." At first, Ariel had blanched, but stayed quiet. Then she'd said, "Oh, honey," as if her daughter were ill.

"They were upset about the marriage outside of Judaism, but they covered it by saying they were offended that Monica, Amy's sister, had been invited to the wedding—when they hadn't even been told. But they were out of the country, and, well, we knew they'd be upset. Amy had decided she didn't want them there—too complicated." Sunil looked away from Premchand's face and kept talking. "Monica tried to rescue us by focusing on Amy's job search. Before we went to DC, she'd interviewed with three nonprofits in Boston. The interviews hadn't gone as well as Amy had hoped—and Ariel made it worse. She interrogated every moment: Had Amy asked the right questions? Listened carefully? It was infuriating. Anyway, there was one place, the Welcome Group, she really likes. She's hoping to get an offer from them." Sunil paused. "The whole dinner was awful. A lot of silence. I could hear myself chew."

Premchand heard distant voices, but no one joined them in the whitewashed room. He waited for more.

"Later, David, Amy's father, started asking all these questions about Nairobi. Ariel, too. I told them that I really didn't know much or what to expect, but they kept asking. Questions I'd never thought of myself, about the older generation—dates—things I know nothing about, and somehow that made things better. It was like they needed to find a redeeming angle, something to feel good about, and they were excited for us that we were taking this trip. That Amy would meet everyone." Sunil shook his head. "I've never seen anything like it. They went from being angry to being concerned, invested, so quickly. They were still hurt, but they were a family. We. Maybe we were a family." Sunil pinched the bridge of his nose, as if pained, and looked at the parchment-yellow maps on the walls. Then he stepped back over the exhibition rope, to the visitors' side, and gestured to his father to move on.

"This is something good," Premchand said. "They have accepted you, and they are Jewish, too."

"Dad, it's not just that they're Jewish. A lot of Jews are like Jon Samuel, your partner—secular and liberal. Isn't he married to a Korean woman? Amy's parents are much more conserva-tive. They're religious like born-again Christians. Anyway, yes, things seem to have healed a little with them, once the initial shock wore off. They weren't going to decide Amy was dead to them."

At the wide bay of windows, they stood together and looked out at the ground where the coffee plantation used to be. A chat-tering European family joined them in the room. Next to the white people, and after a few days in the sun, Sunil was very brown. He was darker than Urmila or Premchand, than anyone in their families, and Urmila had been worried about this when he was a boy. Especially when Sunil came home with bruises on his arm, inflicted on the walk to their house from the bus stop. Still, Premchand had stubbornly maintained their son's dark skin would not matter in USA like it would in Kenya or India. Premchand thought now that he had probably been wrong.

He watched Sunil watch his wife as she strolled across the lawn, away from the house. When they all went out together, Amy looked like a lemon among potatoes. She now reached an outbuilding and pulled at the padlocked door, peeked in the shuttered window. Nosy.

"So, what's new with you and Mom? You seem busy, as usual. Mom has hit her stride with the store. That's great."

Premchand stepped closer, stood beside his son so they took in the same sights. "Yes," he said. Then he thought, *no*, he should tell the truth. No more secrets. "Well. I should tell you, the store is subsidized."

"What?" Sunil turned to face him.

"From my salary."

"How much?"

"Four thousand dollars per month."

Sunil began to pace, around and around the antique din-ing table. The European family glanced at them and shuffled quickly into the next room.

"Four thousand? That's almost fifty thousand a year. That's a pretty costly hobby, Dad."

Outside, the clouds thickened. Gray light filtered into the room, and the romantic warmth of the colonial wood and rugs and paneled walls cooled.

"It's been good for your mother. What other options does she have?"

"What if something happens and you don't have enough to retire? I won't be able to help you guys out for a long time."

Sunil's face was tight, eyes pinched and nostrils flared. A delicate porcelain vase was positioned carefully on a stand just inches away.

"Son, I *have* a pension. We *have* savings. We are not going to go broke."

"I guess I don't understand. If Mom was so desperate for something to do all those years I was in school, why didn't she come to my soccer games, talk to the other moms, pick me up after classes? I just mean that, well, that bus ride was an hour and a half each way. You never drove me either." This was a sore spot, but Premchand had promised himself he would be quiet and listen. "Then Mom wanted to take me out of Pick, just when I was getting used to it. Remember?"

"Your mother was too focused on grades. She did not give you enough time to adjust, I agree."

Sunil shook his head. "We fought so much and you never stepped in. You could have been there more, Dad." His arms burst open then, like furious wings, and the porcelain vase shattered.

Sunil stared at the wreckage. "Fuck," he said. "I'm so stupid. I am so sorry," he said to a horrified-looking attendant who, upon hearing the crash, had hurried into the room. Then both he and Premchand were down on their knees.

Premchand reached over and grasped his son's jaw. Felt the

bristle that proved that Sunil was grown up now, which made his heart contract. "Son," he said. "We are going to be fine. Your job is your studies, your new life. Your good life, your wife, as you told me yourself. Let us worry about the rest. Go——" He gestured to the lawn, where Amy's lens pointed toward the window shedding light on the mess they had made. "Go to her."

Sunil dropped the shard he was holding, nodded, and left Premchand with the pieces.

Despite reports of recent muggings, since arriving in Nairobi Premchand had begun taking walks for the exercise and to get out of the house. He couldn't endure more snacking, more gossipy chats. The sidewalks were narrow, sometimes not more than a dirt path, but it was better than walking at the Oshwal Centre, where he failed to remember the names of the boyhood friends who tacked across the lawn to talk to him——the man who'd gone to America.

Lacing up his shoes, Premchand told Urmila that they'd had a pleasant morning sightseeing in the Highlands. She had complained of a headache and stayed behind. He kept the more troubling details to himself. Amy was a nice, smart girl, he said. She was good for their son.

Urmila was doubtful. She'd heard Amy asking Sarada about email; she was too busy connecting to home and doing her personal things. "An Indian girl would not go in for all the sightseeing."

"The sightseeing is set up by your sister."

"I am telling you, an Indian girl would do the right thing. Especially in a time of crisis."

"She's not your competition, darling. They are happy together. And there is no crisis."

Urmila ignored him. "You know what would make *me* happy? A promise not to take away the money for the shop. Now I am starting a mentorship with this American woman, how would it look if I suddenly closed?" Her face was bare of makeup, her dyed hair showed gray at the roots. Glasses bloomed her eyelashes into thick, dark feathers.

"What will you do to keep expenses down?"

"This is the reason I'm having all these meetings. To find a new supplier and cut costs."

"If you reduce like you say, then you can have the money."

Premchand wanted her to keep the shop, but especially after Sunil's reasonable point about savings, he knew it was time to be more careful. He should start sending larger sums to help Sunil and Amy, and if he was honest with himself, he knew this was a better investment. Being able to give them something extravagant, like the safari, had felt good.

Premchand decided to head toward the ring road with the Westgate shopping center in mind as a destination. Yesterday he'd bought a new watch battery there. But after a few blocks he tired of the route and took another. The late-afternoon heat was drying the roads. He'd been away for many years, but he had never really forgotten the rhythms of his childhood: the cycles of light and dark, hot and cold, wet and dry. Red dust sprayed up under his feet. His shoes would be ruined, but he didn't care.

A spotless black Mercedes cruised by. Then students in blue-and-white uniforms, women in printed dresses, men in suits and pointy shoes, young boys hawking bundles of newspapers, all of them accumulating a layer of fine red clay on their skin.

Premchand felt for the plastic knight in his pocket, pressed it against his thigh, then rubbed the worn nose with his thumb. He turned again, onto a narrower, residential street. If he could drive here, he might have gone to a park to feel a little more open space, grass under his feet. When he was a boy, Jeevanjee Gardens had seemed huge, so many shrubs for hide-and-seek.

He and his brothers used to gather nuts from the ground and throw them at the statue of Queen Victoria, seeing who could hit her square in the forehead.

In his new state of heightened perception, Premchand had felt something worrisomely tense between Sunil and Amy during the drive home from the Blixen house. Sunil had appeared to be urging something on Amy, and she was shaking her head, not ready or willing to accept. At one point she squeezed her eyes shut, and balled her fists on her thighs. Sunil had kept talking in his low, soothing, persuasive tone, until finally her head snapped toward him and she said, "Stop it! You're not helping. I can barely think." Sunil had flopped back into his seat, disappointed and defeated, and Premchand had silently vowed to urge them on, whatever they needed. Because even in this disagreement he had seen that there was love and good faith in both of them; when they had separated into their frustrated silos, their hands had reached for each other, unable to stay apart. The touch calmed them so that they appeared healed by the time they arrived back at the house. He couldn't remember ever having that effect on his wife. When Premchand told Sunil about the wedding gift, he had apologized for pretending to know about the marriage. He'd tried to apologize for Urmila, too, but Sunil had brushed it off. Just that morning he had asked his mother when they would talk about Bimal, about why they had kept it a secret from him for so many years, and Urmila had said, "He was never a secret! He was always there but you never wanted to talk to him." This was foolish and untrue, and Premchand told her so, in front of Sunil. Then Urmila had capitulated and said, "Okay, we will talk. Let us find some time when we can have some quiet and put our heads on straight."

"And I want to see my grandfather," Sunil said.

To which Urmila had gruffly said, "Fine, fine."

They needed more time, Premchand thought. But would

they have it? The safari was drawing close. He saw landmines littered across the days ahead. Each skirmish that passed between
mother and son was another small explosion that weakened the
bridges.

So much healing to do.

Premchand felt responsible for the state of discord between
his wife and son. He knew how much he'd left them alone when
Sunil was young. Maybe each took their anger of feeling abandoned and turned it against one another. And so, when Urmila
had been determined to find something of her own, Premchand
had encouraged it. He and Urmila both had believed that private schooling would take care of Sunil—give him not just an
education but a surrogate American family. Jon Samuel and his
wife had told them that busy American children did not have
time to get into trouble, so Premchand had encouraged Sunil to
take up sports and Boy Scouts. They didn't want to be overbearing parents like the others in their set. And Premchand had to
admit that he never could muster enthusiasm for those school
events, thick with loud-mouthed kids and the other parents
who eyed him warily.

They could not wait any longer to talk about Bimal. Premchand suddenly could not understand why they had kept it to
themselves for so long.

After an hour of walking, Premchand knew he was lost. At
the last corner he should have turned. But when he retraced his
steps, he was not at all sure. There were no street signs, and he
realized he didn't even know the address of his sister-in-law's
house, though he couldn't be far because there were not so many
streets in the area. A hundred yards ahead was an intersection
with a busy road, but when he reached it, he still did not know
which way to turn, so he stopped a taxi and asked for directions
to the Oshwal Centre, but the driver's English wasn't good and
Premchand's Swahili worse.

He did not recognize this pharmacy, this row of greasy shoe-shine stands. Old men in rubber-tire chappals sat on overturned buckets on the sidewalk. Premchand was tired and would have taken a seat if one had been vacant. The city was so huge and sprawling now. When he and Urmila had left, the New Stanley Hotel was one of the most significant buildings on Delamere Avenue. Now the avenue was Kenyatta and had grown three times as many lanes, countless carparks, bus depots, and gas stations. In Columbus it would be easy to find a bench to collect his thoughts, rest his legs. Why had he not been more careful in selecting landmarks?

His underarms were damp and his chest seized. He must not lose his head.

Another group of schoolgirls, with sky-blue collars, passed him, giggling and laughing. *Hello mister! Hello friend! One two three . . . nine teneleventwelve . . .*

Premchand stood still, absorbing the dust flung by car tires, the horns and bicycle bells, the pulsing pop radio flying out store windows. Avoiding eye contact with the double amputees and the child beggar veering toward him.

Finally, he remembered Sarada's phone number, though it took him a long time to figure out how to buy a phone card from a man whose eye was twisted shut, and then to find a functioning public phone.

When Ajay turned up in his smart European car, Amy was in the front seat. "We were worried about you," she said. Her brow was creased and she held out a pale hand to pat his arm—really she was too blond to be Jewish, he thought.

"No need to be concerned," he said. He was embarrassed and touched. "Here I am, safe and sound."

They stopped at a small copy center. Amy was led to a computer where she could check her email. Premchand half listened to Ajay talk with the owner, a friend, about the man's plans to turn the shop into something called a "cyber café." "In London they are springing up like mushrooms!"

Then Premchand saw Amy's head fall into her hands. At first, he held himself back. *Don't pry.* He picked up a newspaper, going first to the international news where he saw Gore still slipping in the polls.

When she lifted her face and it showed tears, he went to her. He said, "Everything is okay?"

She shook her head. "They wrote three days ago. They called, too, and when they didn't hear back, they gave my job away."

"The Welcomers?"

She nodded and looked up at him. "Don't tell Sunil, okay? He'll take it too hard. I'll talk to him tomorrow."

"I thought there were no secrets in modern marriages."

She laughed and bit her lip, but the soft flesh sprang back up. "Not a secret, just delayed information."

"Jews are resilient, are you not?"

She cracked a smile. "You know they call Indians the Jews of Africa?"

Though he ordinarily would never be so forward, Premchand reached out and pulled Amy toward him.

Releasing her, Premchand then did something else he never did in company—he sang a line from *Taj Mahal*, the film he and Urmila had seen on their first date. It had been in his mind for days. *Jo baat tujh mein hai/ taree tasweer mein nahein*, he quavered, completely out of tune. "I am no Mohammed Rafi," Premchand told her, "but he says here 'the substance of you is missing from your picture,' or something to that effect. You are a little bit like a picture sometimes. You can be more flesh and blood. You understand what I am saying?"

Amy looked at him, appearing astonished. "You are a hopeless romantic at heart, aren't you?"

"Hopeless, in any case."

"More to the point," she said, "I think that lyric could also be applied to you."

"Me?" He raised his eyebrows. "No, I am an open book. Let us now go back to those people who love us and eat yet another meal with them."

By the time they reached the house, the sun was setting, and Amy's unease had returned. During the quiet car ride, her fingers had worked roughly through her hair to her scalp, leaving pink scratches on her temples and loose blond hair in her fingers. But there was nothing more Premchand could do.

14.

We used to walk everywhere without fear. Barefoot, like mice, we ran around pulling coconuts off palms and slashing off the tops. Drinking right there in the street. We ate wild blackberries until juice ran down our necks. Our pockets were empty and we lived on top of each other, but we still made something of ourselves.

That was before Mau Mau.

When the terror began, some of the Asians chose sides. Some were angry at the British and fought against them; others joined the Brits to put the rebellion down. But most of us, our family, we were squeezed again between the Blacks and the Whites. It is a surprise we are still Brown and not Gray!

First there were the rumors—secret, bloody oaths. Animal sacrifices, they said. Every Kikuyu man—and some of the women!—they had to make these pledges to kill. The settlers shook in their boots, in those pith helmets we sold them. And for good reason. The Mau Mau began a campaign of slaughter.

But here is the truth. The problem is not that the African was held back by the English, but that he'd been brought forward too quickly. They could not handle such rapid progression, so they turned back to their old primitive ways.

Then came Operation Jock Scott: October 21, 1952. The Mau Mau masterminds, including Kenyatta, were rounded up in the middle of the night. Locked up, every one. Soldiers and big steel vehicles everywhere in the streets.

I kept your mother and all the other children home at night. No one allowed to leave. During the day I still worked in the bazaar. What else to do? We needed the money. And if you close for even one day the competition gets an edge. I banned newspapers from the house, but I know your grandmother managed to find accounts. Stories of bodies hacked to pieces in their homes.

You know Aberdares outside the city? Finally the free Mau Mau escaped there, to the forests. Where they plotted to kill even more. I wrote all my friends along the frontier: *Come to Nairobi! At least send your women and children.* Some did come, but the situation, it was ongoing. Not clearly getting better or worse for a while. And so they went home. I know of three who had their throats cut.

Those months it was so clear that Asians have no place in Kenya's heart or mind. The Africans hate us as much as the whites. And they have the population advantage. The slums are exploding.

Who eats the bones of children? Mau Mau are the flesh eaters! Can you believe I heard this shouted from the jails?

They demanded Kenyatta be released from prison—this man who became our first president. But to release the leader is to give the snake back its head. He was dangerous.

The British were even crueler. They came down like anything, such force you have never seen. But what choice did they have? By this time it is two years later. Springtime. The city was searched section by section. From loudspeakers, they shouted,

Pack one bag, leave the rest behind, exit into the streets peacefully.
They knocked down doors, beat women with rifles. I heard they
modeled this raid on one they did years before in Palestine.
Africans taken and imprisoned behind barbed wire. Separated
by tribe: Kikuyu, Embu, Meru. Twenty thousand, thirty thousand sent to camps. We lost track.

What about us? Well, many of the men were our employees.
Our houseboy was taken. He did come back after six months,
eager to work, but how was I to know if we could trust him?
He had been in prison with criminals, and I was supposed to let
him stay alone at home with my wife and daughters? Not at all.
He disappeared, like so many others.

15.

The rooms were narrow and dark, the rugs and furniture worn. Their footsteps echoed on the tile floors.

When his aunt flipped on the lights, Sunil saw that his grandfather was a wood-colored man crumpled in on himself. Eyes like peach pits, sucking in light. Sarada Aunty had introduced Sunil with a Gujarati phrase he knew well: *You remember this one, the American.*

The old man, whose jaw betrayed a tremor, grew momentarily still, his eyes wide. "Amerikana?" Suddenly Sunil's face was between two surprisingly tensile hands, reminding him of the hard face cradle used during eye exams. And then his eyes *were* examined, from very close up, by the dark and wrinkled sockets, the near-black irises within. Breath sharpened by betel nut shot over Sunil's startled face.

"He knows who I am?" he asked his aunt.

Apparently surprised herself, Sarada nodded, pressing her chin into the wicket of gold necklaces around her neck. "He says he has already been talking to you." She shook her head. "See, I am telling you he is losing it."

"Let him talk," Sunil said.

"He says it is a long story." For a while, she translated. *Too much rain. They were thirsty and then the lights went out.* "Goodness, he is saying something about a hippopotamus!"

"Ask him about the railroad," Sunil urged. "Mom once told me that he worked there for a while. As a coolie."

His grandfather continued, his voice thick with phlegm, pointing first to himself, then as if over his shoulder. Sarada frowned, "He is saying he hardly had anything to do with the trains, maybe just one year, and now he is simply listing a lot of places where the train stopped, all these little, forgotten towns. Wait." She paused and shook her father on the shoulder, asked him a question. "He says it was *his* father who was indentured."

"Indentured? Like a servant?"

She shrugged. "That is the word he used."

He turned to Amy, who was sitting a few feet away to give him space, but he wanted her closer. He pulled on her arm.

"Aunty," he said, "before he gets tired, I want you to introduce Amy."

His mother, who had tried to appear as if she were not listening, now moved closer as well. She sat down on the floor beside them. "Do not tell him you married an American. It will upset him."

Sunil looked in the old man's face, the sunken eyes that appeared to be piercingly active. "Why do you think that, Mom?"

"My own experience," she said quietly.

"But think about how much change he has already witnessed! I think you are selling him short. Aunty, please tell him."

And so Sarada raised her voice and made a V-shape with her arms, one hand on Sunil's shoulder, one on Amy's. In turn, Sunil and his wife grasped each of his grandfather's hands. "Just to be clear, I'm not asking for his blessing!" Sunil said. He meant this as a joke, and to his surprise his mother laughed.

Amy shook her head, smiling, and said, "No, you would never," then pressed her forehead briefly to Sunil's, just as she did when he had a fever, as he knew her father had done for her.

Sunil was sure that his grandfather absorbed this information from the way his tremulous chin swung first toward one of them, then the other. He had no teeth, and his mouth did not change shape—no hint of a smile—but Sunil thought that he gently nodded, a slight bow of the head. It was an endorsement he chose to believe in.

After a few more minutes, Sarada pronounced her father tired. She stood up quickly, as light on her feet as his mother had been coming down to the floor. "It is time for tea," she said. While she set the water to boil and brought out the chevdo, Sunil and Amy stayed were they were, for a few moments longer. Sunil closed his eyes. Let sound and feel and smells come over him: the scratchy carpets over the cool tile floor, lingering spices and floor wax. From somewhere came color memories— a blurry scramble of field, sea, and sky, like a child's drawing. The past and the present swallowed each other, a snake eating its tail.

Sunil's palm landed inadvertently on the soft toe of the old man's slipper, and he kept it there. Perhaps unaware that his translator had left, his grandfather talked on. Sunil began to detect the repetition of certain sounds, the words for *water*, *light*, *river*. *Father*, *fear*, *labor*, *lions* . . . no, now Sunil was inserting, substituting. He would take home the truth, if he was to take anything at all. And the one truth he had found here so far, he was sad to realize, was loneliness. His grandfather alone inside his aged memories; his father's desire to escape to the New World, his mother admitting how little she knew about her own parents.

David Kauffman had said to them, *Be patient. Don't rush to conclusions.* Ariel had instructed, severely, *Remember everything.*

They needed this trip to mean something. Otherwise, what were all of these excruciating scenes for? Except that this last encounter was different from all the rest. For one thing, it had fulfilled the promise he'd made to Bimal.

For another, Sunil had felt seen, not passed over, for a millisecond at least, his wife beheld as well, even if they could never be sure what was really perceived by the withered man with the peach-pit eyes.

His grandfather continued to murmur, barely audible, and Sunil thought it was time to go. He rose to his tingling knees. But his father, already standing, motioned for Sunil to stay put, then gathered the rest of the family in a circle and told them to listen. Sunil and Amy still on the carpet, like kindergarteners; their relatives perched on footstools, the edges of chairs. Premchand cleared his throat, and Sunil swallowed tightly, looked at Amy, at his mother. Both appeared baffled; his mother also looked scared. His father only took charge like this when he was pressed to his limits.

"Being here today, with the elder generation, what remains of it, strikes me as a propitious time to speak the unspoken." Again he cleared his throat, and Sunil's own tightened further. "I am not sharing any secrets when I say that we have had some hard times." Premchand drew a line in the air between himself and Urmila. "Especially in the beginning, the early years in USA. My work was very demanding, I was not a lot in the home. We were struggling with the language, Urmila—your mother—was missing her family."

Sunil glanced at her, expecting her to jump in, but she remained quiet, almost prim, hands folded in her lap. Eyes locked on his father's face like a dutiful wife.

"So, son—"

Sunil's heart beat faster. He was hot. Amy took hold of his ankle. Tethered him.

"—your mother took some time away, back here with her family. It was a very reasonable course of action. She needed some time to consider if we should continue together."

Behind Sunil, his grandfather mumbled faster, steadily, like the hum of an appliance, then abruptly he stopped and his head drooped, and saliva pooled at the corner of his mouth. Sunil's aunt jumped up to wipe it away with a handkerchief, which only caused Premchand to speak louder, as if the entire room were suddenly in chaos. "We did not know she was expecting, okay. And the way things were in USA, we were not ready. It is hard to explain so many years later, to paint the picture, but let us say the uncertainty made us believe Mital and Anup were the best choice. They had no children of their own."

Urmila was fixed in place. Her glasses reflected the sunlight cutting in through a crack in the drawn curtains. Gopal Uncle leaned back in his chair, legs crossed, struggling to keep something like amusement off his face. Ajay pulled threads from the arm of the chair until Sarada slapped his hand.

"It is not much of a story, telling it now, but we don't want you children to think this is some big secret. It is simply something that happened a long time ago, a product of the circumstances. This is the way life goes. The air is clear now, is it not?" Then Sunil's father leaned back against the wall and gently bowed his head.

In the minutes of daylight left before dinner, Sunil and Amy circled Sarada Aunty's property. He snapped a small branch off a hedge and twirled it in his hands. They'd counted two tenant families. One consisted of two women, maybe sisters, a man, and four children. The other family seemed to be motherless. There was a man who looked like he was in his forties, but was probably ten or fifteen years younger, plus an older daughter who took care of the baby and a younger girl who left the compound in a school uniform each morning. "That's one kid out of seven going to school," Amy had pointed out.

Now she walked, hands in pockets. Today it was finally warm enough to discard his mother's sweater, and her shoulders stretched taut her shirt.

"I get five minutes of explanation for a lie that's lasted my whole life?" Sunil fumed.

"Maybe he doesn't understand his own motives, and he's confused and ashamed."

"Then why didn't he say that."

"I think he did, in his way."

"You've gone soft on him," Sunil said, both irritated and pleased. "I'm glad. But still, you can't expect there not to be questions and even anger. And also, you notice it was my father speaking, not my mother."

"Yes, he was trying to speak for both of them. In any case, I think what's important now is getting to know Bimal in this new way, not to learn more about why your parents did what they did. Your questions shouldn't be about why *they* are the way they are, but why *you* are the way you are—the two of you."

"Those questions are not mutually exclusive. Anyway, don't you think this event shaped their lives?"

"Of course."

"So if it affected them, it necessarily affected me."

The boy child was being chased by his older sister. He pulled a wide leaf off a bush, planted it on top of his head, and fell to the ground. Played dead.

Amy said, "It's hard for anyone to imagine their parents when they were young, and with your parents their context was so radically different from what you grew up with. And they are not very good at explaining."

"That's an understatement," he said, wishing he could peel away the layer of hurt that clung to his body, his voice.

When the sister's back was turned and she'd walked several paces away, the boy stood up, wound his arms like propellers, and barreled toward her. She whirled around at the last second and he smacked into her thighs. She scolded him and he burst into tears. Then she swept him up, held him with one arm, patted the back of his neck, and pulled clothes off the line with her free hand.

Adding up the hours of family get-togethers and dinners—the adults talking, the children playing outside or upstairs—and the time in and out of their uncles' shops, Sunil thought he and Bimal had spent no more than two weeks together total. Two weeks spread out over thirty years, maybe half a dozen trips altogether, including when he was too young to remember much more than colors and smells, special dishes he liked that appeared only in Nairobi. It was easy to connect during childhood—they barely had personalities, were just bundles of desires running around and slamming into each other, boys with boys, and girls with girls, all teasing and eating and getting dirty. When the boys started working for their uncles, they were separated by their tasks, often one of them taken out to run errands—usually Bimal because he spoke Gujarati and Swahili—and Sunil left behind to count inventory, clean, and double-check columns of arithmetic with the new calculator brought over from the Service Merchandise in Columbus. Sunil believed he would have behaved differently during those hours if he had known of the bond he and Bimal shared. He mourned what could have been.

The girl from the motherless family leaned over the coals. Her braid slipped over her shoulder and she swung it back with a toss of her head. Forearms darkened with ash and smoke. Onto the circle of stones she hefted a bellied pot, then wrapped something in foil and buried it in the embers. "The rural life of my ancestors, right here in the backyard," he said. He looked at

Amy. "Don't worry, I'm not plotting any scenes."

"You want someone to blame."

"Wouldn't you?"

Soon after they started sleeping together, Amy had woken up one winter morning with a nosebleed. On his blue pillowcase was a map of red.

At first, he was too stunned by the blood to act, then he'd pulled off his T-shirt and held it to her face. "What happened?"

"You hit me," she said. "In your sleep."

"I did?" He was horrified.

"No. It happens sometimes, the dry air."

"Why didn't you warn me?"

She'd responded with a look both confused and disgusted. And then he realized the absurdity of his question, as if she was supposed to prepare him for every possibility of their togetherness?

He hadn't meant to accuse. He was sorry. He'd been so alarmed by the thought of hurting her, of being unknowingly violent.

Her disappointment in his reaction had seared him. Worse than any scolding he'd received as a child. This kind of awfulness, he had realized, was new, was tied up with love and the kind of obligation he desired, did not shirk from, and he needed to learn from it. Act on it: break from the defensive posture that had seemed to him natural, reasonable, but which might instead be an obstacle to happiness.

Amy had taken off her stained clothes, rinsed out his shirt, washed the blood off her face. When she came back, she was naked, and she'd stood for a moment beside the bed, hands on his face. "I love you," she had said, for the first time. "But don't talk like that again."

He had circled her waist, head on her chest. He loved her, too.

For a few months, they jokingly blamed each other for everything—a cloudy day, the deli running out of ham. On February 14, he'd brought home a heart-shaped red velvet cake with the words *My Bloody Valentine*.

Last week, Sunil had said to his wife, "Why didn't you tell me I had a brother?"

"Because I knew you'd take it badly."

He'd laughed. But now, seven thousand miles from home, watching a young girl unselfconsciously make food for her family in front of strangers, peepers beginning their evening song, Sunil realized Amy might have meant it more as a warning than a joke.

16.

The State of Emergency lasted eight years, until 1960. This whole time Kenyatta is in jail, but the Mau Mau fight without him. It is very bloody. Not only black against white, but in some pockets there is civil war: Mau Mau kill the Kikuyu loyal to the British, village against village. There is burning and hacking people to pieces. The rallying cries are about land. It is stealing, plain as day. Even the Asians can see this. We, too, have been denied.

But Mau Mau cannot hold forever, not with so many jailed and disappeared. Not with their top leader in prison, and then the main military chiefs are captured and arrested. One of them is executed. Soon Ghana becomes independent. We are nowhere close to Ghana, hardly we can find it on a map, but we know it is Africa, and that Africa is changing. Everyone can feel the independence movement growing, even though day-to-day we do more or less the same. We cheer the improvements as they come along—the radio broadcasting services, then the big new hospital, Aga Khan, opens in 1958. It is so shiny; we are so impressed. Premchand goes to India for medicine, the first in our family, to bring back what we do not have, doctors of our own, and when he is employed at Aga Khan as a physician, we all boast and go in to visit him like children to a factory where miracles are made.

Finally Kenyatta is released into house arrest. The KANU party is formed by these men, Tom Mboya and the name I love to say, Oringa Odinga. In just three more years Kenyatta will be prime minister. We are on the brink of enormous change.

The British have been so strong, so merciless, these years of the emergency, but the colonials see they have to give some few concessions to the natives. Higher wages, allowance to grow coffee, things like this.

They are creating space for the Africans, and we do not make much of a fuss. Our goal is to hold on. We Asians are now even in the police force, in all aspects of bureaucracy, but we do not know if it will last. The Asians long against the colonials become even more vocal, men like Makhan Singh involved in the unions. Eventually he is arrested.

Even in these days of so much activity, it is hard to believe independence will one day come, and that soon after we will have to choose between two countries, neither of which wants us. By the end of the fifties, I myself am fifty years old. All of my children graduated secondary, knowing no other life, starting jobs. We are arranging marriages, paying dowries.

Your grandmother got very sick one year—1960. A year in the thick of everything, but when illness comes the world shrinks to just you and your family. I wish you never experience this. We were worried for polio, but it was another fever, and she was in bed for three months. The children were not allowed to see her and she got skinny like a stick. Premchand Fua watched over her. I was all the time on River Road, thinking about where to increase and where to reduce. Radios were selling big time. Turntables and records for the Europeans. Do you remember your grandmother? She recovered from the fever, remaining healthy until the cancer was too far progressed, but that was many years later. Anyway, she came out of those fevered months in her room saying *Alam*, enough, determined to stay, a kind of loyalty to this place I had not seen before. She was tired, could not see moving to another continent, again. I kept an eye on the finances. Savings, hand in hand with our low consumption, it is how people get ahead.

Your generation, both here and in America, what has happened? You are buying clothing as if these things cannot be washed!

And so, during this time it is tumult, but feels every day like any other. The bazaar is expanding, because more of our people are coming from the countryside. In the sixties, Africans get on their feet and set up their own dukas in little towns, leaving no space for the Asian originals. Just beyond the edges of our own shops in Nairobi, the Africans are creeping in. Little huts with piles of whatever they can find—onions, bananas, bicycle wheels—at too cheap prices. They begin taking control of the produce chain. Things we used to sell for them they are selling for themselves, to their own people. What, we are going to become farmers, the Asians who were never allowed to own good land? Too late for that. We have been perfecting our role as middlemen, not as men of the earth.

Mostly, we looked straight ahead and up. It seemed the British would be leaving and maybe we could fill their shoes. This is not so much what happened, but it gave us some hope to stay.

17.

Anup grew eggplant, peppers, and herbs in a small garden. Walking Premchand through the rows, he showed off the avocado tree and flowering mango that would bear fruit after his guests went back to America.

They sat on straight-backed wooden chairs under a large blue umbrella. From a wooden lockbox by the back door, Anup withdrew a bottle and poured them each a whiskey. They toasted to Bimal's recovery, to the reunion of their sons. The boys were together now in the house, in Bimal's childhood bedroom. The one son lay recovering and the other hovered, unsure what to do with himself. This is how Premchand had left them. Bimal did not look healthy yet, but his color and energy were better. During the drive over, Sunil had fidgeted and gripped his hands together, stared silently out the window. "What are you nervous about?" Premchand had said. "Already you have been reunited. You are both good boys."

The whiskey pricked his nose and burned on the way down, but it wasn't unpleasant. One's taste did change over time.

"What do you suppose they're saying?" Anup waved his hand toward the house.

Premchand wanted to know, too. How long until he could go back in and join them? Anup's business talk and boasting bored him. He'd already said, more than once, how enterprising Bimal was—how he'd gotten the venturesome genes from Urmila's side instead of the studious ones from Premchand. A few years ago Bimal had joined up with Rushab Patel's oldest son to sell PVC piping, then turned the company into something larger.

But Anup seemed to have forgotten his own question and had returned to singing his son's virtues. "Another good thing about my son," he said, drink loosening his tongue, "he does not enjoy his wife too much. You Americans think all this love going on between husband and wife is okay, but it is distracting. A man should care for his wife, help her when she is sick, give her nice things, but the other is not so important. When they are showing so much affection, this hugging and kissing, the man looks weak and the wife looks like a whore."

Premchand had always thought his brother-in-law was weak-willed, but he didn't remember such crudeness.

Still, Premchand thought of Sunil's arm around Amy's waist, their sitting close on the sofa. Lying down in the grass yesterday outside Gopal's, looking like lovers. Premchand did not care what others thought, but his stomach turned when he thought of Amy being harmed by gossip. Should he caution Sunil? No, there was nothing to say. Let them be as they are. He had raised an American son.

This morning it had rained again, briefly, and a few water drops slid off the end of a leaf. The air was steamy, soft and inviting. He longed to stand and stretch his legs. Another walk would do him good.

Anup talked on, but his face wasn't bright and teasing anymore. Premchand realized Anup was accusing him of "buying into the Hollywood mystique—a son at Harvard, a new car every year." What was behind this? Was he worried Sunil would convince Bimal to leave Kenya, move to America?

Premchand had Anup's opposite concern. What if the stories of Bimal's life in business lured Sunil away from his studies? Sunil and Amy's financial struggle might cause his son's belief in himself to waver. As soon as he got home, Premchand would increase his monthly support.

Yesterday his son had outlined for him the philosophical problem of his dissertation, the role of evolution on moral beliefs, and the intensity in Sunil's eyes had thrilled Premchand, even though his son had admitted he didn't know if he could succeed. In fact, he had looked a little green just speaking about it, like the old days when he eyed tapeworms under Premchand's laboratory microscope.

Premchand wanted to leave, go for a walk, but now, bursting forth, as if from the hedges, was a group of men. Relatives shouting, "Here is Dr. Chandaria!"

They stood against the sun, their edges blurring, all reaching for a glass and a pour. One of the men reminded Premchand that as a newly minted doctor he'd treated him for tetanus. Premchand remembered the incident but hadn't identified this man as the patient, so much time had passed. Was this how Urmila spent her days, reminiscing and chitchatting? The externals of a life—marrying, going places, raising children— did not differ so much from one person to the next, and he saw little reason to dwell on them unless you were seeking advice.

"In the early years we could have used your skills," Anup said. Then, abruptly, "You have seen the new American Embassy?"

Premchand shook his head.

"It is too far away from the commerce section, all the way over to Muthaiga. I tell you, Americans show your lack of faith by putting yourselves so far away."

"Moving was the prudent thing to do," he offered.

"It was the coward thing. Leaving is always the coward thing."

Premchand couldn't tell if the others agreed with him—some were nodding, some staring into their glasses. "When you are smart, you think about all your options," he insisted.

When a loud crash sounded from Bimal's room, Premchand shot up.

"Sit down," Anup said, "The women are in there. They will take care of it."

But Premchand couldn't sit, couldn't remain. "I must go. Excuse me."

In the driveway, Gopal was smoking. "I brought your wife and daughter-in-law," he said, placing a warm hand on Premchand's shoulder. "She's a pretty girl. Too bad Urmila doesn't like her."

"What do you mean?"

"I'm just teasing. The usual mother-in-law teasing, you know. Listen, can I tell you something? My sister has asked me to help her find another supplier. I don't want to interfere, but I can see things are going poorly. You know, sometimes it is best to put these things to a final rest, like with an old animal. The kindliest option."

It was ugly, the way Gopal was going behind Urmila's back. Why did he want his sister to fail? More than that, Premchand hadn't realized until now that pulling out his support for the store would mean setting Urmila adrift. And if she stayed home, they'd be at each other's throats. "Thank you," he said. With the whiskey flowing through him, it was easy to dismiss his brother-in-law and keep walking.

"A good man," Gopal said, in a way that sounded like he was referring to himself. He patted Premchand again on the back and sent him on his way out the gate.

18.

The room was stifling, but Bimal was wrapped in several blankets. "It smells like hospital, doesn't it?" he said. "I ask the nurse to open the windows, and then Mum comes in and closes them all when I'm sleeping."

"So I can open one?" Sunil needed air.

"Please."

Sunil slid open the panes, then hovered near the open window to gulp the soupy afternoon.

"In the hospital I was very groggy and unable to congratulate you on your marriage. Good for you! When I'm out of this bed, I can meet her and have a proper chat. How is everyone taking it? She is American, yes?"

"You mean white?"

Bimal winced in an attempt at a smile—his scar was still healing—and nodded.

Sunil sat down in the metal folding chair next to the bed. He grimaced, crossed his arms, felt the damp cotton of his shirt. "She and my father are getting along fine—very well, actually. My mom is another story. She's resistant, so the two of them haven't even spent much time together. I hope it's just stubbornness and will wear off eventually." Amy was with his mother and aunt right now, picking up last-minute things for the safari, coming back in time for tea. "One more day," Amy had said to him before Sunil and his father left the house. She was visibly steeling herself, making a hard exoskeleton of the shorts and T-shirt already crisp from drying outside on the line.

"Surely it will take time. Listen, Sheetal is Indian and she and Mum still have problems."

Sunil was impressed by how lively Bimal sounded, but he also saw the yellowing bruises under his eyes, the tired creases.

"We saw Bapuji—Nana. I introduced him to Amy."

Bimal brightened, eyes creased at the corners. "This makes me very happy. I know he is losing his mind now, but he remembers a lot from the old days. Things I want to share with you sometime. What did he say?"

"He didn't really *say* anything, to Amy, I think he was getting tired. Sarada Aunty was having a hard time piecing together his words. But he didn't jump out of his chair and shout, 'Naa!'"

Bimal laughed gently. "The important thing is that you saw each other. You know he has talked about you—he is so curious about America, and what you have become."

"Mom suggested he didn't want her to immigrate to the US."

Bimal performed a small shrug. "I don't know about that. He is not saying mean things about her or anything, but surely the separation was hard when it was fresh."

The thought cut Sunil. He nodded. "Before technology, it must have been a kind of death to have a child move so far away."

Bimal pursed his lips. "Yes, I think you are right about that. But tell me, what is it like to be back in Nairobi? You have been killing many cockroaches? You used to smash them with your shoes."

"That's right! I hated them. But now that I live in a city, instead of the suburbs, I'm used to roaches."

Then Sunil told his brother how, yesterday, he had stolen a moment from sitting with their grandfather to visit his old bedroom. At first, lying on the cool bedcover, nothing in the spidery walls had cracked open any memories. "Mostly, I've been preoccupied with seeing you. But the longer I sat there, the smell—mold, I think—crept into me, and—" Sunil broke off for a moment, hesitant. "Honestly, what I remembered was being scared there at night. My mother was staying in another house, at Sarada Aunty's, and I had this fear that I'd been left behind. The house was so quiet at night, I thought I'd wake up and everyone would be gone." Sunil sighed. "I was not the most confident child."

"But you remember in Mombasa when I was stung, I cried like a little boy."

"Understandable—it was scary!" Sunil paced along the foot of Bimal's bed. "That moment yesterday was the strongest memory I've had, when a place felt physically familiar. The rest of the time here, we've been tourists, going to places I'm sure we didn't go when I was a kid. So it feels new, and overwhelming. Nairobi is huge!"

"You get used to it. One goes to only a few places."

"You know what I remember?" Sunil grasped at the images that had come to him the first night, watching cricket with his father and cousins. "Anup Uncle teaching me to bowl. He was so patient, and he knew what he was talking about. After that summer I asked my dad to find a cricket league in Columbus. Once or twice we played together with some families, but we didn't keep it up. Do you still play?"

Bimal shook his marred face. "No time. Maybe on weekends I would, if I had a son, but not with a daughter. Those carefree days are ancient history, don't you find?"

"I have tons of time," Sunil said. "I just don't spend it very well." Bimal's daughter, Raina, must be two or three. His mother had recently forwarded to him a photograph of the girl wearing pink shoes. This girl, he realized, was his niece.

From the chirpy tone of youth—his voice was still high even at fifteen when they were together in Mombasa— Bimal's voice had deepened into that of a smooth radio announcer, but his solemn, attentive gaze had not changed. The way he listened with his mouth parted, nodding encouragingly as Sunil talked. As boys, Bimal would ask about the new sports cars in America, and Sunil unspooled the details of Firebirds, and futuristic Lamborghinis, the petite Ford Pintos that wrapped their drivers in flames. Sunil had been gratified to be the source of entertainment, the focus of Bimal's unwavering attention.

"How are you feeling? Are you still in a lot of pain?"

"It's a bit better. I try not to think about it. I have a great deal of physical therapy ahead."

"Of course." Sunil was the healthy one, the active one, but so far he was not doing a stellar job keeping the conversation running smoothly. After a long pause, he said. "Tell me about your job. You work with your dad now?"

"I started with that, then broke off to partner with a classmate to work in plastics. Eventually we were bought by a multinational. Now I broker medical supplies to hospitals, buying things from USA and India and UK and selling here, and in many other countries." Bimal described a new insulin pump he had just begun to offer his clients, one that had remote-control programming. Diabetes was a growing scourge.

"Did you recognize anything they used on you at the hospital?"

Bimal scrunched his eyes, thinking.

"That was a bad joke, I'm sorry."

"Ah. It was funny." Bimal stretched his arms. With his lower half securely bundled, he looked like a Glo Worm—masked, childlike, a touch comical. "Our parents are insecure about their success. You know how they always talk about Africanization. They're worried about sudden changes in policies. The playing field is more competetive now, too, with Africans getting educations."

"They don't seem insecure to me."

Bimal insisted they were, under the surface. "Mum's always worrying about getting kicked out of the country. Gopal Kaka asks me about foreign investments in the countries I visit for work."

As Bimal talked more, describing how much he traveled— racking up enough frequent flyer miles for first-class flights and free stays at resorts in Thailand and Dubai—Sunil saw that his brother was pleased with his life and its luxuries. But what Sunil heard was a life dictated by work and family obligation. To Sunil, it was terrifying, being reliant on pleasing clients, and the scrutiny that came from living so close to home. Sunil was more like their father; he had to stray to feel he had grown up.

"The hardest thing still is not knowing what comes next," Bimal said. "I'm not as worried as Mum, but the government is unstable, which is bad for business. Life is good now, but something could come along. I think about Raina, and what I want for her. Like she says, 'Here today, gone tomorrow.'" He shrugged. "Something she learned from the cartoons."

As he spoke, Bimal shifted, and the bottom edge of the sheet loosened to reveal feet thin and too still, horned with sharp, alien toenails. On the toes curled wiry black hair, hair missing from Sunil's own flat feet, and he was reminded that he really did not know this man. He wondered how honest he could be with him. When he was a child, he sometimes had the feeling that his relatives were his mother's spies, bound to report back any bad behavior.

Sunil stood up and walked to the window. He ran his fingers down the heavy curtain. "Our dads are sitting out there."

"Drinking whiskey."

"What? No. My dad doesn't drink."

"I bet he is now."

Sunil looked past the garden to the umbrella hovering over a group of chairs. He watched Anup Uncle refill his father's glass with brown liquid from a large bottle.

Sunil could only laugh, laugh at all the things he didn't know—might never. He felt an ease spreading through him, as if he were the one imbibing. Bimal was calming to be around. Sunil saw how tough his brother was, even in this battered, weakened state, how resilient, and how comfortable in his own skin, and he wondered, *Do I have any of this strength?* After a long pause, he said, "I have to ask you. Did you know about us? Even when we were kids?"

Bimal sighed, swallowed dryly, with effort. Sunil poured him a cup of mango juice, and he took small sips. "Yes. But my mother made me promise to keep the secret. I don't know why. I planned to tell you anyway, that time in Mombasa, I felt I should tell you, but we were hardly alone, then you left early. You were a problem child." He tried to smile, his scar lightening as it pulled taut across his face, but the stitches stretched only so far. Bimal then said something startling, something Sunil had never considered. "Aunty didn't want to have her baby at all."

"What do you mean? She came here to have an abortion?" This was shocking. Even during his father's speech yesterday, his mother's forced-still posture, this had not crossed his mind.

"It wasn't why she came. She came not knowing. When she discovered, she looked into it. But it was illegal here. Still is. In India, too, she tried all around, even in the UK."

Sunil was about to ask why his mother hadn't gone to a clinic in the States, but then he remembered how old he and Bimal were. Too old. With care, he poured himself a cup of juice. His fingers were weak. "I can't believe that—I had no idea." His mother must have been desperate. Beyond the pain he now felt on his mother's behalf, Bimal's searing revelation astonished Sunil with the contingency of their situation, his and Bimal's connection that was already so tenuous. "You might not have existed!" he exclaimed. "Do you ever think about that?"

"Not at all. It was meant to be."

"What, like destiny?"

Bimal nodded.

"No, think about it another way. We could have grown up together. Had each other to talk to." A phrase of Lieberman's came to him. "Bear witness, that's what I mean. We both were so alone growing up—in these fucked-up situations."

"I wasn't alone," Bimal told him frankly.

Sunil heard the words, but he didn't pause. Because he couldn't stop thinking about what they could have had, couldn't help spinning aloud the fantasy of having a brother that he'd spent years concocting, before he had any idea his conjuring had a parallel in reality. "You could have grown up in the States! Four of us." Bimal in a bedroom down the hall, riding bikes down the grass-split sidewalks. Following his big brother's silhouette around the corner, pawing through record shops, squashing together in the back seat of their parents' Olds, competing at video games. The life they could have had and the life he didn't.

He willed the cascading images to come to rest, but all he saw now was missed opportunity. And not just for himself but for Bimal. Because even though Sunil had been miserable, he still felt himself to have been given the better circumstances—how could he not think so when his parents themselves had decided to immigrate?—and rising before him was a blunt contrast between Columbus and what he'd seen of Nairobi. He had been able to get lost in America. His house and immigrant parents might have confined him, but the rest of the country always had felt wide and open, and that had been a gift. He said, "Growing up here, didn't you feel constrained? The myth-making about Indian culture, doesn't it drive you nuts? The self-congratulatory talk of money and business?" He began to wonder if one thing they had had in common was being outsiders: brown against black; brown against white. But Bimal was straining to push himself up and speak more forcefully than he could lying down.

"What myth?" Bimal said. His scar darkened to reddish purple, thick eyebrows drew together into a scowl. "Our grand-parents really came here with nothing. Now look—Asians control the commerce. Is that what you mean? That's history, not a myth."

"Overall, sure, but the individual stories are all thin. The ones people remember and have told me, anyway. A couple of days ago I was asking what our grandfather did for work as a young man, and no one could tell me. It's like how things are now is the only thing that matters. You have a good life, but someone else chose it for you. Don't you feel that way?"

"Too many choices are a luxury."

"Exactly!" But he shouldn't have said so much. He had meant to be receptive, a listener, but he was so overcome by what he'd learned that whatever control he usually had, which was not much, had disappeared. Worse, he hadn't said what he meant. He was trying to articulate to his brother what his own outsider perspective had shown him about Indian culture here: the survivor's attitude of defiance, a protective layer that obscured the truth, like his mother's face-lightening cream. He had mistakenly believed that Bimal would want to hear this. "I'm sorry. I'm sure I sound like a jerk. There's been a lot to take in on this trip. I never know what's going on, where the hell I am. You're the first person telling me the truth." Sunil pressed his temples to still the pulsing there. He stepped closer to Bimal's bed. "Can I help you with those pillows?"

"No. Thanks." Bimal's tone was sharp and Sunil backed away. He stumbled and knocked over the metal folding chair, and the crash reverberated down his spine. Some trick of heat or light made the room sway.

He had to step outside, just for a moment. He needed to see his father's reassuringly placid face. He mumbled quickly to Bimal that he needed to use the bathroom and would be right back.

But by the time he made it to the lawn, his father was gone. Sunil looked around, over the hedges toward the road. Cars, rusty air, low brick houses, palm trees, birds flitting across the bluing sky. He'd grown used to it, he realized. The traffic noise no longer bothered him. Out of the corner of his eye, he caught a wave from Prakash, but he quickly turned back and reentered the house. He and Bimal were not finished. He could not leave things the way they had just ended.

Sunil found his mother, Amy, Mital Aunty, and Sarada Aunty in the kitchen, surrounded by the makings of bhajias: chopped vegetables and a bowl of chickpea flour. All of the women had beige dustings on their cheeks. To the side was a stack of fashion magazines from India, open to various elaborate costumes. Sarada and his mother were chatting, mostly in Gujarati, while Amy silently mixed something in a bowl. There was something off about her expression, a terseness that was almost sullen. When she saw Sunil standing in the doorway, she quickly stood up and went to him.

"How's Bimal? How did the bonding go?"

"He's amazingly strong given what he's been through."

Amy opened her mouth to speak again, but closed it when she saw Sunil wasn't finished.

"It was going well, then I think I messed up. I just need to spend a little bit more time with him."

"We have a day here when we get back from the safari," Amy offered. Her eyes were rimmed red, which he assumed was the onions—his own lids were beginning to smart.

Sunil shook his head. He couldn't wait that long. "No, it needs to be now. I just stepped out for a minute to get some air."

"But it's been two hours already." She looked at her watch, a plastic Swatch with a face that dwarfed her wrist. "Two and a half."

"I know, but—well, that's not all that long, considering all there is to talk about, right?"

"I thought we were going to go out with Meena."

"We will, just a bit later. She isn't here yet, is she?"

Amy shook her head, a repetitive movement that reminded him of his grandfather's tremor. "Can you stay out here for just a few minutes?" she asked quietly. "I need you in there." She tilted her head toward the kitchen. "Or maybe I can go with you into Bimal's room?"

Her face appeared flat, lacked its usual curve and liveliness. But he couldn't abandon what he had started. "No, I'm sorry, love. It's delicate. It's what we came here for, remember? Can you stick it out awhile longer?" He put his hands gently on her shoulders.

"Okay." And then she turned away from him and headed, square shouldered, back into the fray.

He could do this, Sunil told himself.

Bimal was resting with his eyes closed, the gash on his face appearing less livid as well. Something about his equanimity, the way he viewed their separation as fated, made Sunil think of his dissertation. Because Sunil believed in the opposite of fate—in agency, accountability. At least he had thought he did. For years he had confidently—happily, righteously—held people accountable for moral decisions. He was justified in doing this because there was a real, and knowable, moral framework. He could say to people: you ought to know better; you ought to know that's wrong. But his thesis about evolution undermined this belief. Even if there were objective moral truths, there seemed to be no reason to think evolution would have shaped humans to be able to know them. "You ought to know better" was therefore a lie, because nobody knew anything about right and wrong. Sunil had described evolution as a used-car salesman out to make a buck. Now he had a horrifying thought. *He* himself was the uncaring salesman. Peddling vehicles he did not believe in because he couldn't be bothered with their inspection.

Sunil knew he used moral reasoning as a weapon. Like the Nietzschean slaves, he used morality as a defense—against his mother, against bullies and usurpers everywhere. But if Sunil's view was right, he was a bully himself, a browbeater, not a philosopher. The thought made him ill and ashamed. How could he move forward with his work, knowing its capacity to undermine a sustaining pillar of his life? If he were a religious man, what he faced would be a crisis of faith, as Ariel Kauffman had suggested: if God does not exist, whom do you trust to guide you? Instead he had a crisis of belief: if there is no way of knowing moral truths, how do you have any confidence in the rightness or wrongness of your actions?

For a few queasy minutes, Sunil stood awkwardly next to Bimal's bed, wondering if he should wake him up or let him sleep. Then his brother opened his eyes, those active, black-coffee eyes, and Sunil saw that they were Urmila's—wide set and thick with lashes. And their grandfather's, before time wrinkled and sank them. Sunil pressed his soles down into the tile floor. They had so much to share and discover and, suddenly, for the first time in weeks he did not feel afraid.

Here was someone, his blood relation, who did not care

about power. Sunil suspected that in his life as a salesman, Bimal had never cudgeled anyone.

And yet, for his part, Sunil could not abandon the path he'd started down. Because his idea was interesting—provocative, at least—the department had said so, and it was the only idea he had. He was sure Bimal would agree that Sunil had to continue.

Sunil righted the chair he had knocked over earlier. He had been prepared to talk more, talk was what he knew best, but he realized he was exhausted. So he said simply, "Do you mind if I sit here for a little while? I promise not to talk."

Bimal turned his palm face up on the sheet, offering it to Sunil. "During my little nap, I was thinking. It's funny, because it seems to me like your life has been the difficult one. Who can you lean on when so few are there beside you? And yet look at what you have accomplished. So perhaps we can start a club of mutual admiration." And the two of them again took each other's hands, and sat quietly in the ensuing, temporary peace.

PART II

1.

The Jain universe is shaped like a man. We live in the waist, where there are many oceans and continents, between the sixteen heavens and seven hells. Each of us hopes to be reborn into a better life, but only if our karma has been good. With each cycle, we try again to attain liberation. Only when we have truly been emancipated do our souls float up and rest at the very top heaven, crescent-shaped like a new moon.

2.

An hour ago, Sunil and Amy had left for their honeymoon. Premchand had woken them at five a.m., telling Sarada he would see the couple off. He fed them juice and black tea and jam sandwiches, and patted his son on his beautiful, bristled cheek just before closing the taxi door. Hugged his springy daughter-in-law. Premchand had followed the car out the gate and realized he was not tired. His travel fog had cleared. Perhaps it was the whiskey, which had poured him into bed early, buzzing pleasantly with images of Sunil at Bimal's bedside. When his son and Amy returned, they would be calm, restored, reunited, and the heart-to-heart with Urmila could begin. Originally, he and Urmila were to depart today, but they had decided to stay and continue to build goodwill.

Yesterday Premchand had come across a troubling scene. At first he was concerned to see Urmila and Mital in such close proximity in the kitchen, the women preparing tea, but when Sarada emerged from the pantry, he relaxed; she knew how to manage the two of them. Then he saw Amy sitting uncomfortably by herself at the end of the table. The women seemed to be ignoring her. So he had invited her to go for a walk with him, and she readily accepted, but Urmila had overruled. "She will stay here with the women. We have many things to discuss." Premchand had stepped away from the table, and his wife, assuming him gone, had thrust before Amy the centerfold of a magazine, a series of bridal saris. Urmila pressed a ringed finger on the page and said, "Aren't they beautiful? The silk, the embroidery. We don't go in for white like the Americans, you can see."

Amy had nodded. "They're beautiful. What was your wedding sari like? Do you have pictures?"

But Urmila had ignored this and pressed on, whispering something in the voice she believed to be low and persuasive but was in fact loud enough for all to hear. "Let us talk about your wedding. We will give you a real one. Maybe your parents can help. Something we can all celebrate in together. We buy you the sari, invite some people for eating and dancing, and you can finally make it official."

"It *is* official," Amy said in the smallest voice he had heard from her. Premchand wondered what she would say next, but he was not even supposed to be here, listening in like this, and soon enough his wife noticed he was still standing in the corner and shooed him away. "Be off with you," she hissed in Gujarati. Amy's eyes caught his for a moment and then released. She was not going to entrap him.

Relieved the newlyweds would now have some romantic time together, Premchand shook out his legs and set forth for what had come to feel like his constitutional. He liked walking best in the morning, when Nairobi still had a touch of fresh air. He laced up his sneakers and waved to the askari at the gate. His knees felt young, and he relished the neighborhood's leafy trees.

The streets were still waking. He bought a sleeve of nuts, inadvertently spilling a few large bills on the ground and retrieving them dusted with red earth. After a few more minutes he reached the kiosk where he'd bought the phone card, the day he'd gotten lost. The same vendor was open now, the man's eye twisted shut, bald patches at the top of his head. Premchand bought a lotto ticket. He would walk just as far as the car junkyard. On the way, he passed a huddle of schoolboys, heads all neatly shaved and carrying string bags.

When Premchand reached the wire fence surrounding the battered cars, he touched the knight in his pocket and lifted his face to the sun. He pulled out the lotto ticket and a coin to scratch it. A gust kicked up a cloud of dirt, causing him to sneeze and cough. When he recovered, he saw that he'd been unlucky. The ticket read, *Sorry, try again next time!* He was thinking that maybe he would play the lottery back in USA, just for fun, just in case, when a knee jammed into his back and pinned him to the ground. Premchand spat dirt from his mouth. He tried to jerk his arms free but the man was strong. He was panting, and the sweat of the man's palms seeped through Premchand's shirt. He tried to speak, to say, *Take everything I have,* but the man was not listening, he was moaning a low string of unintelligible words. What could he do? He tried to shout, but did not have enough air. In this moment, he could no longer control anything. He did not pray, he never had, nor could he believe in reincarnation, in *next*. Like his son, he believed in free will, though he knew there were philosophical problems with this, too—his son had explained. Premchand had always been taught to do right in this life, and some few good actions along the way were the most that time gave you. The man pressed down on him hard and continued to moan until suddenly the words grew rocky, loud, angry, scared. Premchand did not move. Warm metal pressed against the base of his skull. The voice continued to speak in Swahili, but by now Premchand understood perfectly. The man was asking forgiveness for what he was about to do.

3.

The hartebeest had shapely, hourglass horns and a brown stripe down the center of their faces. The streak made them look ashamed, marked out for special treatment that was not necessarily kind. Thomson's gazelles, smaller and lighter-colored than the hartebeest, had racing stripes along their sides. Thimbles for feet. Every now and then they hopped forward, or to the side. Ears wide like donkeys.

"Gazelles are good luck for honeymooners—they bring peace and fertility," their guide Kioko said, his voice both solicitous and bored. Between teaching them the Swahili words for the animals, he twirled a toothpick between his teeth.

They watched, silently. They gawked. The animals did nothing extraordinary, no fights between rams, no skittishness. They bent their heads and ate, then looked up, looked around, lowered their heads again. Sunil ran his fingertips up and down Amy's spine. Urged the knotted length of her back to release.

"I don't care if we never see a lion," she said. "Or a rhino, the Big Five, whatever they are."

"Me neither. I'm happy."

Amy exhaled under his touch, but did not reply.

The horizon's edge was farther away than he'd ever imagined possible; it split the world into two shades of nothingness. Sunil wondered how much of being in love was the capacity—the desire—to be in the same place at the same time, seeing the same things. He could not believe his luck, being here with her.

With his father and Bimal, there had been progress: honest exchanges you could build on; talk he was eager to return to. But he and his mother hadn't found more than momentary peace. After talking with Bimal, Sunil had been ready to try again, more softly, with an eye toward discovery instead of blame and reparation, but they'd not had any moments alone together before he and Amy left for the Maasai Mara.

There'd been a rift between Amy and his mother on the last day. When he walked out of Bimal's room, where his brother had fallen asleep and Sunil had dozed in his chair, nearly two more hours had passed. He'd found Amy silently, rigidly flipping through a magazine in the living room, while the rest of the women were in the kitchen.

"Love," he had said cautiously. "Are you all right? Ready for our honeymoon?"

"Yes, I've been ready for hours," she said. But she had refused to say anything more. She put whatever it was aside, and they had gone out with Meena that night, as planned, but he could tell the after-tension was still resonating yesterday when they landed on the dusty airstrip in Keekarok, with its tin-shack duty-free shop. Still, she said nothing and he determined to be patient and wait until she was ready.

It was a short ride from there to Ngama Hills Camp, where their unusually petite Maasai hostess had wordlessly taken their bags and dropped them in the center of their "tent"—a large, private building of rough-hewn wood—and disappeared. "If this is camping," he'd said, impressed. His father had said the camp was four-star, but Sunil had imagined one star was sleeping on the ground with your jacket for a pillow. The bathroom was stocked with bottled water and soap squares; the shower pressure was strong and even. He hadn't been in a hotel since the Howard Johnsons of his childhood. The light shot sideways across the grounds, pale green leaves turning lazily, and Sunil inhaled the scent of cedar.

They had brushed the journey's dust off their skin. Untied their shoes, peeled off their socks.

They were alone for the first time in two weeks.

"You're breathless," she said.

"That's because I've missed you." He slid her shirtneck down her arm. Bit the salty apple of her shoulder. "If I were a lion, I'd eat you." She dug her nails into his chest then roughly traced through the whorl of black hair, up, around, and over a dark nipple to grip his prickly chin, and said sternly, "We're here now. Be here with me."

When they returned from the game drive today, canvas sheets had been rolled down the tent walls to protect against wind. They quickly washed their hands and faces and walked down the softly lighted stone path to the main building for dinner. Amy shivered under her fleece. Sunil put his arms around her, and she leaned into him. Perhaps whatever was bothering her had been dissolved by their glorious day with the animals, the lucky gazelles.

They ate goat and rice and kale at polished wooden tables on a verandah overlooking spindly bushes and shiny-barked trees. Purity, their waitress, poured their beers and inquired what they'd seen. "Very good," she said, approvingly. "You are counting to the Big Five."

The light turned from lemon to mango to orange to disappeared. The temperature dropped and the staff closed the windows. "The sun does set fast in this country," Sunil said.

Amy smiled and speared papaya with her fork. There were still circles under her eyes, but Sunil thought they were beginning to fade.

After dinner they joined Kioko and the other men drinking Tuskers at the bar. "You are discovering our Mara nightlife," Kioko said. He had a driver's soft body, with a paunch, and a broad genial face trained for tourism. He smiled when he was being looked at, but when he thought no one was paying attention, his expression slackened. Kioko was Kikuyu, from central Kenya. He had been married twice and had eight children. In between safaris, he drove six hours each way to spend one night with his family. "It is little better now," he said. "The government put tourism money into the roads. Before, the drive is eight or ten hours."

The wind rustled the trees. Somewhere out in the dark, wooden things banged together.

A white South African named Rawley introduced himself. With his receding hairline and tanned skin, he looked the part of the weathered, irascible guide. They asked if business was good and he said it was, had picked up after the slump following the embassy attacks. "My father was in the safari game. I inherited his little enterprise."

"Took around Teddy Roosevelt?" Amy said.

Sunil was relieved to hear teasing and casualness returned to her voice.

"If that were true, I'd be older than the Ngama Hills, but we did have a few royals. The King of Monaco after he married your Grace Kelly. She was a beaut." Then Rawley said, "Honeymooning?"

Amy nodded. "And visiting family."

Sunil wondered why she had added that, just as the previous week was easing away.

"Hindu or Muslim?"

"Jain."

"Gujarati?"

Sunil nodded.

"Your people did well for themselves with their dukas."

"Commerce is a cultural imperative."

"Nah," Rawley said. "People think the Indians in this country have some kind of mercantile gift or money lust, but it's because they weren't allowed to own land. A lot of the imported laborers had been farmers in the mother country, but the Brits kept them out of the Highlands. Then proceeded to bugger it up."

Amy leaned forward, tugged the sleeves of her pullover up to her elbows. Her hair lit yellow in the bar's low light. With an easy, forthright smile, she said, "What do you know about man-eating lions, Rawley?"

The guide lit a cigarette and circulated the pack. One match flare after another, as if each lighting depended on the one before.

"It was about a hundred years ago," Rawley said, "while they were building the Uganda Railroad. The Lunatic Express. There were these maneless beasts with an appetite for brown flesh. For all flesh really, but the Asians and the Africans were most exposed."

Sunil shook his head. "People think you'll believe anything if you say it happened in Africa."

"This is true, mate. There's the DNA evidence to prove it. Happened in Tsavo, east of here. The coolies went on strike until the lions were shot. The beasts were stuffed and sent to Chicago. The Field Museum." He took a long drag. "You don't have to believe me, it's all been written about. Patterson was the colonel overseeing the crew that got mauled. The hunt went on for months. All kinds of elaborate traps and ruses. One poor English bastard was devoured inside his railway car." He chuckled. "Does it make you feel lucky to be alive, friend? Could have been your great-grandaddy inside those jaws."

"Then he wouldn't have been my great-grandaddy."

"He's a hard one, your man," Rawley said to Amy, gesturing with his red-tipped cigarette.

"Single minded," she said, the trace of a grimace on her watermelon mouth.

"The Brits were so damn broke after building that railroad they had to find a way to make the country pay for it. That's when the fun really started. Ask these gentlemen." Rawley gestured to the bar, where Kioko had smoked his cigarette down to a glowing stub and the Maasai bartender stood alert but silent.

Sunil looked at Rawley and saw he was the kind of man who'd had success with older women as a teenager and coasted ever since. He was not so attractive now. Classic blue eyes, but one of them drooped, and his neck skin sagged. He wore his khaki safari uniform with the sleeves loosely rolled.

"We've got an early drive," Sunil said. But Amy waved her beer at him; she wasn't finished. She was beginning to settle in and enjoy herself.

But Sunil was tired. "You can stay." He was through listening to campfire yarns, to people telling him stories. The point was to be here alone with his wife, to make new memories.

"No, I'm done. Let's go back." On the path, she said, "You thought I wanted to stay there and listen to Rawley by myself?"

"You started asking him questions."

"Weren't you curious?"

"That guy doesn't know anything."

"More than we do. He's lived here his whole life."

"This is our honeymoon. You said you needed a break. So let's not go around asking strange men to dig up anecdotes that explain my character."

"Is that what you think?" She stopped walking and stared

at him. "That lion story is just that. A great story. I didn't ask for details as a roundabout way of asking for an explanation of *you*. You, I understand just fine."

Sunil felt a hole opening up in front of him. If he wasn't careful, he was going to fall in.

Amy skirted ahead and jammed the key into the lock, entered without waiting for him, and went straight into the bathroom. She brushed her teeth and changed her clothes with the door closed, emerging in enormous flannel pants.

"Where'd those come from?"

"They might be Ajay's. Sarada gave them to me for the cold nights." Her voice wavered despite her efforts to control it, and her face had that furious flatness. Anger made her thinner, two-dimensional. When his own fury rose, it spread through him as something thickening, strengthening, the muscle that filled out his skin and bones. Amy had always been afraid of her anger, but these days—this trip—she appeared to be drawing it closer.

She stood still, deciding something, then said, "You know what I told your mother yesterday? That I'd rescued you. So melodramatic, but I meant it. At the time I meant from her."

The hole sealed up. But behind him gaped a new one. A chasm so vast he couldn't see it all at once, caught only glimpses of its rapid expansion over his shoulder. Carefully he said, "Tell me what happened."

His mother wanted them to have an Indian wedding. In Nairobi. A sari for Amy, a ceremony with fire, all the relatives and friends. "At first it was fine—friendly, generous even. But before I could even consider it, she said that our marriage would never be recognized. She didn't even give me a chance. Just accused me of stealing you. She said I'd always be a stranger, that she wished I hadn't come." Amy released her hair from barrettes, roughly tugging knotted strands of hair out of her scalp. "I tried to tell you. I asked you to help me, to stay with me. I was losing my shit. But you didn't. Maybe you really couldn't, I don't know.

"Sunil, what are you doing? I'm talking to you."

Sunil was rummaging in their suitcase. He knew his mother couldn't be trusted, but he'd chosen to ignore the signs. He was so stupid! Why hadn't he stayed with Amy when she asked? "What was she *thinking*?" He was fuming. He would fix it. It couldn't wait. "Sarada Aunty gave us a phone. For emergencies."

Watch your step. You don't know where the hole is.

"Stop it." Amy grabbed his arm. Her fingers pulsed through his skin. "I'd rather spend the night alone in a cow-dung Maasai hut than here with you if you turn that phone on. It's not worth it. Talking to her will only take you away from here. Put that fucking phone away."

Later, after apologizing, after make-up sex, after lying awake together and listening to the wind, Sunil said, "Can I tell you a story? It's about my mom. Just tell me if you don't want to hear any more about her."

"You know I always like more data," she said. She turned on her side to listen. "Tell me."

It was spring break, he said. He'd come home from school to see the Replacements in one of their last concerts before they broke up for good. "You know how much their music meant to me, right?" She said that she did. The songs pulled him apart and stuck him back together in a way that somehow felt better for the breaking.

The afternoon after the concert he'd woken up late. His mother had stayed home from the store to visit with him, and they ate fresh samosas while he told her about the concert. "She was patient. It was a rare moment—I was telling her about my life and she actually seemed interested. Like when we used to talk about bowling, the plots of TV shows. Stupid stuff, but things we shared those years when my dad was traveling. Actually, the store was a plot we hatched together when she was taking business classes at the community college." At the end of lunch, his mother asked him if he'd take out the daughter of a family friend. "I said yes. She gave me money, and I took this girl Priyanka out to eat. We had a really boring conversation about people we knew in common, and then I brought her home." Afterward he'd met up with the same friends he'd gone to the concert with. Song by song, they relived it. "But when I got home, my mom was waiting up. I guess Priyanka's mother had called to talk about the evening, and they'd decided that I'd been rude. I thought it was clear we'd gone out as a favor to our parents, but maybe I was wrong. Maybe Priyanka had expected something else. We got into a big fight. I stormed out and took their car. I heard this awful crunch when I pulled out of the garage. I looked long enough to see that it wasn't somebody's dog and took off. Drove around for a couple hours."

It turned out that he'd crushed a big jewelry shipment, items for the store. He felt bad, but she hadn't let him explain.

"She thought I broke her things on purpose. I didn't, but I let her think I did." He paused, a grim understanding spreading through him. "We're a lot alike, aren't we?" He'd always known he shared his mother's temperament, but the similarities now felt drawn in sharp relief.

Amy's lips were maintained in a straight line, her eyebrows raised, agreeing with him without saying anything.

"The difference is that I have philosophy. I can articulate reasons that make me feel justified."

Amy finished the thought for him. "What you usually say in moments like this one is that either your mother doesn't see the wrong, which is stupidity, or that she does wrong things knowingly, which makes her a bad person."

He laughed with bitter pleasure. "Exactly! You nailed it.

I'm just going to hand my dissertation over to you."

"Ha ha. That's all you, buddy." She sat up against the head-board. "But seriously, you know I think that's the wrong way to approach your family—most of the time. Yes, your mother can be incredibly overbearing to the point of being offensive—I've seen that firsthand now—but I think the two of you could reconcile *somewhat*, could appreciate each other more than you do."

"You mean *should. Should* reconcile."

"What do you think?" she said.

Outside, the wind picked up, and goosebumps raced up his legs. He imagined them wearing aviator goggles out on the Mara tomorrow.

Soon Amy was asleep, but Sunil lay awake, cracked open to the night. He was bothered by what she had said. And he knew of only one way to discharge the unease. Gingerly, he slipped out of bed and made his way to the front desk where Purity, showing no surprise or reaction on her face, led him to a computer. His email was brief. It neatly laid out a dilemma for the moral realist, a crucial step in advancing his view. On the short walk back to the hut, a strong wind whisked over him. Inside, supposedly protected, he heard a branch scrape the bark of the tent walls, and something crunched the gravel. Then a sound like a mother shushing a baby, followed by a noise so startling and so near he leapt. He'd never heard such a sound, yet it echoed *danger* in a primal part of his mind. A yowl, a growl, a crunch. Amy didn't wake up. Shaking with cold, Sunil found another piece of his uncle's clothing and pulled the shirt over his head, his wrists bare below the too-short sleeves. He shuffled along the wall, straining his ears and listening until nearly dawn. He felt painfully aware of his body, of his thin, falsely protective skin. His thudding heart, the soft loops of his gut, and his vulnerable, curled-under toes. His nerves seemed to cause a separation between mind and body.

He finally fell asleep just minutes before the wake-up knock at five-thirty, when he opened the door to find a tray of hot water, tea bags, hard-boiled eggs, and sweet, dry toast. He was ravenous.

They were deep in the Mara, two hundred miles from Nairobi. They did not know that Sunil's father was dead.

It could have happened anywhere—even in America—but it hadn't. It had happened here. His father had not told anyone where the couple was staying, which camp, and their phone remained securely, protectively off. Sunil had not made his angry call.

No one but the askari had seen Premchand leave. The last man to hear him speak was the groundnut seller who'd happily taken his American dollars.

All this Sunil and Amy would learn on their return.

Their van jolted up and down as they drove directly into the sunrise, the wheels at the mercy of the hardened ruts. The land rolled and they rode the wave. The grassland stretched in all directions. His eyes followed the earth to the thin place where it met the sky, and his gaze lifted him up and out of his body, then deposited him to the side of where he was standing moments before.

He still felt diffuse, sore, and vulnerable. His mind and body had yet not reconciled.

The sun blazed and spotlit the hulking figures before them. Behemoth shadows like nightmares.

"I've never been so close, not even at the zoo," Amy whispered. They were standing with their heads and shoulders out the rooftop window. Now Amy leaned toward the huge forms, magnetized.

The preposterous herd grazed and swayed side to side

among silvery shrubs. Kioko counted off. Twelve. He halted
the van. The elephants roved closer. The upward-arching tusks
made their massive down-hanging trunks all the stranger. What
Sunil had thought were shrubs were actually trees. His sense of
scale was false, unreliable. Everything was larger, more loom-
ing than it appeared. Baby elephants walked at their mother's
shoulders, every part absurd. And yet they *sauntered.* Reaching
out to grasp leaves and branches, stuffing the harvest into their
maws.

"And how do you say *elephant* in Swahili?" Kioko said, keeping up their lessons. "Over there we have *punda, swara, nyati,
kigoni.* Remember all these things?"

"Aliens," Amy said. "Beautiful, incredible aliens." Their
elbows rested on the roof, their hands shading their eyes.

"It's true. They're beyond belief," Sunil said, looked at her
slyly. "That's what *incredible* means."

She rolled her eyes in just the exasperated way he was trying to provoke, and this one powerful look reinstated him in his
body. She made him feel at home in one of the most bizarre
places on earth. He had married her. He needed her. *Almost*
would not be the description of his life.

He would master the past tense. He would make progress.
Sunil closed his eyes and let his lids warm and melt. On the
inside darkness, he saw acacia trees and the stripes of zebras.

*Step back, look around, take it in. You'll never have the chance
again.*

When the Maasai warriors lined up to perform the lion-killing
dance, they carried the oblong leather shields and tall spears
like the ones that had littered the basement of his house as a
kid. Sunil had known, but never really believed, that what his
mother sold came from a specific place, where real people lived.
He suspected she didn't believe it either, that she ordered the

goods from a central warehouse, knowing only vaguely who made them and where. The stories she told her customers were generic, idealized, crafted to ensnare passersby.

This was the last place he'd expected to be reminded of his mother, though of course it should have been obvious from the start.

The young warriors were barefoot. Some heads were shaved; others had long plaits. Some wore faded Western shorts and shirts, others were bare-chested. Their skin all the same espresso. They circled, spears in hand, sinewy bodies urging an arrhythmic, skipping gait. They sang, rich vibrating tones, both high and deep, so it sounded like two pitches from the same throat. Then the singing paused, and from deep within emerged rumbles. Threats and roars.

Paul, the village chief's son and their guide, told them, as he ushered them to the gift shop—a ring of dung huts around a bare patch of dirt—that the women here used no birth control and bore up to fifteen children.

As they handled and released the beaded necklaces, the zebra tail flyswatters, the circular knives that tightly fit a wrist (used how?), Amy said, "Was that a statement of poverty or pride?"

"Good question. Virtue out of necessity?"

Amy could not help viewing the village through public health lenses. The children, she had pointed out, bore clusters of flies in their eyes. Their bellies were swollen, feet and hands riddled with scabies. But unlike the poor in Nairobi, and in the US, the Maasai displayed strong white teeth, which she supposed was the benefit of a low-sugar diet. These were the fiercest individuals on the planet. What were they to make of these lives?

Before leaving, Sunil lingered in front of a wooden stick with a bulbous end. The Maasai craftsman lifted it off the rickety table and vigorously demonstrated its use—to bludgeon things.

"A cudgel!" he said. "I'll take it. If my mother doesn't want it, I'll keep it for myself."

Amy nodded encouragingly and joked that it was the perfect gift to broker peace.

They rode silently back toward camp. Then a voice crackled over the radio. Sunil and Amy perked up for a moment, as if someone were calling them, but Kioko quickly answered in sentences too long and complicated for the rudimentary device in his hand. He said to them, "*Shuee*. You are very lucky indeed."

When they reached their destination, fifteen tense, jostled minutes, three or four vans were already gathered, each one inching closer to a ring of trees twenty yards away.

At first Sunil didn't see anything, his eyes not discerning among the sprouting trees and branches, the encompassing bunches of leaves, until, all of a sudden, it was there, again far larger than he expected. It stretched languorously across tree limbs. Fur sleek and spotted, its paws large as human skulls. A yowling carried on the wind. Not the sound from last night, but related. He had not told Amy about his terror, or his midnight email. He didn't want to burden her. It was time for him to be stoic and carry them along.

4.

In the mornings, before leaving for work, he had always given her a list: shirt cleaned, dentist appointment changed, squeaky brakes examined. If the roof needed fixing, if the heater broke, she was the one who was home and could deal. He left her cash. These things were little effort, but she resented being told what to do. Sometimes she'd given Sunil the tasks, and that had helped somewhat. But now she had a decision before her that she could not make.

Sarada said it was too much money. She'd called five different airlines, and the prices for flying a body back to USA were madness. "Ghastly," Sarada said. "How dare they exploit grieving families!" Then she murmured, "I know it is hard, sister, but we must go one way or another. Already it has been one full day." The impatient little sister who always knew what other people should do. When she learned how to braid, she'd insisted on doing her older sister's plaits, too, because she did it better—tighter, neater, more swiftly.

Urmila felt paralyzed to make a decision without Sunil. He was due back tomorrow. It was hard to explain this to Sarada, who insisted waiting was not how it was done. Was not healthy for the soul, or for the survivors.

Too late, she realized her sister was right.

Her son slumped and crumpled when Sarada told him—Urmila could not yet bear to say the words—and his weakness terrified her.

Tight cords in his neck, a pained hunch in his back, Sunil agreed they shouldn't ship the body back. "Just cremate here," he swallowed at the word, "and take the ashes home."

Yes, fine, take care of the body here. But Sunil was also insisting they hold the funeral in Columbus, and to Urmila that seemed impossible. She felt she had been in Nairobi for months and could hardly remember her home in America.

Outside it was a bright afternoon, but the curtains were drawn in the living room, sealing them inside a gray vault.

"You want to hold the service in America, it's okay," her sister said. "I'll go with you. I understand. The life was there."

Sarada had said *the life*, not *your life*.

"Who should I call?" Sunil said. He mentioned the Savlas, plus other family friends Urmila hadn't seen in years.

Premchand had never talked about Nairobi unless she brought it up, didn't speak to his family unless they called him. He'd decided Ohio over Texas, where a nephew lived; where in Columbus to live (closest to the hospital, but far from their friends); where to send Sunil to school, paying pricey tuition that sucked away their savings. He'd chosen their son's name— first suggesting bland American *Sam* before agreeing to *Sunil*. Of course her husband had been the one to decide they would marry in the first place. He knew her family, he had weighed the options; he'd selected her. Of course her family would agree to a doctor, no matter that he was awkward and difficult and cold. He would provide.

She had been impressed at first by how much he knew, his

years in India adding worldliness to his smart reputation. He was handsome. He complimented her cooking. He did not raise his voice. He didn't care how she spent her free time. Yet he was not as good as people said. Now, abandoned, barely breathing on her own, she could admit that she agreed with her brother when he said to his friends, "Mr. Hollywood left us when we needed him. He could have stayed and helped us improve, but he wanted America for himself."

She couldn't take her husband back with her. Not even the remains. No service in Columbus. She had to take care of him here.

She motioned for Sunil to slide closer to her on the couch. Took his hand, fingers long and smooth like his father's at the same age. They sat like this a moment. "I know this place is not important to you," she said. "Your father agreed. But we are all here."

Sunil shook his head. "His work was there, all his colleagues, our house. That was home. We should have the service there. We can't stay here. It's not what Dad would have wanted. Here it will be religious—he'd hate that. No prayers, he told us.

"And what about his organs—his heart, corneas. Were they donated? Maybe it's not too late to call the hospital. Mom, where is the number?"

Urmila stared at him. She barely understood what he was saying. "We are in Nairobi! They don't do these things here."

"Sister, I must tell you—" Sarada began, but Urmila turned to her and snapped, "Hush up!"

"I know where we are," Sunil said. "Dad moved away from here. He left this country and chose to live somewhere else; we have to honor that choice. We have to tell people at home what happened—he can't just disappear from the face of the earth. He had thousands of patients, maybe some of them want to come."

She shook her head and said with force, "Your father didn't have any friends. He worked morning to night every day of the week and sat home on weekends reading the paper. You don't know. The last twelve years you are out of the house. *I* know." She would not let her son erase her husband's flaws, even in the wake of his death. Why should his voice count more than hers?

For nearly three days her son and his wife had not picked up the phone, had not bothered to check their voicemail. They'd returned last night still flying high on their good time.

"I think I know something about my father," Sunil said now. "I listened when he talked. He told me no prayers!"

"Maybe you are like him, but you did not know him. You were a child. A wife knows her husband best."

Sunil took back his hand. Breathed long, jagged breaths. "You knew him in a different way. Not better. I want to do something that will honor him. He did a lot of good things for a lot of people. It makes me sad that you don't see that."

The ghost of the father in the body of the son? Urmila saw on his face the hot burning of his childhood tantrums. She was sure the hardness had grown fiercer as he continued his schooling.

She would not do what was against her heart on account of her son, not even for her husband. Funerals were for the living, and she needed to live. Sunil had decades in front of him, and she did not. Urmila stood and straightened the hem of her sweater. She told her sister, "Make the arrangements here, please. An Indian funeral, like we do."

Sunil wrote and faxed an obituary to the *Columbus Dispatch*. But there he stopped. He told Sarada *no*, he would not cleanse the body. He would not do any of those eldest-son things. He wasn't even the eldest, after all. He would stay to attend the funeral, but nothing more. Urmila had told him he was free to leave, though she was relieved he stayed. But Amy, what to do with her? The girl was an intrusion. When Urmila looked in her direction, she squinted or removed her glasses, deliberately blurring her outlines.

She had felt liberated when the couple had left Nairobi. After a few days of this freedom, she'd resolved to have a heart of polished stone; getting along was easier then. She had decided that when she got home she would smoothly, unashamedly tell her friends back in Columbus about her son's marriage, no big deal. Talking with Meena, she heard about others, friends of her niece, who'd married out. Urmila had admitted then that Amy was a nice girl—kind, intelligent, pretty enough—it's just that she was not one of them. She would not keep her son close. Maybe not, Meena said, but maybe there was a way to share. She'd seen how it could be with the new couples. Many had two weddings. Yes, Urmila said, this was what she had suggested! They'd stumbled by marrying in haste, and a wedding at the Oshwal Centre would bring everyone together. Make it official.

Urmila told Meena how the day before they had left for safari, she had asked Amy, sweetly, over tea and barfi, if she'd like to get dressed up in a wedding sari. They could shop for a beautiful one, even if not as good as in India. There were plenty to help with the food, the preparations. But no, Amy didn't care to be a part. Jews could be stubborn this way.

Meena had demurred, said to give the girl time—when the couple had babies, things would get easier. "Best to play wait and see, don't you think?"

This morning Meena had found an old picture of Prem-chand in an album Urmila hadn't seen for years. It was dated 1961, when he was recently back from India. Urmila had not known him then, only his name. In the photograph, she saw a narrow, knife-like man; he didn't look into the camera but up and off to the side, as if at a bird in a tree. He wore a white collared shirt, dark pants, his hands in his pockets. Behind him was the Khoja Mosque. It was impossible to tell what he was doing there or whom he had been with. No one remembered taking the picture. Her sister put the framed photograph with the deevo, agarbati, flowers, and rice on a table next to the casket, so people could scatter the petals and grains.

They were introduced in 1963, while Urmila was still thinking about her man in Mombasa. Her first meeting with Premchand was on a sunny, warm, lazy day. She'd gone to see *Taj Mahal* with Sarada and Ajay, and in the parking lot they'd introduced her to a skinny man with a triangle nose. Afterwards, he asked if she'd liked the film, and when she said, *Bina Rai, what a woman, she was radiant!,* he'd smiled and agreed. He liked the songs, he'd said. Six months later they were married. Sometime after that, her sister had revealed that Premchand had slept through most of the movie.

Regarding the photograph, Amy had said to Urmila, "So handsome." The girl appeared folded inward, her nose and eyes red. She said, "I can't tell you how sorry I am, for both of you." She said, "I wish I had known him better." She said, "Tell me if there's anything I can do. Meena said she'd help me find something suitable to wear."

Urmila said, "Thank you for your concern," and stood up to take her tea in the kitchen. She thought instead of her friend Maddy, who would know how to show sincere sadness, who would know how to help the way grown women do. The day that Premchand disappeared, Maddy had emailed her to say she'd quit her hygienist job already and secured a property. She'd come up with a name: Always in Bloom. Still so much to be done—but she had started! She was grateful for Urmila's confidence and inspiration, and she wanted to thank her when she returned to the States.

The note had overwhelmed Urmila, and she was shocked to

find herself crying, her chest heaving in gasps—of relief? gratitude?—and this was how Sarada how had found her when she'd burst in, breathless, pausing—"How do you know already?"— before falling to her knees and weeping, *Oh sister, something terrible has happened.*

First silence, then speaking. A voice filtering in through the whirring of the outside world: *The Jain scriptures reflect belief in the eternal nature of the Soul; conviction that it is a consequence of the Soul being entangled in the material world; conviction that it is a time of bodily change; resigned acceptance of the inevitability of death; trust in the benefit of living a religious and moral life; and belief in the progress of the Soul toward liberation.*

They sang the Namokar Mantra. Or, some sang it.

By reciting this prayer we are aspiring to follow the example of humans who have progressed to monk and nun, above the layperson, and elevate ourselves to the higher stage.

Urmila pretended attention, feigned silent grief wrought by the prayer. Inside, under her white garments, she was in turmoil.

Sunil didn't offer a remembrance. Instead, Bimal rose and testified to his uncle's goodness, his spirit of adventure, his generosity. Urmila could spit. What did anyone here know? They did not know!

When the words and music ended and the visitors had eased out of the building, the casket was closed and the men hefted it onto their shoulders. Ajay, Anup, Gopal . . . her eyes down the line . . . Bimal with his cane—

—and Sunil, jaw drawn ever tighter, desperately pressing his palms into a corner of the weight, tears streaming, the free hands of his uncles patting his shoulders. Brow and ear visible for just a moment more before the doors closed. They descended to the crematorium. At this time the ladies were delicately ushered away from the fire and ash.

Yet Urmila's eyes followed the dark wake of the men's jackets. She was consumed by the desire to go with them, an engulfing, enraging desire that took her down, down. She stumbled a few steps forward, toward the fire, but now she was on the floor. She'd wanted to go down—not down here to the floor but downstairs with the men to the fire to press the button to see it to the end, to see the flames and feel the heat. She wanted to know finality in her core.

But she knew the rules. An exception would not be made for her. Her sister hoisted her to her feet.

"I can walk," Urmila said.

"I know you can."

"I'll take her. Mother," said a man's voice beside her; suited arms supported hers.

"Bimal," she murmured. "My heart."

"No," said the voice, this cracking, mournful voice she did not recognize. "The other one."

No! Not the one she wanted, she wanted the one who did not know her weaknesses, who would love her simply because she had given life, she wanted ease, and this one had never been ease and would never be. And she was so tired. "You," she said, crying. "I don't want you. You are not mine. Go now, and don't come back." As her body shook, she wondered if she was in her right mind, could ever be of right mind and heart again.

Now, in a hardbacked chair, a plate on her lap, she watched the others eat and murmur and shake their heads. She removed her glasses so she could sit without seeing, without knowing. But when she recognized the tender, limping figure of Bimal, dressed in navy blue, cross the room to where his brother leaned against the wall, arms folded, Urmila slipped the lenses back on and the world shifted into place, even if her understanding did not. Bimal's scar was a lightning bolt across his face. It would always be a reminder of their nightmare, the near death that had preceded real death. But perhaps the universe was not so cruel. If someone had to die, it was right that it should have been her husband and not her son.

Urmila stood up, feeling invisible. They were all eating; no one was looking at her. Her sons had their backs to her. She sneaked up on them, her boys. She followed a few feet behind when they drifted inside a room, Bimal haltingly, adjusting his weight on his cane. She stood outside the doorway and leaned her shoulder against the wall. Her older son sat on the arm of a chair, while Sunil paced.

"A few months ago," Sunil was saying. "Before that, maybe six. We were both bad on the phone." A pause—he slipped from view. "You?"

"Years. I am sure of it. Premchand Fua, to me. Not my father. He was only father to you."

Sunil reappeared, his nose sharp. His arms swayed loose, uncontrolled, until they sagged in defeat. He looked at the floor. "He was good. I know he was a good person. Everyone at the clinic liked him, not just the doctors, but the nurses, the staff. He was kind to people." He shrugged and looked into Bimal's marked face, his own skin flawless, his eyes despairing. "But ask me ten facts? Maybe I could give you five."

"Facts change," Bimal said. He smiled.

Smiled! Over what? This untruth? A balm to make the other feel better? Urmila opened her mouth to protest, then quickly clamped it shut. Because there was something here between them she had not expected. Some give and sweetness. Some usefulness. Some softening of shells, allowing the other to talk or stay silent, to be right or wrong. She leaned forward, cupped a hand behind her ear, but the hallway had grown loud and the voices crowded out the voices of her sons.

She watched, as if from very far away, as Bimal reached

into a shoulder bag and removed a worn canvas sack, angular with hard edges, like a short stack of prayer books. Sunil's eyes grew wide. Bimal appeared to insist, thrusting the package into Sunil's hands. Sunil was at a loss—this she could see—but he held the sack to his chest and nodded.

They withdrew into themselves. In the days that followed, anything that needed to be said between Urmila and Sunil was relayed by Sarada or Meena. Occasionally Urmila exchanged words with Amy, but she preferred to avoid her as well. At night she slept and woke, slept and woke, remembered the fact of Premchand's death and forgot it again. After each remembering she expected to feel some change, some reconfiguration of the harsh world, the way its brightness and loudness hurt her eyes and ears, but she did not. She waited for change, but it did not come. Or perhaps she could not recognize it. Or maybe she was beyond change; change was something that happened now to other people. She would remain herself, alone inside her skin, as she always had.

5.

Uhuru, they called it. The Africans won, and Europeans left in droves. We had nowhere to go. India offered only poverty, and Britain didn't want us. Kenya had been the land of opportunity; now it was land of last resort.

It was like the time, did I tell you about the time? The time a hippopotamus waded into the stream that fed the power turbine of Nairobi. The thing got stuck and plunged the whole city into darkness for days. But there were darker times to come.

First came the bitterness. All these years, they think we are cheating them in our stores. Listen, everyone knows about Indian bargaining, but there was no convincing that we were not trying to fleece them. The Africans grumbled about our practices, accused us of using false weights, or writing in our own language so they could not follow. But we had traded with them back when the colonials ignored them, when the whites did not dare venture into the interior. Who had bought their beans and maize and beeswax? Who had sold them hoes to break the soil of their shambas? When people are poor, their memories and tempers are too short.

In sixty-nine, the Africans revoked our trading licenses, our bread and butter. More of us left. Those who could slipped into Britain through the last skinny crack, those men who had accumulated funds in UK accounts. More than one hundred thousand people, you know? But I was too old to start over in a new country, my English limited even then to a few words. Who there would have accepted me as their burden?

And still, most days feel like the ones before. We live our lives. We go to see Raj Kapoor in *Sangam,* and all the ladies talk for months about lips touching on the screen.

And yet, on River Road, all over the city, agents are springing up, promising to help with immigration. Promises to get into UK, which had placed quotas on us. Talk was of the price of gold, the rate of pounds sterling and rupees on the black market. Tourists paid us in foreign currency—who knew what would happen to our shillings?

Maybe you think, from where you both stand, inside your democracies, that this was the time to show political will. Become part of the system and work influence from the inside. After all, the professions and the trades, from lawyer and engineer to tailor and electrician, these were majority Asians. We had many jobs in public sector, too, but after the Africans took rule, they wanted their own in place. There was not the thought that Africans could advance and join us at these levels, but instead that we were standing in their way. They recalled the years of master-servant, and thought all masters must be removed.

Asians had not been active in politics in the protectorate, never protested loudly against the colonials, and in this the Africans saw complicity. When they took power, they wanted total loyalty and nothing but. Dedication to their causes, forgetting our own. So if we cannot represent our true selves, what then is the point?

At a party once, I met a man who was starting in politics.

He was at the temple, maybe trying to raise some funds and pull us to his side. While he is there, we smile politely, but when he is gone, everyone says, *Budhu! What he thinks he is doing?*

Communal representation by race, we used to have this. It wasn't a good system, but at least our people spoke for themselves and most had the vote. These tiny advantages disappeared after independence. We get lost in these big parties that first and foremost must stand up for the African cause. You here, you think you are African? And you over there, American? You see? Indian first, no matter which place we call home.

6.

Once, during the sixty hours he was asleep, Amy opened the curtains to let the sunlight in. But all he remembered were shades of gray, shifting forms and shadows. That was daytime. At night, his dreams exploded in Technicolor. Nightmares on the plains, sausage trees hung with bodies, severed heads. He was chased and half devoured; beasts bit his legs and left him to bleed.

Simama. Twende. Kioko's voice teaching *stop* and *go.* *Simama! Twende!*

He'd been feverish, Amy said, his temperature over 102. "At 103, I was taking you in."

The first day he was out of bed for more than a few hours, Amy made plain pasta with butter and salad for dinner. They sat at the table for an hour, then she scraped his uneaten food into a Tupperware. They watched TV. Amy drank beer and Sunil, Orange Crush, the childhood comfort that was now the only calories he could stomach. Her hair had grown down past her shoulders, tucked flat behind her ears, giving her a religious cast. Her face had lost its Kenya pink. She looked exhausted. Gently, she said, "How are you feeling?"

"Numb. Tired."

"You know, you need to call James."

"I will." Though it was the last thing on his mind.

She nodded and rubbed something off her lips with her thumb. "My parents have been calling. You don't have to talk to them, they don't expect it, but they're sad for you, concerned. They want to know if there's anything they can do."

"They're kind," he said.

"They'd give us a loan, I bet, if we asked. To tide us over."

He shook his head. "Not that. Not now." The interest on their credit card had ballooned—he refused to speak to his mother about covering their tickets as she had originally promised—but being in debt to the Kauffmans was worse.

"They also asked if there's anything they can do for your mom."

"Maybe. I don't know. They should ask her." He thought of his mother alone in their Columbus house; her feet silent on the blue carpet. Pacing blindly past the cola stain, letting the yard grass grow tall. Would she sell the place? Was she still working? She hadn't called. At the funeral, when he'd taken her body to support her, to hold her, he'd called himself *the other one*. He'd meant it as joke, a moment of lightness. Complicit in the unusual past they now shared. But it had come out cracked and desperate, and now he saw that his statement had also been a trial, a test. She'd always thought of him as second. And in one revealing instant, she'd demoted him from *other* to total stranger. She'd been distraught, but her directive hadn't come from nowhere. It had been lying beneath the surface for years. How could the Kauffmans understand that? How could Amy?

Spring had passed them by and now it was summer, though the mornings and evenings were still cool. The distraction of basketball was over, leaving a gaping hole in the evenings. It was eight-thirty, just getting dark. Flickers from the TV on mute lit up their silence. The apartment still felt new to him.

He could barely remember their brief days here before leaving for Nairobi—except for that call from his mother: the phone cord wrapped tightly around his wrist as she destabilized the foundation he'd once thought immutable.

He motioned for Amy to move closer. She slid backward between his legs and leaned against his chest, rested the back of her head on his shoulder. He wrapped his arms around her and felt her ribs. He held her until her breathing fell in with his and they were asleep.

In the morning, Amy poured mango juice, which Sunil suddenly craved. It was expensive, but she insisted he needed the calories. Andrew and Erik were coming by, she said.

"You've been talking to them?"

"Sure. They've called. They've come over. They're good friends." Erik had brought several packages of Norwegian smoked salmon.

Sunil saw in the full light of day that Amy had been busy while he was asleep. The apartment was very clean, the fridge stocked, her sneakers caked with mud. A stack of résumés and cover letters on a corner of the table.

"So those jerks at the Welcome Group never contacted you? I thought that interview had gone really well."

Amy pulled her hair back into a ponytail and tied the drawstring of her running shorts. "It did. They offered me the job, but I couldn't take it."

"What? When? In Nairobi?" She appeared so casual, he couldn't understand what she had said. "That was your first choice."

"I know, it sucks. But there was nothing I could do." She kept her eyes on her bare feet. The nails were scuffed, dark with gray sock lint around the edges.

"Why didn't you tell me?"

They'd been halfway around the world, she said. She'd written back right away, hoping, and they were sorry, but it was too late.

"You should have told me." His fingers drummed the table. He stopped drumming. Shadows circled the bowl of peaches and melons. "It's a big deal that your best prospect came and went, and you're telling me now? Only because I asked?"

She fetched her socks and shoes and shoved in her feet. Roped the laces into double knots. "Do you remember how on edge you were in Nairobi? Do you see how I might not have wanted to give you bad news?"

On safari there'd been plenty of quiet moments when she could have told him. His mood, hers, that wasn't supposed to matter. Was she *scared* to tell him, is that what she meant? The thought was foreign. He'd never come close to wondering that before. And now she'd made up her mind, unilaterally closed the discussion.

He watched her leave the apartment, jog down the stairs, slam the front door, and course down the block, all before she even opened the door.

"Show some self-respect," Andrew said, when he came by to pick Sunil up. He pointed at his gym shorts in disbelief.

"We're only going for barbecue," Sunil said, but he changed into real pants and pulled on a clean shirt.

The unlikely three of them ambled down the street: brown, cream, and paper white. Andrew was the only one dressed decently, who carried himself upright and looked straight ahead. Sunil walked with his eyes on the ground, while Erik, in his own wrinkled button-down, ambled with his head in the clouds, as if scanning for birds.

Andrew asked if Amy might go for a PhD if she had a hard time finding a job.

"No, she says she's done with school. She wants to do something useful."

"That makes one of us," Erik said cheerfully, constitutionally unflappable.

Then Erik and Andrew turned quickly to him, to his problem.

"You can't just quit at this point. You've put in four years of work already. The dissertation is all you have left," Andrew said. "And you know what needs to be written."

"There's no good reason not to see it through," Erik agreed. "Pull yourself up by your Harvard bootstraps, man. We're so lucky here—are you going to throw that away? Erase everything you've done?"

Erase made Sunil think of his father. Vanished into the dust of another continent.

"I want to see what you've written," Erik said.

"No. It's not ready."

They stood in line at Fat Jerry's, the air rich with fry and sweetness. Sunil was glad his feet stuck to the floor, because he felt light-headed. His stomach flipped, growled. They ordered ribs, pulled pork, coleslaw, collard greens, baked beans, cornbread. The trainee taking the order made some mistakes and called over the manager. College-aged, Indian, softly rounded face, she told Sunil her name. Smiled brightly with her American teeth. She asked where his family was from.

"There are Indians in Africa?"

He laughed, the first time in days. "Believe it."

The line built up behind him, but she kept her eyes on him. Her gaze felt good. He felt recognized, reconstituted. Deepa gave them three fat slices of pecan pie and helped carry their food to the table.

Andrew pushed aside the plastic forks and pulled metal utensils out of a case in his shoulder bag. "Tell me about your breakthrough in Kenya. I know you had one because Lieberman told me. I guess you emailed her?"

Sunil pressed fingers into his eyes. He saw what Andrew was doing. Fine. He would talk.

He explained to them how, lying awake in the Ngama Hills (while Amy was asleep, while his father was still alive—in Sunil's own mind), he'd imagined two columns, labeled *Some Effect* and *No Effect*. Those were the two options for the realist, the person who believes that we can know moral truths. Either the realist believes evolution has had *some* effect on our moral judgments, or he believes that evolution has had *no* effect. If he chooses *no effect*, he is driven toward scientific nonsense. If he chooses *some effect*, he is faced with total moral skepticism, or the claim of a totally implausible coincidence. When this formulation had occurred to him in the middle of the Mara night, he'd written it up quickly and emailed it to Lieberman. This dilemma created the more formal terms she had told him he needed for his dissertation.

Andrew nodded, excited. "Yeah, so that's pretty fucking insane. Are you saying all you're left with is skepticism, which is just as debilitating as nihilism? Because skepticism and realism aren't the only two views."

"The other two options are no good. Naturalism just changes the topic, and relativism is incoherent."

"See how provocative that is—you've boxed in the realist. You don't finish this," Andrew said, "someone else will hit upon it and he'll get all the credit. You think you're suffering now. Wait until you get scooped." He rolled up his sleeves and piled more food on Sunil's plate. "Eat. Amy said you're starving yourself. We're not going to let you turn into some boiled-egg-eating Berman. I won't be friends with any Double-D."

Erik's comically thin eyebrows peaked in concern. He said, "We are not joking. You have to finish."

The vertigo started when he left the apartment. Walking up the steps of Emerson Hall, his feet wet from the rain, he tried to imagine the other side: emerging from the meeting triumphant, ready to go on. Ready! He passed the classroom in which he'd substitute-taught for Bernardston, and felt a jittery almost-hope, arms and legs tingling in anticipation. If he could only get back there, back to the students, to puzzling through paradoxes and firing them up.

James offered Sunil a bottle of Poland Spring and waited courteously for him to drink. Something about his office was different. A striking and unexplained absence. Several bookshelves had been cleared; half-packed boxes stacked on the floor. "Are you moving offices?"

"I've been working from home more," James said, his square face weary. "So I've shipped boxes to the house. Not that there's space for them. Drives my wife crazy."

James nearly lived in his office. It had always comforted Sunil to know that in the case of a true philosophical emergency one of the best minds of the generation could be found at a moment's notice. Sunil considered himself to be in the midst of a genuine philosophical crisis and was relieved to be here, immersed in James's calm demeanor, his aura of permanence. But the missing books unsettled him. It was like Andrew wearing a dirty shirt.

"I'm so sorry, Sunil, about your father." James faltered. "Were you close?"

This was the first personal question James had ever asked. He'd never even probed his ethnic heritage, or where he grew up. Like James's steady office presence, his adviser's lack of interest in Sunil as an individual proved the man's seriousness, his intellectual purity.

"Not very close, no. We did have a couple of good talks

before he—was killed. And one that wasn't so good."

"Well, that's par for the course, I suppose."

Maybe James never asked personal questions because he didn't know what to do with the answers. Maybe James relied on platitudes as much as anyone. Sunil removed the sheath of papers from his pack, ready to discuss his paper. He had written up his notes from Nairobi—not as much as he wanted, but something.

But James sighed, looked at him with pained regret. "I'm afraid I have some bad news. I suppose you know you missed your deadline, the extension of your deadline. The department has met, and there are sufficient concerns about your progress to prevent us from funding you for the fall."

"But the deadline was just last week." Or had it been the week before?

"This final deadline was quite firm, which I mentioned before you left. I know you can't have been expected to produce anything since your father's death, but you did have quite a generous amount of time before that. I feel terrible telling you at a time like this." James removed his glasses and massaged the baggy skin under his eyes. "We hope you will sit in on classes—don't disappear—but we can't fund you until spring. And that, of course, is contingent upon significant progress—half or three-quarters of the dissertation. You're working on a very promising idea. I hope you can find a way to continue—talking through it, writing. On the other hand, sometimes a semester off is helpful for students, releases them from some crippling anxiety, something I know a thing or two about."

The backlit vision of the classroom, of bright young versions of himself, of faces to talk to, blinked and fizzled out. Sunil gathered his things. He felt like fleeing but forced himself to slow, to adopt a modicum of dignity. But as he reached the common room, he felt it: the flapping, twisting panic of free fall, of complete fucking cluelessness.

Lieberman's office was empty, but a wet yellow slicker hung over a hook driven carelessly into the wall. Sunil waited in the chair she'd leaned back in and threatened to tip over the last time he was here.

She entered the room still drying her hands on a paper towel. A few brown shreds clung to her palms.

When she saw him she stopped, then jolted forward. "I'm sorry, Sunil. I'm so very sorry." She reached out, as if to hug him, then thought better of it. Her hair was pulled back messily and held in place by a chewed pencil.

"For what?"

"About your father?"

"Oh, of course. Thank you. Honestly, at first I thought you were saying you were sorry about my funding?"

"Oh."

"You said—"

"I defended your project, as much as I could. I used the email you sent from Kenya. But it was a hard case to make because you still do not have enough pages. But you will." She peeled the wet towel off her hands and stuffed the damp ball into her pocket, pushed tangled strands away from her flushed face. When she spoke again, her voice was softer, the softest he'd ever heard it. "I'd like to help you."

But what could she do? He was too far gone for her help. He stood from the chair, feeling only space between his ears. He didn't know why he'd come here. "I have to go," he said. She called after him, but he kept walking.

Outside, the sky was changing. The rain clouds separated from the sky. As Sunil stood motionless, the gray air became infused with a yellowy green light he'd seen only in the apocalyptic glow of movies.

Insects hummed, and with each step, pain registered in every joint.

He thought of his father, of the times in his childhood when Premchand had disappeared wordlessly, leaving Sunil to bear the weight of his mother's irascible temperament; and now, again, as an adult, he'd left, carrying so many unfinished sentences. He was bereft.

The terror his father must have felt in his final moments. The thought nearly knocked Sunil down. His father's stubborn, oblivious, vulnerable head pressed against a merciless gun. Had he cried? Had he felt resignation, or even relief? Sunil was overcome by all that he couldn't know and didn't do, and he stood, weeping, on a busy corner outside the university gate.

Amy wore an apron and checked the lasagna in the oven. Monica had given them a set of kitchen knives as a wedding present, and Ariel had contributed the apron and a stack of cookbooks. Amy looked satisfied now, if not exactly back to her bouncy, goofy self, as if her acts had the power to renew.

Sunil found a corkscrew and popped open the wine. Amy took in his blotted face and embraced him tightly. Her neck smelled of soap and garlic. Her hands pressed into his back. "You miss him," she said.

"I feel so bad for him. He must have been terrified." Again his face swelled, tears escaped, and he sat down heavily.

Large pours for both of them.

There was nothing else for her to say, but he wanted more of her talk. More of all of her, to fill the room, press up against the walls, and squeeze everything else out.

She said, carefully, "No funding?"

He shook his head. "I don't know what we're going to do. We'll have to move." After so many stops and starts, he should be used to this feeling of obliteration. But he wasn't, and no physical action, nothing he could say, could alleviate this guilty weight.

Amy lifted her glass and clinked it gently against his. "Not so fast. I have good news. I got a job today."

"You did?" He hadn't known she had an interview. It was just like her to quietly arrange things then surprise him. "Love, amazing!" He clinked glasses again, with more force, and the liquid sloshed. She'd run the numbers, rent and everything?

She had. She had figured in all their expenses. She'd not included his funding as income—she'd known there was a chance he'd lose it. Amy paused. "You still have to get your work done."

"I know."

"I'm serious. Not just for a job, but for you."

For us, he thought. He nodded. "So what's the job?"

"Executive assistant to a Blue Cross vice president. It will be useful to know how health insurance works from the inside."

"Oh no." He put down his glass. "You're not taking a secretarial job. Not because of me. You worked hard for your degree."

She served them generous squares of meaty, steaming noodles and wedges of steamed broccoli that smelled, as it always did, a little bit like garbage. She looked doubtfully at the plate she handed Sunil.

"I can eat it," he said.

She took off her apron and sat, the picture of competence. "Everything from scratch, except the noodles."

"Impressive," he said. "But love, you shouldn't take the job. It's beneath your skills. You'll hate it. And if it hasn't happened already, you're going to start resenting me and I'll hate myself even more than I do now for putting you in this position."

"I'm young. I can do a stupid job for a year. Lots of people do. And it *will* be useful."

"No it won't. And you know it won't." His stomach turned. This job would be bad for them. He could feel it. "You've already had a lot of lame jobs. Now it's time for a good one. I don't want you to lose hope by working in an insurance agency. Seriously, I'm worried about that."

He saw that she knew she would be bored. She knew what she was signing up for. Amy saw the world clearly, without his warping idealism.

Still, it wasn't right. It wouldn't work. He said, "I'll get a job. How's that for innovation?"

"You? Like what? What do you have in mind? Making cappuccinos?" She had not yet tasted her food. Underneath one eye was a smudge of mascara. She was still wearing the pearl choker she'd worn to the interview, but had changed into a T-shirt and cotton skirt. One of her feet flip-flopped on the linoleum.

She was right, of course. Sunil had no bankable skills. He had only ever been a student. "I could teach, at a community college or something. I actually have some ability there, I think. Or, yeah, cappuccinos, why not?"

"Even community colleges require a PhD. You know that." Amy left the kitchen to wash her face and head to bed. Work started tomorrow.

He did know. He also knew, as she did, that her proposal would allow them to stay together in this apartment for a while.

Water running, soaping plates and forks with an eroded sponge, lasagna pan soaking on the counter, Sunil imagined Amy not as he previously had, in a small, bright room of her own, her worn childhood thesaurus split open on her cluttered desk and a framed picture of their honeymoon on a nearby shelf, but burrowing through a sterile gray hallway lined with ringing phones, carrying coffee for some suited man. She waited patiently, nodding to a stream of instructions peppered with *as soon as possible* and *personnel* and *productivity*. He didn't know what went on in an office, but it depressed him to imagine. *Of course, Mr. Smith. Anything else, Mr. Smith?*

Putting away the leftovers in the fridge, Sunil reached for

a carton of eggs, but his fingers slipped and the whole mess thudded and cracked with a snapping sound that dredged up the breakage of the Blixen house porcelain. Of his father and him on their knees. In his helpless bare feet, Sunil now stepped viciously into the mess he had made, crushing the unbroken shells with his furious, hairless toes.

7.

The shortest distance, bedroom to teakettle, left Urmila grasping the counter for support. Wheezing. She slowed, drank tea, read the paper, too much television. She did not answer the phone, even early in the morning when the callers would only be her siblings.

Urmila left on the radio, and the windows open to hear the neighborhood. She did not enjoy American music; what she liked to hear was talk burbling through the house. By the end of the mourning days in Nairobi, Urmila had felt stifled, craved space to stretch her arms without hitting someone. Yet it was too quiet here, too still. She tossed the condolence cards, barely glancing at return addresses. Floral arrangements arrived from neighbors who'd seen the obituary. None, thankfully, from her Indian friends, who knew better, who knew that Jains treasured the soul of every living thing.

The cut flowers wilted, keeled, and began to rot. Only one gift flourished: the bleeding heart Maddy Forrester had sent, which greened and blossomed on the windowsill where it received morning sun. Urmila followed the plant's care instructions scrupulously.

At the Asian market she bought little plastic trinkets for Raina, cute socks and reflective jewelry, but the items simply piled up on the mail table.

In one swift incident, cut off from both husband and son.

Of course she had not meant *go away*. She had not meant to reject him; she hadn't known what she was saying. She shouldn't have opened her mouth. But still, he should know better! What mother as strong and loving as she meant what she said in such a distressed moment? All the times her own parents had threatened and smacked her, he wouldn't believe. But Sunil hadn't spoken to her after what she'd said, even on the last day when she'd hugged him goodbye. She'd asked him to call her. But he'd looked away. Urmila had even reached out to Amy in a quick private moment, nearly pleading. But so far, silence.

At the end of June, Urmila resumed her routine at the store. As she was settling in, Sharon, who worked at the Gap, popped in: "Thank goodness, I thought you were never coming back!" The cashier at the Wok n' Roll smiled: "Nice seeing you!" More friendliness in two days than in the previous decade. She thought it might be the result of pity, but they did not express condolences, did not appear to know anything of her loss.

Her first shipment from the new suppliers arrived in perfect condition. Flawless soapstone candlesticks. Kikoys and dashikis that had previously carried the odor of human hands were now folded and smelled of incense. Yet the newness, the orderliness, the timeliness were not the balm they should have been. The items did not sell, and each new shipment was another rebuke from that corrupt, violent country, the home that had forsaken her and murdered her husband. The perky wooden animals perched on the shelves, the sharp spears, the loud clothing, the dung-crusted jewelry—she hated it all. Every stitch, every drop of paint, every carving. Yet she could not give it up. The store was her engine. Had been for the past twelve years. And now would be even more so. Like the bleeding heart, it needed attention, and in giving it, she herself was nourished.

She wasn't old enough for Social Security, and in a terrible blow Urmila discovered she had only Premchand's pension to live on. When she got around to examining her stock portfolio, she found that she'd been cheated. The money had nearly vanished. She'd read something about a "bursting tech bubble," but she'd assumed that, like so much economic news, it was exaggeration, that her own investments would be protected—the CNN advice had also been affirmed by their accountant friends, after all. She immediately sold the remaining stocks and transferred the cash to a savings account. She could not afford to let the money out of her sight.

During her long days at the store, she couldn't buy more supplies or spend money, but she could clean. Spraying Windex, wiping in circular motions with a soft cloth, she remembered Bimal's hospital room. Her sister-in-law had never apologized for kicking her out, but in the days after Premchand's murder Mital had brought over a large bowl of rasmalai, strongly spiced, just how Urmila liked it. She ate all of the curd over the sleepless nights. Another day, Bimal brought Raina over and Urmila held the girl tight, walking in circles in the backyard. Braving the driveway, with its gun-wielding askari, was out of the question. She sang in Raina's ear rhymes she hadn't known she remembered: *Mummy na bhai te Mama, Pappa na bhai te Kaka, Mama ni vau te Mami, Kaka ni vau te Kaki.* Songs she'd sung to Sunil, too, not that he remembered.

One day late in the month, Urmila closed the shop early and drove to a suburb on the far side of the city. She passed Taste of India, where she used to eat years ago, before the store, back when she lunched regularly with a small group of women, East African Indian transplants like herself. But once she'd had her store to tend, it had not been convenient to come out in the middle of the day. She'd suggested moving their date to the weekend, but this conflicted with when the other women saw their children. They had to cook two days for Sunday night family dinner, a practice Urmila had abandoned long ago from lack of time but also because she felt it didn't matter to either her husband or her son. This was one way, she thought ruefully, that she had become American, this and playing the stock market, losing out like everyone else.

Craning over the steering wheel, she slowed and sped up, trying to read the avenue numbers. Drivers leaned on their horns. One rolled down his window to swear. Another—a young girl with a high ponytail—smacked the back of her hand through the air as if across Urmila's face. And she felt it, she felt the air move, her face burn. The last few weeks she'd been so low, hovering so close to the ground, no sound could rouse her. Now she screamed into the closed space of the car, the rebounding sound hitting back. The last time she'd cursed, facing down the dreadlocked dashiki thief in the mall in her bare feet, she'd been defending her property. Today she fought just to feel herself alive. And anyway, Americans screamed when they drove. She knew this. She'd seen it. Because sometimes they had been screaming at her.

Just like in her own shop, a doorbell echoed in the back as she stepped inside Always in Bloom, into clusters of woven baskets and ribbons, painted clay pots, cards, and colored envelopes. The strong, tropical perfume of lilies hit Urmila full on, reminding her of all the condolence flowers she'd received that had slowly decomposed in her dining room.

Maddy found Urmila leaning against the rose case, mascara running under her glasses. Maddy gently led her to the coffee shop next door. Ordered chai and coffee cake. She said soothing words that Urmila could not hear but whose tone she appreciated.

"I'm so glad you finally came to see me. I didn't want to bother you at home, and during the day I've been so overwhelmed, though that's not a good excuse."

Urmila sipped the terrible chai and ate all of the cake.

Maddy looked different than Urmila remembered. In her mind, the woman was disheveled, in baggy clothes, skin splotchy like an infant. Hair only the suggestion of blonde with gray roots poking through. Today her hair was a bright, natural-looking yellow pulled back into a low, neat bun. Her skin shone a healthy pink. She wore a fitted V-neck sweater and black slacks that traced the outlines of her thighs.

Urmila shook her head. "You're a good friend. The email you sent me in Nairobi made me cry. I received it the day he died."

"Let me help you." Maddy said. "What do you need?"

"Oh, today, just stopping by to say hello. To see that your business is booming and that *you* don't need any help."

Near their table, a mother bundled a baby into a carriage, but the baby fought back. Others talked on phones and typed into computers. Happy, occupied people.

"Things are busy, that's for sure. I know they're talking about the dot-com bust, but around here people still like to send flowers. I'm just so grateful, you know?"

Urmila stressed again how she desired to help Maddy, drawing on her many years of working in import and export, knowing the American market, but Maddy only nodded silently, not understanding. Nodding was sometimes the opposite of agreement, as Urmila had discovered talking to Amy, who nodded as if she was listening, but did not accept. Urmila finally came out with it: "I need to work more. You have something for me?"

The café's cash register jammed and made a terrible cranking noise; the cashier muttered under her breath. Urmila had never asked for help from someone she was not related to. She didn't know how it was done. She felt awkward and foreign, struck with a deep sense of unbelonging—her hair, her speech, even her way of sitting. Yet she hoped. Hoped she had understood this friendship.

She thought of Sarada, of the two of them and their cousin-sisters going in a gaggle to Whiteway and Laidlaw, where the ceiling and walls of the foyer were mirrors. They had stood underneath and looked up at themselves, skinny as pencils, their heads black erasers. They kicked their feet and whirled their arms, performing dandiya raas without the sticks, craning their necks to see themselves from as many angles as possible. "When you grow up, you're going to look like the Pink Lady," Urmila used to say to her sister, using their private name for the sketched, elegant woman in the choli advertisements. To Urmila, the girls said, "How will you get a husband if you scowl like that?" Once in a while, Urmila had stopped at Whiteway by herself during the quiet hours—when she was supposed to be studying at MacMillan Library—to practice her demure look. She pinched and stretched her cheeks to soften them, rubbed her lips to red. Tried to appear as others wanted and expected.

Maddy shrugged back into the plastic chair, her hands loose and open on her lap. "Oh, honey. Oh. The shop is still so new."

Shame tunneled down into her body like a frantic animal. Urmila stood and gathered her purse, said thank you too many times.

"What did you have in mind?" Maddy said. "Please sit down. Talk to me."

Urmila stood still, had not managed to gracefully exit. "I am just saying that I have some experience you are missing. I could be helpful to you."

Maddy was quiet for some time. She then explained that she'd taken out a loan for a large greenhouse. But it would be built slowly, over the next couple of years. "Right now I have only one employee. She's going back to school at the end of the month and I'll need to replace her, but, Urmila, I pay her minimum wage." For twenty-five hours a week, the girl took home $168.25.

"How can I run my shop if I'm over here twenty-five hours a week?"

"I don't think you can."

"When they gave me the bank loan for the store, I felt like a citizen. The American dream, you know?" Urmila's knees trembled. "Mostly we used our savings, but I *wanted* to do the application. Recognition from the bank. He didn't understand. He was already a part of it. My son is the same way, not seeing how lucky they are. Men, I am talking about." So small already, she shrank more. "My husband leaves me nothing, savings have disappeared; my son, too, has abandoned."

Maddy looked down at Urmila's hands as if to take them in her own. Some part of her wanted to be touched, but Urmila clasped her wrists behind her back. The mother with the baby had succeeded in strapping it down into the carriage. Its face was red, but it was no longer screaming. Despite the warm day, the mother spread a blanket over its squirming body.

"I felt the same way when I was going through my divorce. The house was falling down around me, there was green mold all over the basement, and I thought nobody cared, that I would have to do everything myself." Maddy sat forward, looked up at Urmila with clear, blue eyes. "Listen to me. We'll figure it out, I'll help you. I know that right now you have two big expenses, the store and the house." She was saying Urmila couldn't afford to keep both.

8.

You both were alive when, to the west, the gates of hell burst open. Always we kept our eye on Uganda, and our people there looked at us, knowing that anything ripening in one place could easily burst over the thin border. The seeds were sewn with the trade boycott back in fifty-nine. Still, it was a shock when that dictator Amin seized the country with machetes and machine guns and erased the Asians overnight. All in the name of *national economic development*. Just as the British had kept us down while hiding behind the claim that they were protecting the natives.

In this country, just three years before, Tom Mboya was assassinated. He was a government minister, close to Kenyatta. Terrible, though we all were aware of the tribal rumblings. Kikuyu suspected Luo and vice versa.

Asians stole away in the night, in the cargo holds of planes and boats and trains, the boots of cars. Families split apart— men here, women there, children another place. Cash and gold sewn into coats, just like the rupees carried on the dhows from India years before. Some of them escaped as far as America, and they are over there now with you, grandson.

Of course we in Kenya saw our own faces in their open mouths of terror.

In August, when Amin began his so-called economic war, the rains fell and fell here, drowning us in mud. Over there, in Uganda, properties and businesses were taken. Imagine how we felt, like old men sitting down to eat, having given years of life to the household, only to find that the wives have abandoned and taken all the food.

How were we *cheating, conspiring, and plotting*? What we earned, we put back, in schools, hospitals, and temples. Amin wanted to hold on to the doctors, the lawyers, but no Asian in his right mind would stay with that madman.

There was madness in our own country too, of course. After the Africans took power, they made us choose the color of our passport—did we want to stay British or change over to Kenyan? Oh, that was a hard one. If you chose British, the Africans would not allow you to work! So in some families, we split. The mothers, who were not working anyways, took British, as a safeguard. Fathers like me pledged our allegiance to Kenya, because Britain was cold and far away, and in truth the British did not want us. They limited how many nonwhites from the colonies they would take—they did not put it this way, you understand, but the rules amounted to as much. It was all a scam. Kenya-born Asian men took British passports, then the new government went after them. Arrested them! Then Britain said, no, they would not take them in. Such duplicity, I am telling you.

You were just babies then.

When Amin started his expulsion and his witch-hunts, no one came to our defense. Not the Africans, not the British, not even India. Not a peep.

Bimal, your parents talked of sending you away to America. Very expensive telephoning! But it was a reasonable idea. Good for your English. Some time with your cousin-brother. I still think it would have been a marvelous time for the two of you. For a while everyone was enthusiastic, but your parents were worried, you were so young to be so far away, and who knew for how long. Once you went there, maybe you would never come back? And there were so many more of us here to take care of you, aunties and uncles, many cousins in the same boat. You didn't know, eh? Well, it amounted to just some talk. No one put you on a plane now, did they? Really, it would have been too hard on your mother.

I went to the store and sat with the other men, helpless, listening to the radio. We bet on how many days before we fell, too. We knew those stolen businesses would fail under the Big Men, and we were right.

Here, more and more money was salted—you know, over-invoicing the imports and underdoing the exports—the difference going into a Swiss account or some such. Not me, but many others.

I don't blame those who fled, but we here have turned out all right. I say what I have always said, We will live until we are gone. But in their defense, for those who managed a voucher, who had the money to leave, things did get worse here before they got better.

9.

The wind-scrubbed expanse in his chest, an enormous vacancy called *missing*. Sunil had existed only in some small corner of his father's life, the boy his father found in his house every night. The memories cropping up now—his father saying *funnily enough*, or fingering bills as crisp as his starched shirt to buy them hot dogs at a football game—were too gossamer to embody or examine. They were just scenes, a vision, missing heft and consequence. Even if there were more details to be mined, Sunil would never know the most important thing: how his father *thought*.

And Bimal? Did he feel more like a brother now that their father was dead? Now that they'd lost the man who'd imparted their narrow faces and girlish legs, hair that sprouted like thick Ohio lawns. The man who'd given them, more than anything, silence and privacy. Sunil was grateful; these were not small gifts. But, in the end, they were not enough. They had not protected Sunil from his mother. They'd not given Sunil and Bimal each other.

To feel this now, these layers of lacks, filled him with sorrow.

In the days surrounding the funeral, Bimal had shared Sunil's loss without hogging it, without needing to own it. Bimal had loved Premchand, but not as a father. He left that to Sunil. Sunil had felt this generosity in the silence Bimal had allowed him in the sickroom, even after Sunil had offended him. Like their father, Bimal was sometimes too calm, unmoved when he should be angry or upset or full of awe, but Sunil was filled with admiration for his brother's strength.

Where could they go from here? They'd traded a few emails, but sporadically and brief. They wouldn't see each other again for years and years—probably not until another death, maybe even his mother's, perhaps another two or three decades. Who knew if they'd even live that long? Maybe knowing that their brief days in Nairobi were a rare window was what had spurred Bimal's parting gift. A gift to be unwrapped, or rather, decoded. Because the tapes, a series of brief interviews with their grandfather that Bimal had recorded for a college oral history project, were not in a language Sunil could understand.

Sunil was left with a pared-down image of his father, and this slim, dark older man haunted him. He had appeared an hour ago at the grocery store, then disappeared around the corner of the cereal aisle. He'd even shown up in Emerson Hall, just down from Lieberman's office, and the proximity of those two visions was overwhelming.

Sunil unloaded the grocery bags in his kitchen. Amy would be home soon. Yogurt, eggs, baby carrots, hummus. Paper towels. On impulse, he'd bought a small African violet, which he now set on the kitchen table.

When he first started doing the shopping, he'd made some mistakes, bringing home celery instead of leeks because the labels had been switched, but Sunil liked procuring things. He was grateful for the assignment. He'd shop all day and mow lawns all over town, for free, if that would help ground him. Cheerios, apples, bananas, pasta sauce. Laundry detergent.

Amy had not complained about her job. Not once. The crude

Blue Cross boss of Sunil's imagining was an elderly Mr. Ricci, and he was pleasant, agreeable, appreciative. The other assistants were friendly. But on weekends, Amy slept more. Talked less. She still rode her bike along the river, still read novels on the porch, woke at four-thirty to get to the pool, but she asked few questions about Sunil's days, lost her cool when he failed to wipe down the table after dinner. She didn't shout, as he would have, but issued lengthy, exasperated sighs. He'd urge her to the couch to watch TV at night, but she begged off to read journal articles, to keep up on the research in her field. Sunil often went to bed before her now. The annual road race for cervical-cancer screening was coming up, but Amy said she was too tired to participate.

Salt, chicken broth, soy sauce. He didn't know where these last things went. Opening cupboards and drawers, he found only plates, glasses, silverware, Tupperware, spices. He made a rough triangle of the items, placing the blue salt canister in front. Stacked and unstacked. Squared items into the wrong cabinets then removed them.

The phone rang. He thought it was Amy calling from work. "Love?" he said.

But it was Ariel.

"How are you feeling, duckling?"

"Better. But I still see him everywhere, you know. My father. Yesterday he was the seller at the newsstand—what a stereotype! Has that ever happened to you?" Ariel's father was still alive, but her mother had died years ago.

"I used to see my mother at the pool. There was an older lady in the water-aerobics class who got me every time."

Ariel said she was glad to hear Sunil's energy was coming back. That he was spending time at the library, trying to turn his inventory of notes into arguments and pages. "And holding up the housework, too!" Then she paused, "But listen, duckling,

I hate to say this, but this job Amy has isn't good for her. She should be getting her career off the ground."

"Ariel, I know. I've tried so many times to tell her."

She continued in a more accusatory vein that skewered him, but not because it wasn't true. "It's an enabling situation. Maybe for both of you."

"You do realize that we really love each other, right? I begged her not to take this job." He thought of the opportunity with the Welcomers that had passed Amy by while they were in Nairobi. He owed her so much more than he had been able to give.

"But she felt she had to."

Ariel had a plan. And when she was finished, he was in complete agreement, even though he was not sure if he could bear it. He would have to.

A memory painful to him now. The first time they talked about marriage. On a stairway, in the Gardner Museum, where the works of art snugged cozily together on the walls, and the rooms were how he imagined a maharajah's palace—overflowing with paintings of all shapes, sizes, and colors; polished furniture, expansive rugs, gleaming silver and candlesticks.

Amy was talking about her friend Lena, who'd wanted her to be a bridesmaid, but Amy wasn't happy about the wedding. "She hasn't even started her first real job, and Alex has never liked her music, or tried to understand why she writes these weird atonal pieces. He thinks she should compose some pleasant Mozart rip-offs so Starbucks will sell her CD by the cash register."

They'd stopped in front of the gilt-framed portraits of the Gardner family, then crossed the sun-limned courtyard and headed up the stairs to see the Titian.

"What's the rush? We're still so young." Her hand rested

lightly on the banister as they climbed, opal ring glinting. A turtleneck sweater cupped her chin.

Sunil agreed. He said he didn't believe in marriage.

"Because you're a feminist?" She didn't show her teeth but her lips rose at the corners.

He didn't think marriage was wrong, just unnecessary. Relationships were about trust, honesty, reliability, caring, all the abstractions.

"What about passion?"

"There are different kinds of passion. Wait until you're old like me." His fingers walked up the banister to touch the tips of hers. He didn't know precisely what he meant, just that he didn't mean lust, as she did. When he thought of passion, he thought, disturbingly, of his mother, her emotions always at a near-boil. The touch of his and Amy's fingers, the stuttering brush of their softly ridged skin, thrilled him, stirred him, made him want her, but he didn't think of their relationship as passionate. That was one of the things he liked about it. He'd been with passionate women, insane women. An attraction to steadiness was part of what he meant by being old, though he was then not even thirty.

They reached the painting, in which cherubs peered down on a gleaming woman in disarray, a coral scarf whipping overhead.

"It's a rape," Amy told him. She pointed to the shiny white bull at the right of the frame.

An older woman in a peacock blue scarf turned to look disdainfully at Amy. "That takes all the magic away," she complained.

"What do you see?" Amy asked gamely. Sunil would have retorted, and then regretted it.

"I see a magnificent painter at work."

"Of course," Amy said, "But this is a scene, there's something happening. I mean, look at the energy of that scarf!"

But the woman simply shook her head. "I choose to see beauty—the gorgeous supple colors. You young women and your sexual politics. It just gets in the way of pleasure."

The woman began to walk away from them, but Amy had to have the last word. "Truth and beauty are not mutually exclusive. Also, the word *rape* is in the title!" she called after the woman, who was striding purposefully into the next room, shaking her head.

Sunil laughed into his hand, as Amy turned to him and, trying to keep her own mirthful scoff inside, said, "Well, that was a total failure."

"You were saying about Lena, my bra-burning feminist?" he prodded.

"Right!" With renewed energy, Amy said, "If Lena got married, it would be an obstacle to her leaving Alex if it didn't work out. Marriage would be a reason to stay."

"A bad reason," Sunil said.

But marriage would make Lena feel differently about the relationship, she insisted. In that way, marriage mattered. It put a finality on things.

"But aren't you undercutting Lena's agency here? You said she *wants* to get married. She sees that 'finality' as a good thing. Maybe the emotional stability she'll get from marriage will actually help her find her way as a composer."

Amy was skeptical. "I just don't see it playing out that way."

"Aren't you being kind of judgmental? Getting in the way of Lena's pleasure, like that wise woman just said."

And then she had turned to him, so emphatic she actually stamped a Ked-shod foot. "That's my job! For me to judge the things she can't see herself." Softening, she added, "Maybe what you mean is that when things are good, marriage doesn't make a difference—doesn't make things better."

Maybe, he said. Maybe that was what he'd meant. So why did it matter more when things were bad?

"No," Amy said. Ariel had called her, too, at work and explained her "plan." "I'm not moving back in with my parents. What self-respecting person would want to do that? I told her this was just a stopgap, but she doesn't listen." Unbuttoning her shirt, she walked to the bedroom to change into her summer evening uniform— the gray skirt, red T-shirt (braless, nipples edging through), and flip-flops. She continued to wear her hair long and straight, like a missionary. "We're having stir-fry for dinner, so take out the rice?"

Sunil took out the rice. Pulled out onions, peppers, and a cutting board.

Amy measured the grains and water and stirred them together. Chopped and sliced. Told him to set the table.

But Ariel had found Amy a good job, an interesting job, a résumé job. It was at the NIH in Washington, where Amy had long wanted to work, and she'd had to pull some strings to get it. She had told Sunil she needed his help convincing her daughter.

"Look how tired you are after just six weeks," he said.

"And what, you live here by yourself doing nothing? Where's the garlic?"

Sunil retrieved a papery bulb from the windowsill, and she plucked it from his palm with an authority that reminded him of his aunt with the vegetable vendors in the market.

"I have James, my friends; I'll audit a class." He'd not seen James recently, but he had added ten pages to his dissertation. He told Amy about his progress.

"I know."

"How?" Then he realized. "You snooped on my computer? You're checking up on me?"

She shot him a look. "What would you do if you were me?"

He took a deep breath. Huge. Let go.

He'd move. Amy shouldn't spend any of her earnings on him. The summer before grad school, he'd worked in a socialist bookstore in Cambridge called All Together Now. He'd actually loved the battling politics, the shouted conversations between the aisles, but they were too loose in their thinking. He had needed a system, and philosophy was nothing if not systematic; there were rubrics for how to think about the most troubling questions. Even if the answers to those questions remained in doubt. It was time for Sunil to say to philosophy, *All in.* To see if he could succeed at the thinking, the language he loved. Sunil still patronized the bookstore occasionally, though, and the owner might give him some hours.

What worried Sunil most was that when he'd asked Ariel how long the job was for, she'd told him that what her daughter did when the job ran out was Amy's choice.

Amy flattened her cheek against his chest, wrapped her arms around him, and breathed him in. Her heart pulsed through his skin. She was flooded with guilt. And yet he knew she was fed up with him. And who could blame her. "I can't leave you now," she said, and he knew she would take the job. She wanted to.

He swallowed hard. His jaw resisted what he was about to say, the making light of desperation, his panic and resentment that she'd caved so quickly. Even if it was for the best. "I lived alone before I met you, remember? I'll get a parrot to keep me company, to talk back to me. You need to do this for you. I'll finish my work. I promise. Then we'll be together again." Sunil was not in the habit of making promises, but at the moment he'd promise anything he could.

The view was expansive, the sea sparkling, the sun high, and the breeze soft. The air heady and inspiring. She met him, sleepy-eyed and smelling like hotel sheets, on the white porch the inn was named after. Sunil poured coffee from a French press the owner had delivered to his side. "Is it hot enough? I'll get you some orange juice. Fresh-squeezed."

She brushed her hair from her creased cheeks and faced the ocean warily. She'd slept for almost ten hours. "A second honeymoon," she said.

But it wasn't a honeymoon. It was the opposite. It was a separation gift, the last they'd see of each other for a while—they didn't know how long. When Sunil had called Ariel back, to deliver up her daughter, she'd given them a long weekend on the Cape. She'd already made nonrefundable reservations, so Sunil couldn't refuse.

Doors opened and closed, and water rushed through old pipes. At the breakfast bar, Sunil met an older woman from Philadelphia who told him it was going to rain tomorrow, so he and his lovely wife should enjoy the beaches today. How had she pieced him and Amy together? He was momentarily relieved. Their life problems—their shock and grief at his father's death, their differing reactions—had sometimes pushed them physically apart. They did not often exude togetherness anymore, not since coming back from Nairobi.

"What did you think the first time you saw the ocean?" Amy said, peeling back layers of croissant.

"Boston Harbor? It seemed kind of small and smelly."

"You never saw the ocean before you moved here?"

He shook his head. "Midwestern boy."

She pulled him to the white railing and leaned forward over it, resting their twined forearms on the bar. "Do you ever think that getting married set off this bad chain reaction? If we hadn't married, we wouldn't have gone to Kenya, your parents wouldn't have stayed so long at your aunt's, your father wouldn't

244 THE LIMITS OF THE WORLD

have died, you wouldn't have broken off with your mother . . ."

He had thought that, yes. He couldn't help it. But it was a mistake. He said, "If my parents hadn't been born in Nairobi, they wouldn't even have gone back there for a visit."

Another breeze brushed the side of his face, rushed under his nose a floral scent Amy had last night called sea lavender, but there was an undercurrent of something dark and spongy, some kind of seashore muck, an odor of rot.

"But getting married, we had control over that," she insisted. "We're responsible."

"Then we should also regret not keeping my father from going on a walk the day he died. We had no reason to keep him—we didn't even know he'd gone—but you can always stretch farther back, impose counterfactuals." Hadn't she herself told him that thinking this way was both useless and wrong? "Why are you doing this?"

"Because I feel it! I feel regret! It feels awful."

He didn't know how to talk her out of it. And what did it matter, she'd soon be so far away.

The inn gave them a brown paper bag with picnic lunches. They pedaled through wooded paths, up and down, around smooth curves, straining to hear the promised tremor of birdsong. When they reached the dunes, they sweated in the humid sun and stared, again, at the ocean.

"Sort of the same view as from the inn," Amy said.

Sunil stretched his legs; the ride had done him good.

They left their bikes and walked along the water's edge, ate their sandwiches on a grassy knoll, beachwalked some more, holding hands but not talking much. He couldn't help thinking Amy had given up on him. Then again, if he didn't finish his dissertation, he'd give up on himself. And then how could he expect Amy, or anyone else, to have faith in him?

For a while she lay with her head on his stomach and they read their books, pointing occasionally at clouds or dune birds, but they couldn't sustain this until sunset, so at dusk they headed back in the direction from which they came.

Nestled in the grass near the parking lot, they noticed a bizarre spat of graffiti etched into a piece of driftwood: *fuck-honeys*. Sunil laughed, but not fully, not all the way to joy. Amy pulled out the small L-shaped wrench they'd loaned her at the bike shop to adjust the height of her seat and drew a long, confident line under the word.

Sunil remembered this on the third and last night of their long weekend, as they floated next to each other in the most delicious and billowing bed they'd ever slept in. The plump pillows molded to his head and the sheets were soft and the blankets not too heavy nor too thin; each morning he had woken up feeling mournful that his time in this bed was shorter than it had been when he'd gone to sleep. That last night they made love, and afterward Amy slept like a log, like a deep dreamer, like a woman determined to make the best of it. Sunil kissed his wife at the corners of her eyes, and he lay on his back feeling the fleeting support of the perfect mattress, his eyes closed but his stomach flapping with the constant, anxious wings of a honeybee.

10.

If her husband were here, he'd remind her of what she already knew: Nairobi had been her home once, but its rhythms were no longer first-hand. Columbus was home. It was not a question of belonging, but of making the best of it.

She missed these gentle reminders.

Urmila didn't realize she'd fallen asleep standing up by the register, braced with a cramped arm, until the phone rang. A small, buried hope dusted itself off: Sunil? What she wouldn't do for his pure laughter, his impish joy reading a misprinted sign, his slim beautiful face.

"I'm closing up for the day and thought you might want help packing. I can bring dinner. Or ice cream?"

Urmila said she'd already eaten. "Come over this weekend. I'll make lunch." Maddy's food was too plain, everything tasting somehow sweet like bananas or potato-starchy, and her friend didn't quite understand being vegetarian. Last week she'd triumphantly brought chicken: "White meat!"

"Are you sure? Tonight's no trouble. Extra pair of hands in that full basement. Going once, going twice ... Hon, I know it's overwhelming. When Jim moved in with his new girlfriend, and Connor at school, every day I woke up and walked through the house and made lists, so many lists, but until my sister came, I couldn't do the work."

"The weekend is better, please."

It was true that Urmila had not made much progress. Little more than putting things in piles and dragging these piles, plus to-be-filled suitcases and boxes, into the center of every room. But she'd done the hardest part: Premchand's things. Yanked all the clothing off the hangers and into garbage bags. Shoes, medical books. When the clinic called to ask if they might deliver to her home a box of "personal items" from his office, she had told them to throw them away. What would he keep there instead of here?

And then she was done with his part. He had saved no cards or letters or photographs, no souvenirs. The two of them had never exchanged birthday or anniversary gifts. It made sense a bullet in his brain had killed him. A bullet in his heart he could have survived.

When the time came, one week from now, professional movers would pack up the furniture that would fit in her new apartment, a carpeted block of rooms in a shabby suburb. But there was an Asian grocery and a video store, and the new place was a shorter drive to her store. This had been Maddy's advice, and she had followed it to the letter. It was the store she had chosen to fight for. She would slim down, shape up, tighten everything. See if she could squeak out a living. While Maddy was supportive, Urmila wished she were more confident about the odds—the likelihood the store could be saved. Once or twice her friend had asked her, "And what would you do if the store can't succeed? Just hypothetically."

Tonight Urmila would tackle the kitchen. She drove home and changed into loose black pants and sandals and the only sleeveless shirt in her closet. She'd found it in the back of a drawer, left behind by Meena when she'd visited the States years ago. Urmila never showed her shoulders in public, and her exposed armpits now felt like embarrassing holes, prickly with hair, yet this evening she loved the defiance of reaching an arm over her head in front of the window and showing, casually, her savage side.

She microwaved a samosa and ate it at the counter, leaving the crumbs and grease to clean up later. The house was quiet, except for an insect buzzing on a window screen. One by one, she sorted pots and pans, serving dishes, wooden spoons, tea strainers, tins of leaves and spices. Clear baggies of turmeric and cumin sealed off with twist ties; jars of cinnamon sticks; rainbow sacks of dal. Her new kitchen would be an "efficiency," which meant, she understood, very small. Maddy had suggested she keep only one of everything. But how could she give up these tools of her life? Watching her sister bustle about in Nairobi, Urmila had realized just how attached they were to these implements, like a butcher and his knife. When she held the handle of the strainer, in some small but important way her body remembered all of the many moments before that, standing against the sink the way her mother had stood in her kitchen. But now she made tea only for herself.

Urmila selected one frying pan, one pot with a well-fitting lid, one wooden spoon. Two mugs. She had Maddy, after all.

The insect on the screen buzzed again, maybe a third time, loudly now, and so insistent she realized it would not cease until she let it go. Urmila followed the sound to the door, which she pulled open and said, "Shoo!" Shoved her arms into the screen—and hit a man in the nose.

"Oh!"

"I'm so sorry!" he said. "I rang the doorbell, but . . ."

He looked a little familiar. The stork-like face and flapping ears topped with hair completely gray. Light-brown suit without a tie, the collar open at the neck. She smelled the lilies before she saw the bunch wrapped in cellophane in his hand.

"What is it?" she said.

"Do you remember me? Jon Samuel? I worked with Dr. Chandaria? He hired me, actually."

"Haa, yes, the broken thumb, the baseball game," she said.

"Right! You have a good memory. That was the softball game in Cheshire Park. Gastroenterology versus infectious disease. Must be twenty years ago."

"It was comical," she said. "You ran into the fence." It had been a good laugh. For months, Sunil had mimicked the doctor crashing into the wooden boards, hamming it up. During the game, Premchand had stood aimlessly in the outfield, mild amusement on his face.

On the sidewalk beyond Jon Samuel, a teenaged couple was crossing in front of her house, ice cream cones in hand. Contented smiles. They were absorbed by something in her direction. Her—they were looking at her. Urmila remembered her appearance with a pang: her exposed jellied shoulders, the gray hair under her arms!

"Come in," she told Jon Samuel. "Sit down. Clear a space—just a minute." Metal mixing bowls were displaced to make room. She ran to the bathroom, hurriedly splashed cold water on her face and ran a cloth around her neck, across her back and chest and under her arms and toweled off. Ran a brush through her hair and exchanged her indecent shirt for one with sleeves, and pockets over the breasts.

The way the doctor sat, unbalanced, amid her kitchen rubble made her want to laugh. Baking sheets clanged when he shifted his weight.

"Tea?" she said.

"No, thank you. I don't want to trouble you. And I'm sorry for coming by so late, but I heard you were moving, and I didn't know where I'd find you again."

"I'm not going far," she said.

"Moving in with family?"

"No."

He looked down uncomfortably at the flower stems gripped in his reddening hands.

"I can't take those," she said. "Thank you, but I have no place to put them—you can see. And let me tell you, for the next time you want some very nice flowers, spend your money in Always in Bloom. A new business owned by my good friend. I am like a consultant there."

There was something else in the doctor's hand, Urmila noticed as he looked around at the walls, as if he expected to find some information embedded there. He said, "I came by to deliver some personal things we found in Premchand's office. I know you said to throw them away, but Lisette worked with your husband for a long time and she felt sure he wouldn't want us to toss these." He waved the manila folder in his hands. A folder neither thick nor thin.

"Lisette?"

"Fiske. Our office manager. She was going to bring them by herself, but she's on vacation this week, and as I said, I heard you were moving. Also, I'm terribly embarrassed, I feel as if I must have missed the notice of his funeral. We all did."

"We held the service in Nairobi. Where we were born. It was too much to have another here."

"I see. I could help you organize a memorial service here. Should I do that?"

Urmila shook her head. He didn't see, but it didn't matter. If she didn't get him out of her house very soon, he would begin to apologize again. "Thank you for coming by," she said and stood up.

"I miss him," Jon Samuel said as he followed her to the

door. "I want you to know that. He was an excellent colleague. Conscientious, generous, always pleasant." He stood unmoving on her steps. Shook his head. "Isn't there anything I can do? A scholarship fund or charity the office can contribute to? We'd be honored, really—"

"No. Thank you."

He nodded sharply. "Good luck with the move. Please call if we can help in any way."

After he'd gone, she remained in the driveway, hands on her hips, the humid heat of the day rising up from the asphalt. The sky was finally beginning to darken, but the relief she had expected when she'd looked forward to sunset an hour ago did not come. *The shade on the day is drawing*, her father used to say, some proverb. She said it now out loud. *The shade on the day is drawing*. She waited for something to happen, for the blue-gray to be suddenly eclipsed and the lights of the neighborhood to switch on in unison; some nights it felt like the other houses acted in concert, knowing the unwritten rules. Then she noticed that Jon Samuel had set the lilies on her doorstep. Urmila tossed them, glass vase and all, into the bushes.

She made a cup of tea and ate half a Hershey bar. Scanned through the evening's television programs. Checked her email and the economic reports, stared at the unringing phone. She ached with loneliness.

Whatever she had expected to find in the folder, it was not these simple mementos of Sunil's childhood. School report cards, pencil drawings, newspaper clippings from high-school athletics. A few soccer goals had launched his name into the paper. Because they were boys' games, she had never considered going; she didn't imagine any mothers had been there. Had her husband gone? She found also Premchand's certificate from medical school in Ahmedabad, and his board certification. Paper-clipped to this was an envelope, and, inside, a letter.

Dear Dad,

I'm going to call you again next week, but I first wanted to give you some warning. I'm quitting pre-med. I'm no good at it. It's both boring and far too hard for me. I've tried to call, but you've been too busy. Mrs. Fiske said you read your mail. Mom is going to be furious, so I hope you can soften her up for me. The last thing the world needs is another miserable doctor, right? I'm hoping to make a go of it in philosophy, a field where I might be able to contribute. I can at least see if they'll let me try.

Your favorite son,
Sunil

Urmila left the loose square papers on the counter, in the center, clearing a space for these life moments that felt now like bricks of grief. Pushed all the things she didn't want to the floor. Tomorrow, she'd stuff all the rubbish into Hefty bags.

There was a sale on color printing, so Urmila requested ten large signs with red ink and posted them throughout her store, including several in the windows. It was back-to-school season, which meant a pickup in foot traffic. Mothers ventured in looking for interesting decorations for their children's dorms. White girls like the one who'd tried to steal from Urmila bought much of the loose, printed clothing, and the kikoys, which she decided to market as a wrap skirt after seeing one of the teenagers try it on that way. Maddy brought friends who purchased dozens of olive-wood salad bowls and matching tongs. Urmila was touched, and energized. What should she do with the revenue? Maddy advised her to restock her three most popular items, spend a little on marketing, and sock the rest away in the bank.

Urmila kept an eye on the store mail, listened for the phone. She had sent the folder of papers from her husband's office to

Sunil in Boston. She did not expect to hear from him, but still she hoped.

The strange thing, she told Maddy now, was that a few days ago she'd received a message from Amy's mother. They sat in two folding chairs at a small round table—all her new kitchen/dining space could accommodate. Last week, they'd scrubbed away every speck of mildew. Urmila shook her head. "Now she wants to talk! No, she did not want to talk *before* the marriage. We could have fixed things then."

"There was nothing either of you could have done. Kids make their own decisions these days." Maddy ran a fork through the mung dal and sampled a tiny bite. Mostly her friend ate the breads, the pooris and parathas and rosemary naan; the other things she poked with polite curiosity.

"Why should I want to talk to her?"

Maddy put down her fork. "Why not? She is the mother of your son's wife."

Urmila stared at her, surprised, a bit hurt by the reprimand.

"Let's go for a walk, check out your new neighborhood," Maddy suggested.

They slipped on their shoes and took the elevator down two flights, then cut through the complex's parking lot. Urmila made sure her car was still there, though Maddy had assured her that the people who lived here were other seniors with grown children who had downsized, so there was nothing to worry about.

Walking alongside a new strip mall with a Walgreens, Maddy pointed out *Opening Soon* signs in the storefront of a hair salon and Chinese takeout. "New businesses coming in, that's a good sign. No pun intended." She smiled.

"I bet she is disappointed," Urmila said.

"Who?"

"Her mother. Jewish mothers want their daughters to marry

high achievers, smart boys, other Jewish boys. Boys who love their families."

"Sunil's getting a doctorate at Harvard, he's no slouch. She wants the same things we all do for our kids."

"Yes, Harvard is very good. But how many jobs do you know for this field? He will struggle forever."

"Every college must have at least one or two philosophy professors. Don't they still teach it? It's not a dead language like Latin."

"Some men are gifted to be leaders and others learn. He is a learner, but he lacks ambition, that is what I am saying. A mother-in-law cares about these things. Also, he is very dark."

Maddy's yellow hair fell across her face. She stopped and stepped aside to let a man with enormous hearing aids push by with his walker. "What is that supposed to mean?"

"You know. You don't need to ask," Urmila said quietly, knowing this would silence her friend.

The sun was warming, concentrating on them. Urmila felt conspicuous, and wondered if Maddy did, too. Or if everywhere felt natural and normal to her. Coming down the street was the bus Maddy had told her about, the transport that would allow her not to drive in the winter. Urmila said, "But where is the green? I thought you said there was some park."

"I said there were athletic fields near here, soccer and baseball. I never promised you a park. I never said this would be easy."

Urmila again felt herself on the edge of tears. "I have no one to help me now but you! Naturally I do what you suggest. I don't know what I'd do without you." She straightened her glasses, smudging them. "You are an American, you have lived in this place longer, you know the way things are." Sunil used to be the one to guide her through this place.

"And who are you?" Maddy stood, arms crossed. Behind her squatted low garages and mid-rise buildings. The sky shone blue over the flat land.

"Just an immigrant," she said. "Just a woman. Once the store is gone, there will be nothing left of me." *Just a mother*, she thought, though she did not dare say it.

Maddy looked down, chin doubled. Sometimes, with her blond hair pulled back and a bright T-shirt on, she looked like the high-school girls that had volunteered at Premchand's hospital, souls bursting with goodness and light, but today she looked middle-aged and brittle and irritated. Maddy said, "One thing I definitely don't suggest is self-pity. Do me a favor and see your son. Call him at least."

"He can call me."

"But you said . . . you told me what you said to him. I know you regret it. Did you apologize to him?"

Urmila shook her head, feeling desolate and removed from everything she cared about. She did not understand how love was not a given, how it constantly needed to be reaffirmed. Why did she need to apologize when it was so obvious her grief had gotten the best of her? Of course she loved her son! With her whole heart, with a heart larger than her body.

Maddy looked at her watch, signaling her impatience. "Have to go home and do laundry, my sister is visiting this weekend. Come and join us some night."

But Urmila saw the invitation was halfhearted. Better to let Maddy go.

Back in her apartment, Urmila considered the telephone. She itched to pick up the receiver and dial. She wanted to know what he thought of the papers she had sent. No matter what Maddy said, if her son truly cared, wouldn't he have called her by now? She knew Sunil thought she could be overbearing, and so, this time, she would prove him wrong. She would show she could respect his silence. She would step back and let him come to her, no matter how much she wanted to hear his voice.

11.

The shower was rusted, the paint ballooned from the ceiling. Sunil closed his nose against the lingering grease smell and turned his back on the armies of ants that marched across the windowsills with enviable determination. What he liked was the twenty-minute, litter-strewn walk to the T. One of Amy's wishes had come true: he was enjoying the exercise, the fall air. He'd found this tiny apartment before Amy left, but he hadn't told her. Didn't want her to set foot in it. When the Kauffmans had picked up his wife in the Volvo that signaled her entry into a gleaming professionalism, Sunil had pretended to have a meeting with James. He was a coward; he couldn't have borne their scrutiny or the loss of her; he might have cried.

That was three weeks ago. This was the first September of his life—since he was three—that he had not been in school.

More than the grime and the roaches, it was the silence that corralled his misery; silence was the hunter that took aim at hopeful forms and picked them off one by one. The apartment's one grace note was the kitchen window that at night offered a full-on view of the moon. Otherwise, the apartment's sparseness settled in him so deeply that the car horns and television, even other people's love murmurs and angry outbursts, did nothing to alleviate the Amy-less loneliness. During the two years they'd lived together, Sunil had begun making noise as soon as he awoke—his tuneless rhymes, his mumbled dreams and midnight thoughts, stats and developments in the NBA. He riffed joyfully, ridiculously, into the morning air while Amy laughed, swatted him away, told him to shut up, ignored him. She was his loving ear.

Erik bought him a nighttime companion, a teddy bear with an "I ♥ Harvard" T-shirt.

Over the phone, Amy told him that she and her epidemiologist boss were investigating strains of multidrug-resistant TB. There had been terrible outbreaks in Russian prisons, so some of her work focused on underfunded American jails, places where the disease was likely to go undertreated.

"During the day I'm a detective," she said. "And then when I go home I'm a captive. So really, I see both sides." Her parents' religiosity, which had been subdued during their May visit, was on full display. The continual blessings and prayers, rigidly observing the Sabbath, their attempts to drag her and Monica to synagogue. "I don't want to leave my room because I might succumb. It feels unfair that I have to say no to them, when I feel like they're the ones who broke the contract. They're the ones who changed."

Sunil lay on his bed, phone to his ear. Tried to feel the warmth of her breath. "What's the worst thing that will happen if you don't do what they want?"

"My mom got me this great job. I'm living here for free. I feel like I owe them."

"She got you the job because she's your mother and she cares about you. There's nothing wrong with saying thank you and living your own life. Like you said, they didn't consult *you* before deciding to live religious lives." In the bathroom, a faucet dripped. Scratching in the walls. Sunil squeezed the spongy bear around the middle with savage force.

"When are you coming to visit?" she asked every time they talked. Sunil waited for this moment. He craved it. Some days he didn't understand why they had to be apart—why she couldn't have stayed to help him through. But it wasn't realistic for her to stay, and he knew it. Love was simply not enough to get them through this next difficult stretch. They were adults, and they owed it to each other to pursue their individual goals, or they could never be happy together. Yes, they were obligated. *Committed,* as Amy had said in the Nepalese restaurant the day they—she—had announced they were engaged. And Sunil believed this to be right and true. For they were equals and had committed each to the other.

But Sunil had decided that he didn't want to visit DC until he had something to show for himself. He had begun working in earnest in her absence. He now had sixty pages and guessed he had sixty or eighty more to go. Philosophy dissertations were not nearly as long as those in other areas of the humanities, so that was a blessing at least. Still, Sunil undersold his progress because he was not yet confident he could keep up the pace. They would see each other when he had a draft. Which he would! He just needed more time.

But he said, instead of all this, that they didn't have the money since they were saving for another apartment.

"I'm worried about you. My parents are worried. They want to see you."

"Sure, to convert me."

She laughed, but his jokes wouldn't hold out much longer. He hoped they wouldn't have to. He had sent Lieberman his sixty pages two days ago and had barely slept waiting for her response.

"We need to see each other," she said.

Something sharp in her tone, some undercurrent of warning. He said, "That doctor you work with, what's his name again?"

"My boss is a woman," she said evenly. "I told you that."

What about the other people in her department, he wondered, the men in the staff room on her lunch break? Who walked her down the hall to her lab? Their concrete, purposeful walks echoing side by side.

"Soon," he promised.

"I know you don't want to hear this," she said, "but you should call your mother. I know she's at fault for a lot of things. She hurt you and went against your father's wishes. But you don't even know if she has any money or how she's getting along. Maybe the store is failing."

It was a painful thought. His mother needed her African bazaar more than ever to keep her life together. He said this to Amy, then added, "But that doesn't make it easier to reach out to her. Love, I feel like she disowned me. Because that's pretty much what she said! Can I really pretend what she said was just fine? No consequences?"

"That's the way diplomats at the United Nations talk, adversaries like the US and Russia. She's your mother and she made a big mistake. But I can't believe she meant it."

"Do you think she didn't mean those cruel things she said to you?"

Amy sighed. "I think her temper got the best of her. And anyway, I'm not her child. Now she has no one but you. And even if you don't want to forgive her, at least make sure she is okay. Women do better than men after the death of a spouse, but the data is pretty clear that widows need social support."

"Like you said, we're talking about two people here, her and me, not abstractions. Why don't *you* call her?" he suggested, knowing this was a terrible idea. He deserved the heat that came next.

"She doesn't want to talk to me. She wants to her from you. Her son!"

"Okay! You're right. You're right! I'm a stubborn jerk. I'll call her."

And then something happened that changed how he thought of both his parents. An envelope arrived in the mail. There was no return address, but his name was in his mother's hand. It had been forwarded from his old apartment, the gloriously light-filled one in Somerville; the place that was supposed to be his and Amy's home for years. Feeling the loss of those cheery rooms made him morose, mad at himself all over again.

He stared at the envelope. His mother had written in large block letters across the seal: PRIVATE. SUNIL CHANDARIA ONLY. He remembered her doing this when she sent packages to Nairobi, thinking she could scare off the meddlesome, and underpaid, Kenyan postal workers. It made him laugh to see her carry on the habit. But he wondered what could be inside. Perhaps it was the copy of the autopsy he'd requested—mistakenly sent first to next of kin? He now regretted asking for it; he couldn't imagine wanting to read it. And so he let the envelope sit on the counter for days, then a week. In the meantime he kept up his new routine, basic but fruitful: Dunkin' Donuts, Widener, Au Bon Pain, All Together Now (ten hours a week steering weedy, unpromising youths like the one he had been toward the philosophy section), Widener, and then, when he was too blurry to see the keyboard or a page in front of his face, he went home. He walked everywhere, to save money and to make his wife proud.

One night Erik swung by to take him to a movie. Sunil had been turning down invitations for several weeks, and his friends thought he needed a break. Waiting for Sunil to put on his shoes, Erik pulled the envelope from under a pile of junk mail. "What's this?"

"You're a worse snoop than my wife," Sunil said. "I don't know what it is, but put it down, we have to go."

After the movie, they retired to Rosie's. Starting in on the first pint glasses from their pitcher, Erik said, "You know what your problem is, old sport?" Erik had recently read and admired *The Great Gatsby*. "You have to get over yourself."

"This is what I get from a philosopher? Barbershop advice?"

"What I mean is that no philosopher is expected to live the way he outlines in a stupid paper. Philosophical reflection is insulated from ordinary life, thank God. We puzzle over *oughts*, what makes for a good life, but none of us believes those theories should have that much power over how we actually live." Erik grinned. "When Hume got overwhelmed by skeptical arguments, he played backgammon, and his doubts evaporated."

Sunil understood why Erik had a hard time with women. There was something both of the devil and the clown in his smile, and it was sometimes hard to tell which was which.

"Hume was weak," Sunil said.

Erik laughed. "He did like his claret."

"That fat dude also got himself stuck in a bog."

Like Hume, Sunil had to work hard to keep undermining thoughts at bay. As a human immersed in daily life, he found the idea that we lived in a world without knowledge of independent moral truths unpalatable. He had to remind himself that as a philosopher he *should* be exploring what scared him. Because it was fascinating, and because if he didn't see this idea through, he'd lose not only his direction and his friends, but also his wife and his self-worth.

When was he going to hear from Lieberman? He'd sent her his most recent pages, and her silence ate at him. So he ordered a plate of fries and stuffed them into the void.

When the fries were gone, Erik cleared a space and pulled from his jacket the envelope he'd taken from Sunil's apartment.

"Open it."

"What the fuck? That's my private mail."

"I think it is something important," Erik said, unapologetically.

"Yeah, I think it's my father's autopsy. You want me to open that now? Here?" A sickening feeling rose in Sunil's throat.

Erik did look regretful for a moment, shamefaced but endearing like the hartebeest Sunil and Amy had loved in the Maasai Mara. "I'll open it for you, and if that's what it is, we can set it aside." Erik took a clean knife and slit the top. Sunil looked away, peering into the dim recesses of the bar, then forcing himself to look further, higher, toward the door, where the autumn evening light was still bluely visible.

Erik said, "I think you're going to want to see this."

His friend handed him a stack of papers, varied shapes and sizes, many of them stuck together. Sunil began to peel them apart, one by one. On top were red construction paper hearts folded in half, crusted with dried glue stick: Valentine's Day cards made at school for his parents. Then a jumble of his report cards and teacher's notes, names he hadn't thought of in twenty years. His eyes picked up phrases remarking on his generally good disposition but noting, too, "recalcitrance" and "tempers." He was often alone and easily distracted. One teacher had asked if perhaps Sunil watched a lot of television at home? He laughed out loud. "They didn't know the half of it," he said, mostly to himself. Usually he'd watched TV from the time he got off the bus until dinner, and then from after dinner until bed.

There were ten or twelve drawings flattened and pressed in a stack. Some of the older, stickier pages had to be pried carefully apart, flaking off decades-old bits of crayon, pencil lead, finger paint. Clearly, his mother had not already gone through all this. Here was a crayon sketch so big it had been folded in quarters. He spread it out on the table and saw that the scene was populated with animals, some fantastic and some copied from their 1970 *Encyclopaedia Britannica*. Elephants, a spotted cat, a shakily striped zebra, a lyger. A lyger! In the corner the date, 1979, and the name of his fourth-grade teacher. And this was not even the most surprising. Stapled to his Kenyan recreation of Noah's Ark was a second drawing: a brown crayon stick figure with a swirl of gray turban standing next to a glossy cutout of a train. This one also had a title: "My Grandfather."

"A veritable Edvard Munch!" said Erik, never missing a chance to pump up the reputations of his countrymen.

"My father must have kept all this," Sunil said softly. "I had no idea." His father whom he had believed to be as unsentimental as a polished spoon.

In Kenya, his father had told him about the large number of Somalis he saw in his infectious-disease practice; they carried African fevers and variants that American-educated doctors didn't recognize. "It is very difficult being an immigrant," he'd said. "They do not know the language, the system, and all of these procedures are very frightening to them. It's my job to convince them the tests and so on are necessary. Their lives depend on it. Also, they look to me to comfort them." He had sighed. "I am less effective at this part." Sunil had understood then that his father no longer thought of himself as an immigrant; maybe he never had. Coming to America was his due as an educated man. He'd lived in several American cities, owned a series of American cars, made down payments on American apartments and houses, each bigger and in a better neighborhood than the last. When his father returned to Kenya, he, like Sunil, felt more American than ever. And his safeguarding of these papers from Sunil's childhood confirmed what Premchand had valued just as much as his own freedom: his son's education.

"There's something on the back of your portrait," Erik said.

It was a postcard, a Nairobi street scene: women in saris and salwar kameez leaning over a grocer's abundance of oranges. Above, a handwritten sign: *Chandaria Stores Ltd.* Only one word was written on the back, in Gujarati, and somehow Sunil's brain recalled and recognized: his grandfather's name. It would have been his mother who, years ago, had affixed the drawing to the postcard; the taping was a particular black electrical tape she was fond of using for everything.

The vertiginous feeling that had begun its ascent when Erik first withdrew the envelope from his jacket now rose higher, lodging in Sunil's throat and inhibiting, for the first time Sunil could recall, his powers of speech. The two of them finished the pitcher in silence. Erik looked him in the eyes and nodded sympathetically, while Sunil felt his throat close up and his eyes fill. He covered both his eyes with his hands and leaned his elbows on the table.

Sitting up straight, Sunil inhaled sharply. Looking around the bar, he spotted Liza, with whom he worked at the bookstore. Committed lefty, funny, smart, and not unattractive. He waved her over and introduced her to his friend, saying, "I think you two might like each other. Erik is from a socialist country. He also likes Fitzgerald." And Sunil slipped away.

The sky was black and blue and, above the clot of city lights, abundant with stars. Sunil found the moon and followed it all the way home.

The next week, as his momentum snowballed, Sunil increased his trips to Dunkin' Donuts to twice, sometimes three times a day. He took time to look around him while he walked: signs in Spanish, the salsa music bursting from bodegas as early as seven in the morning, the lingering aroma of fried rice, the passed-out drunks using their arms for pillows. Sunil thought coffee would help his constipation, which had been plaguing him like a terrible metaphor come to life. Because although he was producing more and more pages, he was running headlong into fierce objections—many of them in the work of his advisers. Though he knew one standardly "killed one's fathers" in a dissertation, it felt disloyal and awkward and like biting off the hand that fed him. He drank the supersized cups greedily. For a couple of days he was high enough to overcome this new angst. Aside from morning bagels, he did not need food; hunger helped push him through from morning until night. He thought of Double-D Berman. Of Bimal selling plastic parts to businessmen around the world. He loved his brother, but such could not be his life. He wanted something that had sprung from his own mind.

On the third day he felt weak and dizzy, but he charged on. Ignored all but the words. On the evening of the fourth day, he kneeled on the floor and vomited a thin stream of bile into the toilet. He splashed his face with water, pulled the towel rack down on his head. What seemed like hours later, he found himself in bed, strapped down by a nightmare. There was blood, but from where? Shots rang out continuously, almost musically, and the maggots of his dreams feasted on mounting corpses. He was beaten to a pulp by a stick-wielding Maasai.

When he woke up, he called Lieberman's office. No answer. A glass of water later, back on his butt on the floor, he tried again, and she picked up.

"It's Sunil," he managed to say. "I'm just wondering, did you get the pages I sent you?"

"Yes. Why? My father was ill. I had to fly to Tel Aviv to nurse him."

"Oh. I'm sorry."

"Me, too. He's declining." After a pause, in mock corporatese, she said, "How may I help you?"

"I really want to know what you think of those pages."

"When can you come in to talk?"

He put a hand on his belly, which rumbled, then to his temples, which throbbed. "Um, good question."

"Tomorrow?"

"Not sure."

"Sunil, are you all right? You sound sick. Out of it."

"You could say that." He was beginning to regret calling, feeling uncomfortable with the intimacy of the telephone, her voice so close.

There was silence, and he hard her slow breathing. "Where do you live?" she finally said.

He told her.

"Fine. It's on my way home."

She showed up an hour later with a ramen cup of soup. "It was all I had in the office." She looked around his dingy apartment and took a tentative seat in one of the hardbacked kitchen chairs. "I read your pages on the plane ride home. They're excellent. The only reason I'm here is because you sounded in danger of giving up, and that would be a tragedy. Now," she said and put her elbows on the table, leaning forward, "the problem you lay out for the realist, your demonstration that whichever way he turns, he is faced with an implausible conclusion, this is exactly right."

She smiled, yet her eyes were serious, a contrast that made him smile; and she took this as encouragement, perhaps a compliment, maybe even a flicker of interest, of desire, and smiled back even more widely and invitingly. In this moment, he thought her beautiful. She readily understood the challenges he posed to the moral realist, and why they made him queasy. Why not knowing if objective moral truths existed would turn his world upside down. She didn't know how important it had been to him, in particular, to believe in a morally correct course—

he had not told her anything about his upbringing, about his mother—but she was sympathetic to his crisis of belief.

She told him now, as Erik had, and as she had once before, when she had warned him about anarchy, to ignore the qualms about how he lived. But she said it in the forceful Israeli voice he associated with her seminar, and not in the irritatingly sensible and passionless Norwegian way Erik had of putting things. He had to try to blinker himself to anxieties—to any thoughts at all—about his life. When he voiced his worries about potential objections in the literature, she said emphatically, "Those are not insurmountable." And he believed her.

Then she did something even more suprising than coming to his apartment in the first place. She sent him to his computer. "A thousand words. Just to get you going. Then you take a shower and we go for a walk." To show she didn't mind waiting, she pulled papers out of her sleek leather satchel.

As he sat at the desk in his bedroom, his whole body was aware of her presence, just as the back of his neck and the tips of his ears had always known what Amy was up to—and if he'd not known for sure, he'd called out to her. It was sexist and said something weird and terrible about his independence, but he felt relieved to have Rivka in the apartment.

When he was finished, they headed out his front door and into the warm evening. Exhilarated, he told her what he had written, and she nodded vigorously, interposing suggestions as he outlined further how the realist was boxed in at every turn.

To Sunil's relief, the glimmer of attraction that had been sparked by her arrival at his kitchen table gradually faded. When they passed Szechuan Garden, and Sunil mentioned that it was good, better than it looked with its cafeteria bright lights and split-leather seats, she said, "Let's go in. I'm starving."

Over burning-hot eggplant and a fiery cumin lamb dish, as well as several beers, they talked not only about Sunil's dissertation but Rivka's own new project, which she was just beginning to sketch out. Then she walked him back to his apartment. She looked apprehensively at his front door. "Good night!" she said with awkward brightness, and Sunil was flushed with gratitude. And struck, too, that tomorrow, Saturday, he would have to again face his work alone. He fidgeted with the keys in his pocket.

She eyed him closely. "Tomorrow, should we meet at a café?"

He nodded, relieved.

They met at ten in the morning and worked, separately, through lunch. Sunday they met for dinner to talk about what he'd written. The following afternoon, they went back to his apartment so he could retrieve and reread part of Gibbard's *Wise Choices, Apt Feelings*. As he found the right passage, he was again overcome with appreciation for Rivka's fine balance of intelligent insistence, threats, assurance, and warmth. This feeling kept him going all afternoon, entering a kind of fugue state, while she, sitting with bare feet tucked under her, worked as well. He had never felt so good, so optimistic. He did not fear another overcaffeinated crash once she left—though he did not want her to leave just yet. Every now and then, when he came into the kitchen for more water (he'd learned his lesson about hydration), he caught her looking around nervously, as if someone might be spying on them. But their easy rapport appeared to wash away her concern. In these moments, their arrangement struck him as so necessary as to be natural.

Still he knew that after today she could not come back. Her time with him was indefensible. Many leagues beyond inappropriate. Just as he knew that there was no earthly excuse for him kissing her back when, after a final, parting beer, she packed up her sleek bag and said goodbye, standing in the doorway of his apartment building, half inside, half on the stoop leading to the street, the pinkish sunset clouds tingeing her hair red.

"That's not what I meant," he said, pulling away.

She looked startled, distraught, yet somewhat hopeful. About what, he was not sure. Because the way she'd looked behind him then, at something over his shoulder, then turned to the street, to the scattered chip bags and cracked concrete, made him think that she not only understood him but also agreed and was admitting that the force of his gratitude and relief had momentarily overwhelmed her as well. But then she found his eyes and gripped his gaze and told him in a tight voice that he was remarkable. Rather, his project, his work—not him. Right? But then why was she still standing so close?

He'd delayed, irredeemably. He wanted her close. Did not want her to leave. Took unforgivable pleasure in the intensity of her approval. In the still-present feel of their talk. Her dedication to his project, to him, to his fulfilling his requirements—he knew it was not selfless.

His acceptance of it, obviously, had been entirely selfish.

12.

Some were surprised by the violence, but not me. This country has always gone through cycles of pain. You know how the sun first parches the land, then the rain clouds drench it? Sometimes there are only shallow puddles to drink, other times we are drowning.

Africans grew bolder and more desperate after Independence. Nairobi burst its seams as people moved in droves from the countryside. And when there are more men than jobs, men with families to feed, ruthlessness takes hold. The education system started off with a bang, free for all, really a thing to be proud of, but then it unraveled. You know, you have seen it. Thievery increased, then the violent crimes and murders. Yes, people to whom we gave opportunities!

When the rage boiled over, you were already teenagers. 1982. You remember? Your mother took you out of the city, to the coast.

The morning of the coup, all of Nairobi woke to a commotion like we had never heard. Your grandmother rushed to the window, and I had to take her to the floor, out of sight. Hold that stubborn woman down by her plait. She thinks she can protect herself, and I have to say, listen, these are *soldiers*. Soldiers ran through the streets, took over Voice of Kenya, announcing their new government was in charge.

After locking the women inside, I went to the store with some others to protect our goods, and there were soldiers all through the bazaar, running, pulling men out. They stormed into the shop, shouting, guns smacking, arms flying. A young man, a skinny thing, face black as night and eyes wide with power, gripped me by the shoulders and threw me against the wall. Sweat rolled down his head and his teeth shone. *Mwizi!* He cursed at me, spit in my face. But I saw in his eyes that he was ashamed of what he could not do for his wife and children. While the men with guns pinned us and accused us of national theft, the gang wreaked havoc. Not selecting for items of value, simply to destroy. They looted all over the city, leaving the African shops untouched. The damage was more than five hundred million shillings.

The Africans had been put down for so long that they did not have the proper time to learn to operate democracy. The British had taught nothing but segregation and force. And they were too suspicious to allow Asians, outsiders of any kind, to assist. So they bumbled, reinventing the wheel. Followed tribal divisions the British had enforced because a divided people is easier to rule. Even now their minds are still set in that way, one group pitted against the other. Moi proved to be a decent leader, though. He came down hard on those who revolted—after all, the coup had been against his government, the one he inherited from Kenyatta when the Old Man died. The coup masterminds, some members of the Air Force, were put to death. Moi understood that instability in the economic sector was bad for the country.

Our people are understanding, you know. We know what it is like to want but not to have. So we put this incident behind us. In fact, after the coup, Asians began to support the government more strongly than ever, donating to campaigns and showing our faces at rallies. You remember the time I took the grand-children to hear that speech by President Moi? What was he talking about, something about the Cold War . . . My mind is so slippery these days.

When twenty-five years of Independence came around, I myself made a donation to show national spirit.

No, I am not finished.

Because there is one thing about that day, August 1, 1982, that you were too young to know at the time, but no one has for-gotten. On that day, not only was my own throat squeezed, but many of our women were assaulted. You know what I am say-ing. In the months after, there were suicides, poor things who could not live with the shame. It is terrible even to mention these and so we do not. But I want you to understand why we give only silence when they say to us, when they clamor, Why do you not marry off your daughters to the Africans and inte-grate?

13.

Their father had taken a turn for the worse. Three days in hospital, a day home, today back again, trying another antibiotic for the pneumonia. Her sister said, "He waves his fingers in the air as if trying to snatch insects. Other times as if he is swimming with them, or paddling a boat. And yesterday as if shooting a gun. Imagine!"

"Do you think it is the end?" Urmila had called Sarada from the store, after-hours. She was surrounded by clothing drooping like dead leaves, the little animals pretending to keep watch. She used to enjoy the way it looked like a board game in here, a safari fantasyland where exotic adventures could happen. When the light was low, the mall quiet, an earthy scent that reminded her of Kenya's red clay wafted up from her goods.

"The doctors say he can recover, but, you saw, he is muddle-headed. You know something strange? The other day he was asking for 'the American' and I think he meant Sunil."

"He could have meant anyone. He could have meant me."

Her sister laughed. "Who thinks of you in that way? Not even you!"

Urmila clamped a hand on the soft flesh over her dia-phragm, where once laughter came from.

"It is difficult to see the decline, even though he was so hard on us," Sarada said. "He wouldn't let us girls do anything. Even when I was twenty I had to go to the movies with you."

"Sometimes I would go by myself. I didn't tell anyone."

"No!"

"Yes, and take walks in Jeevanjee Gardens before picking you up. I found a private corner where I could enjoy the grass, without shoes."

"This explains the stains on your socks?"

"Those came out in the wash. I was the one who did the scrubbing anyway."

"You were not alone with the scrubbing!"

Urmila shrugged, though her sister could not see. She asked about Meena—was she going to marry this boy, the engineer from Kisumu whose parents worked with Ajay? "She would not move out there?"

"He is looking for a position in Nairobi, one of the factories outside the city."

"She is in love?"

"This is what she says, but who can say, they have hardly spent any time," her sister said. "And what about you. Are you missing him?"

Urmila had been considering this, and she told her sister that she hated to be alone but her husband had been such poor company, walking around in his own silent world like an astro-naut in a bubble suit. Again her sister said Urmila should be liv-ing with family; they had a room at the ready. Could she really bear another Columbus winter?

"There is a bus from my new apartment, if I don't want to drive."

"Who are you seeing? What friends do you have?"

"I have told you about her before. The one I inspired to the flower business. And there is much more to life than a few friends." But Urmila knew what her sister was thinking, that Maddy was just an acquaintance, a new one at that, someone who might see the surface but knew nothing of the past. In a way, this was true. But friends came in different kinds, and Urmila had long ago proved herself to be self-sustaining, able to carry on with little help from the outside. She would make it through again. There was work. And there was Sunil. She was still a mother, and she thought now, for the first time, with her sister hanging silently on the line, and nothing from Sunil in response to the package, that the way to her son might have to be through his wife.

The quiet was so long, Urmila thought the connection had been lost, and she raised the phone to make sure it was still plugged in.

In a circle of furry dust, she found a scrap of paper with a scrawled phone number and the name *Lillian Ross*, the old rich woman who had wanted to buy ivory for her husband. Urmila had been looking for this.

"Gopal has told me about your business. He says you cannot sustain, now with Premchand gone."

It was true that sales were not high enough to keep going. Already she had discounted deeply the pieces that were not moving. Maddy told her she had only a few weeks of savings left to run on. Then a decision would have to be made: either raise more capital, or close up shop.

"Why are you poking and prodding? What help was he ever to me?"

"I don't care about the love lost, I am talking about the money! Did you forget that you told me about all the financial arrangements? I know you are the elder, but age has no hold on perfection."

"Never in my life have I said I was perfect."

Urmila pictured Sarada huffing into the phone, cheeks red, heeled sandals stamping into her servant-swept floor.

"Exactly my point. Let us do what family is meant for."

Urmila bit her cheek. She was remembering the day, now so long ago, when her father had told her bluntly that she could not keep the child she was carrying if she was to remain separated from her husband. Even Sarada, whose house she was living in, had agreed. They had said they were protecting her and the baby from the shame. Maybe they had even believed what they said.

She scanned the dim rooms. The trappings of her African childhood were now the remnants of her American old age. All these useless, inglorious things.

On her way out of the mall she waved to Sharon inside the Gap, to Omar polishing jewelry he could never afford. The speaker nearest the Wok n' Roll sounded fuzzy, and she stopped at the information desk to pass this along, as if she were just a regular shopper. A goodbye wave, too, from the round and smiling teenager who scooped Urmila's vanilla, chocolate, and strawberry afternoon dessert and always complimented her jewelry, today a chain of bone beads with a diamond-shaped centerpiece of coconut shell. Where just five months before she'd pulled a girl's hair and called her a whore, a man now held open the door for her. Urmila stepped purposefully out into a beautifully clear September day carrying a single wrapped box under her arm.

Lillian Ross, who presented herself in the din and bustle of Ohio's Best Coffee, was more ordinary than she remembered. She was taller than Urmila, plain gray hair brushed away from her face. Exhaustion in the purple circles beneath her eyes.

"My husband is now very sick," Lillian Ross said.

"My husband was murdered by a thug."

As if these bald, tragic facts were all there was to say, at least all they could manage aloud, they stood for a silent moment, occupying an invisible silo of grief. Breath rose and fell inside Urmila's chest. The air smelled sweet and bitter. At least this was the second time Urmila had been at this coffee chain, so she knew what to expect—noisy mothers, bad tea—and she relaxed a little bit. This was a sure thing. "Someone is helping you, with your husband?"

"My daughter came last weekend but she is gone now." Lillian looked around calmly, tiredly—an expression Urmila knew from the mirror—and led them to a table by the window. Urmila offered to buy her a coffee but Lillian declined. More people were leaving the café than entering. The sky was still bright, but the sun lowering. It must be the dinner hour. If she were on the equator now, very soon it would be dusk. From under the table she took the box of brown paper and ribbon and offered it up. "Two thousand dollars."

Lillian Ross shook her head. "Five hundred."

"Naa, that's a steal. You said you were rich!"

"That was before. Now he is sick."

"I am doing you a service, you said it would make your husband happy, but obviously you care less about his happiness than I thought. Forget it." Urmila waved her hand.

The woman gave her a penetrating stare. "If you think your son is going to want this, you are wrong. If he has not claimed it already, he's not interested. I am older than you. This husband is my second, I have been through the death of one already. The fate of your things is in your hands."

"I see you are an expert," Urmila said coldly.

"I know what I know. I know you need the money."

Urmila was silent.

"It's nothing to be ashamed of," Lillian said gently. "Anyway, I will give you a thousand."

Urmila stood while Lillian Ross wrote out the check.

"Thank you."

"I'm glad we can help each other." Lillian Ross looked up into Urmila's face, the pity gone, replaced with a soft sympathetic smile. "I'm being serious. Thank you for calling me. And it will get easier, I promise."

Urmila gripped the flimsy check between finger and thumb, nodded politely, and walked away.

On her way home she took in the landmarks of her thirty-five years here, the various stores—one with better fruit, another cheaper dry goods; the intersection where she had once run out of gas; the Italian restaurant where Sunil had insisted they eat one freezing December day, where he spilled an entire plate of red-sauce spaghetti on his lap; the travel agency owned by one of their friends where she'd secured the best prices for their Nairobi tickets; the Sears where she'd bought her husband's suits and Sunil's back-to-school clothes. These places belonged to a life so far removed from the one she was rolling through now that she could not recall what it had felt like to enter their doors. Without going anywhere, she had somehow left all this behind. Just past the Sears, the red light enlarged and brightened to an impossible size and colored the thick watery lenses of her tears.

She squeezed her eyes shut and saw the silky white ivory of the elephants inside the brown paper package she had left on the table top in the coffee shop. Fingertips running over the bumpy, warm steering wheel, she tried to recall their beautiful reassuring smoothness.

Pulling into her driveway, she saw that the lawn had been freshly trimmed; the air smelled of the cuttings. It wasn't until she saw, buried deep in the hedges, the glass vase containing the long-rotted stems of Jon Samuel's lilies—the glass uncracked but clouded with mold and moisture—that she remembered she no longer lived in this house.

14.

Sunil leaned across the Volvo gearshift to kiss her and catch her cottony warm scent. He had missed this; her sweaty scalp smell, too. Sunil realized he'd never been a passenger with Amy driving. They didn't own a car, and Sunil had driven the rental to the Cape. There they'd both been strangers, experiencing the salty, grainy beach together for the first time. Now, he was acutely aware of being her guest, and of needing her faith and favor.

She'd shaken the plain missionary look. Today her hair was pulled back, high and professional. Makeup on her eyes, color on her cheeks; her mouth, thankfully, was untouched. It was Thursday, she'd come from work. She gestured to a briefcase in the back seat and said she'd have to do some work from home tomorrow morning before they went out for the day.

"That's fine," he said.

Then she told him the good news. She'd been promoted to assistant research director of their small lab—basically the same job, but more money.

"And status," he said.

She was flourishing here. Now would be a good time to tell his wife his own good news, but he wanted to wait for a more celebratory moment, one filled with ease and openness, rather than bumper-to-bumper horns inching forward from the train station. Also, he had not yet decided how, or how much, to tell of his story of accomplishment. His friends had offered opposing advice.

She pointed out the capitol, where they'd go tomorrow, and then they were cruising down avenues so wide and straight it was like Ohio.

In her blue button-down and pencil skirt, even Amy's voice was polished in a way he didn't remember, that he hadn't heard in their phone conversations. Yet she appeared to be nervous, too, hesitant to see him, touch him, which he didn't understand, given how much she'd pushed for his visit. They'd been apart only two days at a time before this cavernous separation of nearly three months. When you didn't know the little things about each other's days, the big things got bigger.

"My parents are so excited to see you, they're almost nervous, it's very cute. You might even get a train set out of my father, early Chanukah. He always wanted a boy." She turned down a narrow street and added, "I thought we'd go straight to the restaurant." Because he'd expected to go first to the Kauffmans', Sunil was underdressed, but Amy assured him he looked fine in his wrinkled T and jeans. Worn sneakers and third-day socks.

The place was neither a grad-student dive nor an upscale retreat, but some kind of fancy pub where you had to squeeze past a well-dressed horde—men his own age in suits, several with cell phones—at the bar to get to your seat. Where you had to shout to be heard. He wondered why she had taken him to such a raucous place when they hadn't seen each other in so long. All he wanted to do was look at her, from every angle, and touch all the soft and hard curves. Listen to the stories of her success.

"Who are all these people?"

"Congressional staffers, White House assistants, future senators. Pompous asses."

As the evening blew out a few pink-tinted clouds, Sunil took her in his arms and pressed his temple to hers, felt the heat of her face. Amy led him by the hand to a booth in the back. Wooden tables and brick walls. She looked at him with soft, almost sad, eyes and continued to hold his hands. "You're thinner," she said. "God, I sound like my mother."

He'd stopped weighing himself at the gym because he'd stopped going to the gym. But he was eating better.

Sunil scooted forward on the leather banquette. Their drinks came and he told her he'd been thinking about her parents, refining an idea on the train. It had been obsessing him, this puzzle of their motives and beliefs. He wanted to present an idea he thought would help Amy be less frustrated with them.

Because they were good people, he said, not inclined to dislike or shun, he thought their initial hostility to his and Amy's marriage was more a show of hurt feelings than a serious objection to his not being Jewish. "They were offended, but not for religious reasons. They didn't want to categorically reject me."

Amy shook her head. "You don't understand how much they've invested in the idea of themselves as religious people." Like all fundamentalists, they saw themselves as following not just any code, but the right code. She wrapped her hands around her wineglass, her wedding band clinking in a momentary pause in the noise. "I think it's easy for journalists to feel self-righteous. Their vocation is serving up truth to the public. And at *Moment*, there's a culture, a cohort, they can be a part of and feel good about." But they didn't go along with everything Orthodox, she pointed out. "They don't discriminate against gay people—I don't think they even believe it's a sin. My gayest friend from high school has been over a lot, and they couldn't be nicer to him."

"Yes, exactly, another data point, as you would say." It felt so good to be talking to her again, face to face. "They adopted externally justified moral principles—Jewish moral codes—but some parts of this code conflict with what they know to be right. So then, why hold on to the code at all? Forgive me, I've been thinking nonstop about external moral codes."

"This has been a sore spot between you and my parents in the past. My mom saying you were amoral and anti-God. The look on your face."

"Was I rude?"

"On the arrogant side," she said.

He shook his head in dismay. "I'm not planning to bring up any of this, I just think it's helpful to think about it this way. Don't you?"

"What I want to know is why they have to believe their moral code comes from God."

"Right, that's just it. An external justification, in this case a transcendental one (from God), seems to be irrelevant for them," he said. "See, the way they know some principles of the transcendental code are right is because they're supported by their own confident moral judgments. When the code conflicts with their own internal judgments, they say, 'Fuck the code.' This rejection shows them that they don't even need support from an external a code. It's irrelevant. See what I mean?"

"I think so. Yes. You're saying that you're like my gay friend, in my parents' eyes. They're good people so they really don't want to discriminate. Their initial reaction to our marriage was like a hiccup. They *thought* they should object because of their religious code, but in the end they really couldn't because it wasn't fair or right to exclude you, to keep us apart." She leaned back, her dolphin-sleek profile pale against the red leather seat. "I think that does change how I think of them. Of course I know they love me, and they love you, but it's a relief to see them as flexible in this way. More flexible than I thought, anyway." She leaned over and kissed him. "To choices," she said. "To us."

Amy's blonde head flashed in the mirror behind them, and he thought of her steadfastness in Nairobi, her yellow amid their brown, how she was both slender and unassuming like his father and a fistful of steeliness like his mother. Sunil had told Amy about the envelope his mother had sent, but he had not gone into much detail. He had brought it with him and was waiting until they were back in her house, secluded in her room, to linger over the pages with her, for they still felt intensely private. Although every day since the receipt of the package he had woken vowing to call his mother to thank her, to tell her what it had meant to him, he had not been able to do it.

During their quiet drive back to the house, Amy played him a few minutes of Beethoven's Ninth, whose movements bridged her daily commute.

Rivka, too, listened to symphonies. Had played Mendelssohn one evening.

He did not have feelings for Rivka Lieberman. None beyond gratitude, anyway. He was still baffled and distraught by how those moments of gratitude and intellectual understanding had felt forcefully, however fleetingly, like some kind of love. He had run into Rivka just once since she left his apartment. She had been outside the library peeling an orange, white pith under her nails, and had pointed to a green apple poking out the top of her backpack. "Fruit?" Then assessed him in her unnerving way. "Remember, the brain needs sugar." He had accepted because he could not remember if he had anything but popcorn in his apartment.

"I finished my dissertation," he said to Amy now. "I've been approved for spring funding."

The car slowed softly, as if braking into a featherbed.

They were on her street, almost at her parents' house. The road was recently paved, completely smooth, with no center stripes. This was the kind of street where lines were not needed. Here was successful self-rule and self-control. Where everyone behaved as he ought.

Amy steered the car into the driveway and put it in park and turned off the ignition and clicked off her seatbelt. She leaned into him and hugged him very hard. His arms wrapped her narrow back, and he pulled her as close as he could given the seatbelt still locking him in. Amy took his head in her hands.

Inside the potpourri-smelling foyer, Amy released her briefcase onto a bench. She slipped off her shoes. His own shoes were the largest in the neat row against the wall. Very close to them was a small, very worn, pair of black sandals that looked like nothing Amy or her mother or sister would ever wear.

"We're in here!" Ariel called from the living room deep inside the house.

Amy took his arm, as if with pride, and walked him down the hallway. Warm lamps lit the people in the room. Three people.

He did freeze for a moment, but he did not buckle. No, after a first startled hesitation, he moved steadily and silently across the plush carpet to greet his mother-in-law and father-in-law and embrace them before facing his mother.

She hugged him fiercely, desperately, as she had in Nairobi the first night they arrived. He was surprised to feel relieved to see her, and to be held by her; to know that she had survived the last few months; to feel her strength and believe in her desire to be with him. Because there was little give left in his bony, grief-soldered body, his depleted mind.

On the table in front of his mother was a small dish containing a used teabag, the brand she filled whole suitcases with in Kenya and carried back to Columbus. She'd brought the Kauffmans several bags of the Indian equivalent of Chex Mix, snacks that turned your fingertips orange. Also in front of his in-laws were wineglasses, a half-empty bottle, and dishes of flawless green olives. Jazz from the local public radio station gently buzzed the air. Then the Kauffmans stood, and all three of them quietly filed out of the room.

"We'll leave you alone," David said.

As Sunil watched Amy's firm back and bare legs walk away from him, he realized: she had brought them together. She wanted them to find peace, just as she had been advocating for months. But could he do it? Could his mother? She was here; she must want it as much as he did.

"Mom, how are you?"

"I have been worried sick about you! Me," she sniffed. "I am fine."

They sat on the Kauffmans' springy new couch, awkwardly turned to face each other. Right away, Sunil pulled the envelope out of his backpack, the edges now worn from his repeated opening and closing. "Thank you for sending this. It means a lot to me."

"I have been waiting for your reply," she said quietly. She had recently dyed her hair—no gray at all was visible. This, combined with the elegant sari she was wearing made her look severe, like an old-fashioned portrait. He was touched she had dressed up.

"I can imagine. I'm sorry. I know it doesn't help much now to say that I really did try to call. I even tried to write a letter, but I just couldn't. Seeing all these mementos that Dad kept, that I had no idea still existed, it made me feel so empty and sad. I missed him too much to talk about it."

"It was his secretary who did this, who preserved them."

"What do you mean?"

"Mrs. Fiske."

"Yes, I remember her, but what does she have to do with it?"

She shook her head and burst into tears. "Everything is upside-down, that is all. I had forgotten who she was—you know, I barely knew anything about that part, the office. So," she said tentatively, "you do not think they were having an affair?"

"Definitely not! Dad was too low-energy to have an affair. Not that he would have anyway—" He was moved to wipe a wet blushy smudge from her cheek with his thumb. He began to ask her if seeing him was the only reason she'd come to DC, when he caught sight of the cluster of enormous suitcases in the corner. Of course. "You're moving back there," he said.

She nodded. She explained how, earlier in the day, she had visited the Kenyan embassy. So the nice clothes weren't for him, but no matter. Her paperwork was now in order. "There is now nothing for me here," she said.

"Aside from me, I guess you mean?"

"Of course! I meant the store is closed. It was a failure in the end."

He knew how much it had meant to her, and he felt as if his heated conversation with his father in the Blixen house had willed its demise. "I'm proud of you, Mom. I'm sure it wasn't easy to make that decision." He was glad she was going to Nairobi, he said. No more Ohio winters. She had always hated the itchiness of wool and thought fleece an abomination. Sarada Aunty would take good care of her, he said. "And Bimal," he added, his voice thin and frayed, "of course he is there."

She waved her hand at this. "They do not want me near him. They are too protective." She appeared to be bracing herself. "But I have to be respectful because everyone is healing."

He poured himself a glass of wine, refilled his mother's tea, and they awkwardly clinked glass to porcelain. Sunil had never imagined reconciliation would take this form, in this place foreign to both of them. But perhaps all they had needed was neutral territory and some clear time and space.

Headlights cut through a Venetian blind and swept across them, gleaming the gold rings on his mother's hands. Sunil thought of the one photo he had seen of his parents' wedding and wondered how his mother had felt that day.

"So, have you and Amy had a chance to talk, since you've been here?"

She shook her head. She had arrived at the house while Amy was picking him up from the station. "Why are you asking?"

"I just think it would mean a lot to her if you showed that you accepted her. She was upset when you were being pushy about having an Indian wedding, and the things you said about her being a stranger. You could tell her you're sorry."

His mother was quiet, clasped and released her fingers. Her eyes drifted over the tea set. "You know, a long time ago when your father went away on one of his trips, he came back with a gift for me. A brand-new set of pots and pans. He bought them at a factory outlet for a very good price. I was so happy! The old ones were from Nairobi and were too scarred and scratched. I cooked elaborate meals in the new pans, and, oh my, everybody loved it. A year goes by, maybe two years, and he asks me, So, darling, do you like your present? And I laughed because it was so obvious!"

Sunil stared at her. "I'm confused. What are you trying to tell me?"

"That all of this please-and-thank-you politeness, this needing of this emotion and that one, is for the birds! Such sensitivity, as if we are all children. He gave me a gift and I gave back to him, and what is the more to it?"

Was she saying that the best he could ever have would be

288 THE LIMITS OF THE WORLD

to understand that her outbursts—in her own mind, at least—
were trivial? Did not mean what they appeared to?

"Don't you see, Mom, he wanted to know that he made you
happy. To know that the *reason* you made those meals was not
some wifely obligation but because you were appreciative. Just
like with Amy. I don't know why you said those things to her,
but I don't think it was to hurt her. She should know that."

"I am entitled to my opinion," she said in an offended voice.
"Everybody is."

He gripped the seams of the sofa cushion.

After a moment of silence, he said, "I have some good news."

"Yes? What is it? You have found a job?"

He smiled. "Not exactly. Not yet. But I did finish a solid
draft of my dissertation. I still have to revise, and get feedback
from my advisers, and then I have to defend, which should happen sometime in the spring. So someday I'll have a job and you
can finally be proud of me."

She nodded eagerly. "We are all waiting for that day!"

And if they had said good night right then, perhaps the
wine and the tea and the tasteful, cushioned room would have
caressed them into, if not comfort, then acceptance.

But his mother then asked if Amy had found a job. She
remembered that in Nairobi she had been waiting to hear the
results of some interviews.

Sunil told her about his wife's admirable position at the
NIH, and how she was thriving there. She had recently been
promoted and would soon have her name on a paper coauthored
with her supervisor.

His mother appeared confused. "NIH is here in DC, isn't
it? But you are in Boston. Wait, you have been there all alone?
Without your wife?" She was getting upset. "Where is the support? She should be with you!"

It was well intentioned, he told himself—she was concerned

about his welfare. Yet her words only revived her dismissal of Amy in Nairobi. Sleeping dog to jackal. "It's just temporary," Sunil explained. "I'm the one who let *her* down. She needed to come here to get a good job."

Urmila threw up her hands. "Yes, I know something about difficult people, people for whom the job is everything, the job is life, and so this is why I am urging you to think again about your choice of wife. It is not too late! You need more than someone who runs away at the first difficulty. I have known this about you your whole life." Her feet shushed agitatedly across the plush carpet, her nose wrinkling, her voice growing louder and more adamant.

"Mom, please at least be quiet," he urged. "I don't want the Kauffmans to hear you. What you're saying is unkind and untrue. And I want you to respect my decision. And to respect Amy."

But his mother had only been gathering momentum. Something had set her loose and Sunil could do nothing but watch her unwind. How many times had his father done the same? "I am warning you. Because I wish I had known this about myself, about *him*," she continued. "I wish I had not been duped. You know they said he was perfect, not one flaw! Why did they not tell me about his cold side? His always-out-of-the-house side."

"Think of all Dad did for you," he said, his voice thickening, coming up in volume. "Beyond the stupid pots and pans, think about the store. The biggest and best example of his caring for you. You told him that having a store was your dream, and he agreed to help you."

"It was a good investment!"

"No, Mom, it wasn't. That's the point. Dad helped you not because it was prudent, but again, because he wanted you to be happy." He put his head in his hands. This was supposed to be his area of expertise, and yet he could not even convince his own mother how important it was to make motives clear—to do right *because it was right*. Because he himself was convinced— if not on paper, if not in theory, then in action: he knew how he ought to live his life.

"I just want to be clear about one thing. Amy didn't abandon me. I encouraged her to take a job here *because* I love her. Just like Dad sacrificed for you. I don't know how to put it any other way."

His mother was silent, her shushing feet slowed. She looked at him through her large glasses, the metal sidepieces shining through her brittle, dark hair. "Naa," she said, shaking her head. "He set me up for failure. And I will not hold back in telling you that the same will happen to you if you keep up this dream of being married to someone who doesn't understand us."

"What are you saying? Are you telling me to get divorced?"

"What is the big deal? You are American first and foremost you always say, and the Americans do it all the time."

He felt the furnishings in the room fall away. Sunil stood, leaving his place beside his mother, and taking a seat on the couch opposite. The jazz was still playing, a sax solo, and it thinned his nerves further. He leaned forward, elbows on his knees. She was forcing him to choose. He said quietly, enunciating every word, "That's the last time you give me an ultimatum. And the last time you talk that way about Amy. When you're ready to apologize, you let me know. Until then, I don't know how we can have anything more than a superficial relationship. But maybe that's enough for you." He shrugged. "It will have to be enough for me." This last utterance had exhausted him, and he lay down sideways on the couch. His ear pressed again the cushion, which mercifully subdued the jazz, his mother's spiky breathing.

She had made it clear she did not believe in her own fallibility, in apologies, and so he would never know if she was sorry for anything, or if she ever meant what she said. And that was a terrible thing to consider.

A moment later his mother was waving a piece of paper near his shoulder. "I almost forgot this. I want you to have it." It was a check for a thousand dollars.

He could not take money from her; he was sure she did not have enough for herself. "You keep it," he insisted. "You'll need it for your new life."

Sunil barely ate anything at dinner. Urmila had begged fatigue and an early flight and had gone up to her room. The Kauffmans talked among themselves. He couldn't bear to tell Amy about the disappointment, the fracture, that had come of the meeting she had planned out of love. He excused himself before dessert and went upstairs to lie down. Sometime later, he heard Amy talking to someone. His mother. They were both in the adjacent guestroom.

Sunil crept out of bed and put his ear to the wall.

"You're crying," he heard his mother say.

Amy had not been crying at dinner.

"I was." A pause. Then, "When you wrote me asking if Sunil had received the envelope, I invited you here. I risked a lot for you. And there's something I deserve to know. Why didn't you apologize for telling him to go away, that he didn't belong to you? You're here, so you obviously didn't mean it."

"'Open your mouth and flies will enter,'" Urmila said. "This is what my mother always told me. "Too much talk is no good. Don't you say that actions speak louder than words? And I am here! I came here." There was a rustle of bedclothes, a creak in the floor. Downstairs dishes clinked into the dishwasher. "No one can say that that my heart is not in the right place."

"I think I can say that."

Sunil inhaled and held his breath. When his mother spoke,

he could almost hear the shrug in her voice. "If you think it is so important, you can tell him I feel regret. I do feel it. But what does it matter? He will never change his view of me. When you are old and abandoned by everyone, you will understand."

The next morning she was gone, up in the air. What she left behind was a neat pile of boxes filled with Maasai jewelry, soapstone candlesticks, batik wall hangings, and rusted knives sheathed in stiff leather.

He looked out Amy's bedroom window onto rain-splattered leaves. The sun had just come up, which was a relief because he'd been awake for hours already. The lengths to which Amy had gone to help him astonished and humbled him. Feeling the immensity of her love and effort, his hip weighed against the windowsill, and he pressed it harder until he felt a slow bruise blooming around the bone. Rays of sunlight began to angle through the tree outside the window, warming the side of his face. The forecast promised several days of Indian summer.

When Amy yawned and said, "What time is it?" he pulled up a chair beside her bed and kissed her warm forehead. He said, "I have to tell you something." He told her then, in as straight a manner as he could, exactly how his dissertation had come to be written. Unabridged, unlike the rendition he'd given his friends—he'd told them about the kiss but not about how sick he'd been, not how Rivka had found him shriveled on the floor.

"It sounds like you needed her," Amy said uneasily. "You needed an intervention, like a drug addict." Users and recidivists were a group she knew well, though she did not say this. "I couldn't have done what she did. I don't have the tools."

"And you shouldn't have to. This was my fault, not yours."

"I know," she said. "Doesn't mean it doesn't feel awful. But do you want to keep seeing her? I mean, beyond her role as your adviser?" He saw her prepare herself for the worst, the final withdrawal, and it eviscerated him.

"No," he said. "Not at all. I only want you."

She reached out and pulled him into bed, with all her strength, under the covers in all his clothes.

After breakfast the four of them piled in the car and drove to the Lincoln Memorial. Monica was already at the library, studying. Sunil stood before the thirty-six columns and the inscribed Gettysburg Address and inhaled the damp, staggering lawn. In the afternoon, the zoo. Straight to the primates—the baboons and gorillas—where Amy said, with a soft touch on his arm, "A different kind of safari, isn't it?"

Gravel under his feet, glass panes between them and the animals, monkey-shaped stuffed toys and balloons for sale— nothing was the same. He said, "Now that I know that my father was already dead while we were on the plains, looking for rhinos, those days feel impossible. Like I made them up in order not to think about him."

"They were real," Amy said firmly. "We had a wonderful time."

He knew this. Sometimes he could summon their joy, and he fed off morsels of recalled elation. As they watched the tufted orangutans now, all Sunil could think was how they could best be together. Stay together. He would go back to Cambridge, back to his hovel, and grit his teeth through the rest of the semester, sitting in on seminars, revising his dissertation, preparing for his defense and to teach in the spring. He wanted to ditch his paralyzing fellowship for the living work of the classroom. Amy encouraged this plan. She would stay put, too, at least until the summer. Commuting the next nine months would not be easy, but they thought they could do it.

Sunil watched one orangutan, off in the corner of his artificial world, sullenly stare at his own reflection in the glass. Reach

294 THE LIMITS OF THE WORLD

an arm toward the glossy image then bare his teeth. With rubbery fingers, he plucked things off the ground and threw them down at an increasingly rapid rate.

For years Sunil had tried to exile his parents from his private life, to separate his problems with them from what he desired and loved most. And yet his mother had still landed herself squarely in the middle of the only relationship that had ever spoken to him of the future. The threat had been real, but it had not toppled them.

Behind them the orangutan screeched. The day was warming up, and Sunil's back and wrists prickled with sweat. He submitted to a bench. David sat beside him and clasped his clean, lean hands in his lap. Crossed his runner's legs. *Love each other* he'd once said to them, before Amy had met anyone in Sunil's family, when she knew only what he'd told her about where he came from. "What about your brother? Will you keep up with him?" David asked.

"I hope so. I think about him a lot now."

"That's no small thing."

"I do know that. I absolutely do." Despite last night, despite the loss of his father, who still haunted the margins of his vision, Sunil felt his world to be larger now. Even if it was an uncertain one that caused his head to buzz, his knees to twang.

The women now flanked them at the bench, Ariel beside David and Amy beside Sunil. Their palms touched their husbands' shoulders.

"I'm sorry it went badly yesterday," Ariel said. "But I hope you can see that we all thought there was a chance it would do everyone good."

"It was a long shot," Amy admitted.

Sunil gave a sad laugh and pressed his palm to his wife's face. "But we need long shots for breakthroughs, too, right?" Because in the world they had created for themselves, the success or failure of this particular experiment didn't matter to their future. What mattered was that they paid attention; that even their mistakes were motivated by love.

15.

Her relatives did their best. They brought small, welcoming presents: a battery-operated radio for blackouts, a new silk scarf, embroidered slippers, a coupon for a new hair salon. "Treat yourself!" they said. But Sarada said, "The sooner you are used to not being coddled and treated like a guest, the better." Urmila exchanged frequent emails with Maddy, who promised to visit Kenya someday, as soon as she could afford the ticket and to leave her shop for a couple of weeks. As long as the weather in Columbus was dry and not too cold, the workers could continue constructing the greenhouse. There were a dozen different seedlings she wanted ready for sale by Easter.

When Maddy had told her to accept her family's kindness, Urmila said, "May this never happen to you."

To the Kauffmans, whom she had promised to call when she'd settled in, she was breezy, maybe, but also true: *You know what they say about Africa? The dirt never washes off your heels.*

For weeks she resisted Sarada's entreaties to join the morning meditation class, but finally they drove the few blocks to the Oshwal Centre, and Urmila smiled weakly at the women she recognized in the candle-lit room. She sat on the cushion as she was told, piling the blankets high under her seat to avoid compression in her joints, but soon her knees pulsed violently, and staring at the black insides of her eyelids made her dizzy. She thought she would faint. She left Sarada to finish on her own, and for thirty minutes she walked in circles around the cinder trail in the sports yard. Before she left USA, the doctor had given her medicine for high blood pressure and instructed her to take two walks per day.

Her husband had tried walking in this city, and look what happened to him.

What would do her the most good, she thought as she circled, pebbles lodging in her shoes, was seeing her son and granddaughter. She craved the girl. Saw Bimal's face on the young men in TV movies. But she had not asked about seeing him, had not even inquired for news. In another month she would reach out to Bimal, once she had been reabsorbed into the fabric of this place. And she would write to her Amerikana just to tell him she missed him and wish him good luck on what came next—at the moment, she could not remember. A breeze picked up and cooled the back of her neck. Beyond the high walls of the Oshwal Centre hung laundry strung between smog-stained sandstone.

Today Urmila was home alone. She opened the novel she had bought with one of her welcoming coupons, but the street noise in the front room was too distracting to read. Something jostled at the edge of her hearing, and she peered nervously out the windows at the front of the house. There was nothing to see through the hedges. She circled to the back and watched the sister, the tall one living in the far shack, scold her younger brother. He immediately started to bawl, so she picked him up, sighing, and kissed his tears. The young woman seemed to sense that she was being watched because she looked pointedly toward the house. Urmila hastened back to her chair and sat, unreading, unmoving, with her feet up. Then the doorbell rang.

Mital wore a new turquoise sari, her hair pulled back in the same severe way as always. Face still long and horse-plain. The two women had not spoken since Premchand's funeral. But now here she stood, empty-handed, unembarrassed, as if there had never been any disagreement. She inquired about Urmila's health. Could she accustom herself to this Kenyan life after such a long time in America?

"All going very smoothly. Of course there are many modern conveniences that I miss. Not things you would notice if you never had them." Then she swallowed her pride and invited her sister-in-law to stay for tea. While the milk warmed, Mital apologized for the cloudy days.

"I think the weather has been fine." Urmila found cups and saucers and spoons and made the tea very strong and very sweet. There was a tin of biscuits that she brought to the table, where Mital waited patiently, as if this had been an afternoon ritual for years. After some moments of silence, thinking of nothing else to say, wondering if there was something flawed and idiotic about them all living so close together with their mixed-up problems, Urmila finally said, "And how is your son?"

"Like you, he says he thinks the change will be for the better. He is looking forward to all the new opportunities."

"Change?"

"You didn't hear the news? He has a new job in America, a place they call the research triangle in the Carolinas. He left the day before you arrived."

Urmila sipped the scalding tea, trying not to choke on her dismay. "I see. When you next speak to him, please pass along my regards."

16.

[7 h: 35 m]

I will read you just this bit from the newspaper. "Asians in Kenya, to talk from experience, are very tribalistic. Just try to enter their temples or mosques, impossible because of the *rungu*-wielding askari. I have a friend who is very much in love with an Asian girl. Why is he not allowed to see her? Why can she not ride the bus with him?"

This is a laugh, don't you think, in this tribalistic country? We welcome anyone to visit our temples, as long as they observe that they are sacred places. I would not demand entrance to some Christmas ceremony without first knowing about it. Why does the Golden Rule not here apply?

We have certain rules of respect and purity, grandsons. Alcohol is not bad because it makes you drunk—though this is a big problem—but because it causes unnecessary life through fermentation. Ease happens between people who have grown up in the same culture. Don't you think this is so? Those one or two who have married English women, we have accepted them with all our hearts. But it takes getting used to. Each side has to give.

After so many years, it is tiresome still to account for ourselves. All we have ever asked for is a little freedom. To be allowed our lives according to our beliefs. To take care of our souls; each man to try and rid himself of the karma tying him to the physical world and the cycle of life and death. The ascetics rid their karma by practicing austerities. This perhaps is not so practical for all of us, but we do aspire. Our people are so far away from things that few ascetics come to visit, and our idols are unconsecrated, but we get along with our lay community. My father was not a very religious man, but he read his sacred texts each morning in front of the shrine with the murti of Mahavira.

Do you know, grandsons, when the ascetics achieve enlightenment, karma drops away and the soul is released—never to be dirtied again? But no divine being can help emancipate your soul—no short-cutting. Only you can do this. And this emancipation is only possible when happiness and unhappiness in the world are balanced.

Stay now, you here, share our food, and watch some cricket with me. I enjoy watching the most when there is someone at my side.

17.

Douglas Berman's beard was gnarled and hung to his chest, but his hair was recently cut. His shirt untucked but not overly wrinkled. Sunil had last seen DD-36 outside the library in mid-summer, the last vision Sunil had wished to encounter after ingeniously squandering several hours walking between the stacks, chewing off the end of a pen, while his wife worked eight hours at Blue Cross. Perhaps that was why, as Berman approached their table, Sunil joked to his friends about a phantom white shell buried in the hair below the man's chin.

"And I thought we were gathered here to reboot your normal condescension," Andrew said. "Apparently our services are not needed."

"He finishes one dissertation and *poof!*" Erik said.

"I shouldn't have said that," Sunil said. He had drunk too much. He felt he was still decompressing from the months of caffeinated thinking and typing, and the emotional crucible of DC. He had promised Amy he'd take good care of himself, and he would. He would continue to walk everywhere, eat three times a day. He just needed some downtime with his friends.

"Libation, old sport?" Erik asked Berman, who accepted the plastic cup of yellow beer.

Berman said, "I saw you all walk in here on my way to the talk, three hours ago. Sunil, you should have come. It was in your bailiwick."

"I'm off this semester."

"Never off," Berman said. "That's the first thing I learned. Philosophy is a worm that burrows inside you. Dormancy is the most you can hope for."

"So what did Morgan have to say?" Andrew asked.

Sunil was too tired, too distracted by the thought that in Berman he was staring at a very nearly missed future, to pay close attention, but he did notice that in a few short sentences Berman had laid out the speaker's argument, then demolished it with an objection. It had been so long since he'd had an actual conversation with Berman. He'd forgotten how precisely and clearly he spoke—an ambassador of the short, declarative sentence. And as Berman talked on, Sunil thought that if this haggard, hangdog, arrogant, sorry excuse for a graduate student could marshal his resources so quickly and impressively, Sunil, too, had to press confidently on. His defense was scheduled for April.

"Let me ask you something, Berman," Sunil said. "You're an awfully smart guy. Why the fuck are you still here?"

Berman drank the warm beer and dispassionately eyed the waitress as she squeezed past him with a loaded tray of scavenged dishes on her shoulder. He stole a fried potato wedge off a plate of demolished food.

"Being a critical philosopher isn't so hard," Berman said, gesturing with the wedge. "Taking down other people's positions. What's hard is building up a positive view, something creative that explains what others haven't. I guess I'm still searching for that. I'll keep trying until I find it. What else is there?"

Berman was a seeker, Sunil realized. From beneath his beard pushed a smile, and his shoulders shrugged, meaning, yes, this task might take the rest of his life.

Yes, that was right. And for the first time, this thought was freeing. Sunil had been approved to teach in the spring. His fellowship had been given to a Pakistani-American grad student named Ahmed. Sunil had another shot at forward.

Sunil slid over, making room for Berman. But their bearded friend turned around now and left the bar, tossing his cup in the garbage at the door, as if he had better places to be.

Sunil shopped for a few items every day, a few small reasons to get out of the house. He did not clean the apartment with soap and water, but every night after heating his dinner he straightened up a little. Recycled old papers, cleared the dust off the TV, aligned the kitchen table neatly against the wall, folding cardboard under the short leg as he had seen Amy do in their old apartment. The mornings were cool, and he resumed his walks to Dunkin' Donuts. He'd expected some of the younger, college-aged staff to turn over once the school year started, but they hadn't. One guy with a horse tattoo on his neck said it was nice to see him again, and Sunil said, gratefully, "And you."

There were a few brilliant leaves left on the trees, slumped scarecrows hanging on in front yards, but the wind these days had an arctic undercurrent, and Sunil wore a hat in the mornings. The days grew shorter and they set the clocks back. One brisk afternoon, Sunil walked the four miles from Emerson Hall to his apartment just to prove that he could.

He called Amy every night at eight. Sometimes she was home, and sometimes she was out, still at work, Ariel said, or having dinner with her sister or her colleagues. Ariel suggested he try her new cell phone, but he could wait. He was not going anywhere, and neither was she.

One morning in the Maasai Mara, Sunil and Amy had made a mistake. Waiting for a young herder to cross the road with his bony cattle—trademark red cloth hung over his shoulder, gaze hard yet passive—Amy had pushed her camera out the window.

The herder had turned and run toward them, shouting, wielding his club, threatening, darkly silhouetted against the golden plains. Kioko, in his calm, round voice, explained you had to pay for pictures, but he arranged for them to make it up when they visited the herder's village.

After paying their debt to the Maasai, late in the afternoon they'd crept alongside a wild and burnished pride of lions, seven or eight adult females and a handful of fully, incredibly maned males, whiskers thick as rope. They stretched and rolled and padded from one spot to another, releasing long glistening tongues and dull roars. Shockingly at ease. They belonged utterly to that place, to the grasses and cracked earth.

That night Rawley told them that there were lions around the camp. Purity had verified. "But do not allow that Mr. Rawley scares you," she said.

"Now do we believe it?" Amy had asked Sunil. Did they believe in the man-eating lions?

Her look of genuine curiosity. Her patience. Their joint consideration of what to believe.

"Yes and no," he'd said.

Me too, she'd said, *me too.*

One night Sunil met Rivka Lieberman for coffee at a busy café off the square. She would be taking a job at Hebrew University next year. Her father was weakening, and she wanted to be closer to him.

One night, Sunil fell asleep on the couch watching TV and woke up in the morning to the ringing phone. He answered immediately.

His accented name, exclaimed with enthusiasm. "I am so happy to hear your voice!" After a pause, "You don't recognize me. Because I'm so much stronger now."

"Bimal?"

"You remember you have a brother? At least a cousin-brother?"

"Is my mother okay? What time is it there?"

"She is fine, I think. But I am here, in your city. I'm inviting you to lunch today. Can you meet me in Harvard Square at one o'clock?" Bimal named the restaurant where the department took candidates after job talks.

Sunil dressed hastily and fretted while he waited for the T, regretting he hadn't sprung for a cab. He kept checking his pockets, wondering what he might have forgotten. He had not had time to shave, and his jaw was thick with stubble. Bimal wore a suit, and Sunil felt embarrassed arriving without a jacket. The last time he'd eaten on a white tablecloth was the day he and Amy married. Six months had blinked by.

All the tables were packed. The brick-colored walls resounded with talk. Sunil balanced on a high wire, nervous and excited. Look at them—brothers! The scar tracing from Bimal's eye to his chin had faded to pink. It was a line that would always remind Sunil of the place that sliced time into before and after.

"I am looking recovered, yes? Not the invalid you saw. Or even the one with the cane at the funeral." He ordered bottled water for the table. Bimal explained how quickly and surprisingly the job offer had come in and they'd moved—all in three weeks. "I think you were the inspiration. You are such an American cheerleader."

Sunil said how healthy he looked, how glad he was to see him. "But I thought you liked Nairobi. And Sheetal, doesn't she miss her family?"

Between tastes of tomato soup, Bimal said, "Nairobi is a very fine place to live. Nice community and good business contacts. Family is there, of course. But Raina is so smart, we want her to have the best education, and education is the best in America—the most options, the least cost, especially if you have residency for state schools." He set down his spoon. "I don't mean to bring bad memories, but the death of Premchand Fua was a great shock. Raising children, you want someplace safe. America has violence, but it is a big country—just as you said." His hands rested on the table, his fingers slender like their father's, gold wedding ring catching and throwing the light. Sunil fingered his own ring in his lap. If he closed his eyes, he could hear in Bimal something of their father's voice, its taut instructional quality, which Sunil had always found comforting. Bimal added shyly, "And we are not alone. You are here. And I think we can be good friends. Don't you?"

"Yes. Yes, I do." Over the past months, in the moments when Sunil had expected to be most in control, directing his own work, he'd been powerless. Bimal, on the other hand, had executed something radical and impressive out of disruption and trauma.

How did you grow a brother as an adult? What could they learn from each other? What could they give and what should they take? Well, they would discover.

After dessert, they walked down Brattle Street. Bimal, something of a dandy, Sunil realized, wound a scarf, pulled on a wool hat, and tugged his hands into snug leather gloves. Walked the mild Cambridge streets with confidence, alert, taking everything in. Sunil tried to see things from a foreigner's point of view: the smooth stones under their feet, the shiny storefronts and clean window glass, the disarming variety of people. Clumps of pigeons ravaging a crust of bread, though there was nothing so local in that. Bimal had been around the world, far more places than Sunil had ever dreamed of visiting.

"Listen, there is something I have been meaning to tell you.

Those tapes I forced on you at the funeral. Nana addressed them to both of us. I think he knew his mind was getting weak, and he wanted his story told, especially to his American grandson."

Though Sunil had been careful to move the tapes to his new apartment, he was embarrassed that he'd forgotten all about them in the last several months. "To both of us?" Sunil felt a jolt. "I had no idea. But I can't understand them."

"*Hakuna matata*," Bimal said with a lopsided smile. "We will translate them together."

That night, Sunil called his wife on her cell phone. She didn't answer, but over three messages he unspooled the whole story of his afternoon. The strange reassurance he'd felt just walking down the street together. Sunil wanted to confirm Thanksgiving, that he'd spend it with the Kauffmans—maybe Bimal and his family would come, too—but he had already gone on too long. He ended by saying, simply, "There's more, love. So much more." Which she already knew.

18.

When Urmila was a girl, once or twice her father had borrowed a car and driven to the game park outside the city. In those days it was informal, you hired a local guide at the gate, a man with a gun, and he drove you around. She had loved all the animals, but most of all the antelope. They were nimble and beautiful and never alone. Out there, under the wide sun, she felt such relief from the city and the bazaar. To be out in the wild where the beasts roamed free and dangerous was a thrill she had remembered all her life.

She had the day off from helping Gopal in his store, expanding the souvenir section. She'd been dismayed to realize she had to deal with the suppliers she'd spurned, the fat president and his son, but she managed. Whenever they made a mistake, she recorded it. In time she would report to her brother. Today she would have beauty and space. Just go and enjoy. There was something uplifting about these sun-scorched plains.

In traffic, the driver had tried talking with her, first in Swahili, then in English. But it was her day, and she was not obliged to be polite. Small talk was for tourists. At the Langata Road entrance, he escorted her to a Jeep with big tires and open sides.

The new driver lifted and spread his hands and explained that from the back seat she could stand and look three hundred and sixty degrees.

Vast sky was what she was expecting, and yet her breath caught to see the stretching, stretching world. For miles and miles rolled away grasses and trees until they were too far to see. She could almost see her childhood, that's how vast it was. Because from within the park you saw the animals against the backdrop of the city, its skyline of scrapers big and small.

First, the scampering Thomson's gazelles.

"No camera, madam?"

"No." She lived here now—again. No need for pictures.

The guide pointed to the small herd. "Always they are watching for predators. The plains are very dangerous place."

"Life is dangerous," she said. She had bought two lion postcards at the gift shop and would send one each to Sunil and Bimal, her American sons.

As they drove, the guide told her the names of trees and plants, but she was here to watch the things that moved. Soon giraffes appeared. The Jeep slowed, crept along, and she craned her neck up and up and up and thought that her gaze would never reach the top. Way up in the sky, the giraffes circled their jaws.

"Where are the elephants?" Last week Lillian Ross had emailed to report the death of her husband. The ivory elephants had been on the shelf beside his bed until the end.

"Very sorry, madam. No elephants in the park. Too small. For elephants you must visit Sambura, Meru, Tsavo East—"

"Yes, yes, okay, I understand," she said, but she was disappointed.

Here now were zebras and a herd of wildebeest. Urmila began to count but they were too numerous—fifty, sixty, or more. Some grazed, some ambled along, not a care in the world.

Then, in a single, rapid movement, the herd lifted heads. Halted. The landscape quieted, and Urmila's breath slowed.

The Jeep jerked and the driver, in an excited voice: "Madam, madam, you are about to witness something extraordinary. Look closely now. In those bushes, what do you see?"

"Nothing. I see nothing." She craned her neck.

Sounding satisfied, he said, "Now we wait."

"For what?" she said. "For what!"

"You will see."

Urmila heard the wind in her ears. Sun pulsed on her skin. For the first time since coming back, she enjoyed feeling utterly alone.

The wildebeest released their attention, and Urmila watched them walk to the edge of a large watering hole.

The attack happened so fast she nearly missed it. First the grass rustled, then from many directions lionesses leapt. They had agreed on a single, weak target and lunged toward it with astonishing speed. Beasts scattered, a flurry of legs and hooves like a quiver of arrows released all at once. Urmila urged them on. *Flee, flee*! But then she turned back to the sacrifice. The cats were too skilled, too determined. Yes, they had felled. The fleeing ones screamed; the captured one writhed.

Urmila strained on her toes to see all she could.

The driver smiled knowingly and eased them forward. "Your first live kill?"

Gleaming white teeth ripped meat from skin and bone. Everything red and slippery; insides turned out and exposed to the driven, hungry world.

"The beasts eat the heart while it is still beating."

Haa.

Looking up from the carnage at last, onto the plains, into the still, yellow grasses and beyond into the burning, lowering sun, she felt another heart, in a different place and far away, catch fire.

ACKNOWLEDGMENTS

When you work on a book for a decade, there are a lot of people to thank.

I am grateful beyond words to my agent, Duvall Osteen, for being a true friend and advocate, for buoying me in every possible way, for expertly finding this book a good home. Deep gratitude and appreciation to Jonathan Lee and Scott Cheshire for sending me to Duvall and supporting me along the way.

Many large and sincere thanks to my editor, Joseph Olshan, for his unending keen attention and excellent narrative suggestions, without which this would be a much floppier book.

Gratitude to my dedicated and brilliant Bennington teachers and mentors: Alice Mattison, Brian Morton, Amy Hempel, Askold Melnyczuk, Bret Anthony Johnston, Paul Yoon, and Wyatt Mason. I frequently return to your letters and our conversations. To my Bennington classmates for good times and excellent writing. For literary support, mentorship, inspiration, and friendship, I am grateful to Claire Messud, Lauren Groff, Karen and Jim Shepard, Ted Conover, Suketu Mehta, Martha Cooley, Judith Frank, Lawrence Douglas, Diana Tejerina Miller, Ilan Stavans, and Harold Augenbraum.

Philosopher friends have been indispensable in discussing both story and morality: Casey Perin, Katia Vavova, Alejandro Pérez Carballo, and Sharon Street, who has been more than gracious as I stole and simplified nearly beyond recognition her own original and fascinating view. Heartfelt thanks to David Velleman and Kitty Bridges, who have become my extended family.

Unending gratitude to my dear women writer friends who have helped me weather storms both personal and professional: Hannah Gersen, Krista Hoeppner Leahy, Elizabeth Witte,

Katherine Jamieson, Mindy Misener, Alicia Christoff, Katherine Hill, Megan Tucker Orringer, Emily Everett, Nancy Pick, Elisa Mai, Sara Brenneis, and Karen Latuchie.

Big thanks as well to the entire staff and intern team at *The Common* for being such hard-working, inspiring, funny, and smart writers and readers.

For time and space and companionship, thank you to Writers OMI and Vermont Studio Center. To Curtis Bauer for being there at the beginning and staying with me.

Gratitude to Timothy Wangore and his mother, Elizabeth, for welcoming me to the sugar cane fields and harrambe school of Mwira, in Kenya's Rift Valley, with open arms in 1995, and again, with my father, in 2007. I have gained so much from being your American sister and daughter for nearly 25 years.

Barbara Mayer and Charles Acker have been the best possible parents, far better than I deserve. Their love and interest in my work and in my life have kept me afloat in countless ways. I want to acknowledge the early love and support of my grandparents, Eleanor Mayer and Malvin Mayer, *in memoriam*. Gratitude to my family in New York, Los Angeles, and Canada. I thank my parents-in-law, Bachu and Surya Shah, for sharing their stories and their son, and for welcoming me to their family. To the Shahs of Nairobi and London for their welcome and hospitality.

To my beloved husband, Nishi Shah, I owe this book. You have taught me to laugh at myself, to take disappointments in stride, to be silly with joy, to think harder and longer, and to love fiercely.

A note on research: This book is a work of fiction and cannot be traced to any particular individuals, but it is inspired by some real events and stories. My reading has encompassed numerous invaluable volumes and scholarly works. I am particularly indebted to the following books and individuals: Dharam P. Ghai and Yash P. Ghai, Yash Tandon, Agehananda Bharati,

Marcus Banks, and Mubina Hassanali Kirmani; *We Came in Dhows* by Cynthia Salvadori, *Asians in East Africa* by George Delf, *A History of Asians in East Africa c. 1886-1945* by J.S. Mangat, *A Short History of the East Coast of Africa* by L.W. Hollingsworth, *The Man-Eaters of Tsavo* by J.H. Patterson and *Ghosts of Tsavo* by Philip Caputo, *North of South* by Shiva Naipaul, *My African Journey* by Winston Churchill, the many novels of V.S. Naipaul, particularly *A House for Mr. Biswas*, and the works of Isak Dinesen.

ABOUT THE AUTHOR

JENNIFER ACKER is founder and editor in chief of *The Common*. Her short stories, essays, translations, and reviews have appeared in the *Washington Post*, *Literary Hub*, *n+1*, *Guernica*, *The Yale Review*, and *Ploughshares*, among other places. Acker has an MFA from the Bennington Writing Seminars and teaches writing and editing at Amherst College, where she directs the Literary Publishing Internship and organizes LitFest. She lives in western Massachusetts with her husband. *The Limits of the World* is her debut novel.

www.jenniferacker.com